Memories of the Théâtre - Libre

Books of the Theatre Series

H. D. Albright, General Editor

Number 5   *August 1964*

A Rare Books of the Theatre project of the
American Educational Theatre Association

ANDRÉ ANTOINE'S
"Memories of the Théâtre - Libre"

translated by
Marvin A. Carlson

Edited by H. D. Albright

UNIVERSITY OF MIAMI PRESS

International Standard Book Number 0-87024-034-X
Library of Congress Catalog Card Number 64-8734
Copyright 1964 by University of Miami Press
All rights reserved
Printed in the United States of America

Second Printing, 1977

CONTENTS

André Antoine's *Memories of the Théâtre-Libre* (*"Mes Souvenirs"
sur le Théâtre-Libre,* Paris: Arthème Fayard & Cie., 1921), translated by Marvin A. Carlson.

FOREWORD

Up to the present, the American student or general reader without a confident knowledge of French has gathered his impressions of André Antoine principally from such works as those of Miller and Waxman. Now for the first time an English version of Antoine's famous *Memories* is here made available, as the fifth volume in the Books of the Theatre Series, jointly sponsored by the American Educational Theatre Association and the University of Miami Press. First issued as *"Mes Souvenirs" sur la Théâtre-Libre* in 1921, the book has been translated and published in this country with the permission of Arthème Fayard and Co., of Paris, the original publishers.

If critical estimates of Antoine's influence on the drama and theatre of modern Europe range from "profound" to "debatable," the weight is certainly in the direction of the former. In any case, the man's own testament of his childhood and early adulthood in 19th-Century Paris makes delightful and even fascinating reading; and, since it deals so directly with the prophetic events in the European theatre of the 80's and 90's, it is both stimulating and revealing as well. As the translator's introduction suggests, the book is not properly viewed as a journal, and its author may well have been overly cautious in deciding which profile he displayed to his audience at any particular moment. But for the most part the theories, the events, and the personalities that made up this most remarkable of the "free" theatres are there for all to see and—in a way—to know.

In these pages Barny and France, Mévisto and Gemier, join Antoine himself in demolishing the stereotypes of conventional acting and production. Zola is there, and de Banville and Daudet, and Jullien and Sarcey. Antoine moves to "the wrong side of the Seine"; he is investigated in the Senate and debated in the Chamber of Deputies;

he tours his troupe in Belgium and can not afford the fare back to Paris. But he survives, is talked about all over Europe, succeeds more often than he fails. His first biographer, Thalasso, is later moved to declare: "The Théâtre-Libre was the cradle of the dramatic art of our times. The history of the Théâtre-Libre is the history of the contemporary theatre."

The original edition of the *Souvenirs* was without illustrations; and those appearing in the present volume have therefore been supplied by the translator. In each case specific credits are given in the captions accompanying the several plates. The photographs specifically credited to Matei Roussou's *André Antoine* are reproduced with the permission of the publishers (L'Arche, Paris).

The observant reader will note that the entries throughout the volume are arranged somewhat differently than in the original edition, being clustered in six- and twelve-month periods. An index—i.e., of names most frequently mentioned in the text—has been added, and Antoine's own index has been dropped. In a very few cases, short passages (of generally irrelevant material) have been removed from the original; these infrequent omissions are clearly indicated with a series of asterisks.

Special acknowledgement for support and assistance is again offered to the Rare Books Project of the American Educational Theatre Association, of which David G. Schaal has most recently been serving as Chairman.

H. D. ALBRIGHT
Editor

TRANSLATOR'S PREFACE

One can not work closely on Antoine's *Memories of the Théâtre-Libre* without having from time to time an uncomfortable feeling that their presumed spontaneity is forced. Matters fall out rather too well, circumstances seem a bit too pat for real life. Foreshadowing and juxtaposition of events altogether too often suggest artistic arrangement of material rather than the random progression one naturally expects in a diary. The impression is inescapable that a serious amount of editing, even of rewriting, went into these pages before they were put before the public.

Of course, there is nothing strange in this. Even if as scholars we would prefer such notes in their original purity, as human beings we must accept the fact that Antoine, like most of us, was probably not wholly candid in exposing his thoughts and experiences to the public. Indeed, in mentioning the publication of a part of the Goncourt *Journals* (January 9, 1891), Antoine notes: "I am sure M. de Goncourt was careful to exclude everything from his memoires which might lead to recriminations." Since Antoine expected such editing from Goncourt, it is not unreasonable to assume that he himself exercised similar "care."

Another characteristic of Antoine's manuscript sheds further light on this problem. The inevitable checking of other materials for substantiation of questionable references or clarification of ambiguous passages yielded unexpected results. Time and again Antoine errs in the names of theatres, plays, and performers. Even more strange, except where it is a question of actual Théâtre-Libre presentations, he is frequently mistaken about dates—erring sometimes by a day or two, sometimes by a few weeks, and in a disturbingly large number of cases, by a year or more. Surely such errors could not be the result of editing for publication; on the contrary, careful editing would presumably have reduced their number. Another possibility, however, would explain both the strange factual inaccuracies and the unmistakable arrangement of material—that Antoine actually wrote this book long after the dates it covers, and probably just before its publication in 1921.

The form of the book, of course, argues strongly against such a possibility. The log arrangement is hardly suited to recollections of thirty years later, and in his preface Antoine himself states: "All the details of the birth of the Théâtre-Libre will be seen in the notes *which I began to take at this time*" (italics mine). So direct a statement is difficult to disbelieve.

Happily, Professor Francis Pruner of the University of Dijon has just published external evidence which sheds much light on the apparent method of composition of the *Memories*. Working in the 33 volumes of Antoine's clippings preserved in the Rondel collection of the Bibliothèque de l'Arsenal, Professor Pruner discovered that aside from the various anecdotes clearly conjured out of Antoine's memory, all the factual information in the *Memories* was derived from press clippings of the time, carefully arranged by Antoine. Using such clippings as a framework, Antoine adroitly slipped in anecdotes as he recalled them, assigning what seemed to be suitable dates to each. His method is further betrayed, notes Professor Pruner, because the clippings used in the composition of the book are all circled in red crayon. The result is a diary which seems most rigorous in arrangement but which is in reality extremely arbitrary.

A warning is therefore necessary for the reader of this book. Its importance in theatre history is indisputable, but it is not, as it appears, a day-to-day log in the manner of the Goncourt *Journals* (the dates where the two overlap clearly substantiate this). One should always remember that Antoine did not call his book a *journal* (diary), but *souvenirs* (memories)—a term which is literally true, despite the book's misleading form. What is presented is not, therefore, the true story of the first years of the Théâtre-Libre—a story which may never be wholly told—but the story of those years as Antoine wished them remembered. Both stories are fascinating for the student of theatre history, but they are of course not always the same. Especially where Antoine's own motivations are concerned, the reader of the *Memories* should view Antoine's words with suspicion. Again and again, for example, Antoine emphasizes the role of chance in his venture, protesting that he little realized where he was headed. His recently published *Lettres à Pauline* (Paris, 1962) tell another story, and show him consciously planning his future path—surely a more reasonable picture of what actually happened. Antoine was an actor in life as well as on the stage, and he presented many faces to the world during his long career. The naive young man of the *Memories* is only one such face, and should be accepted as such.

What, then, can we gain from a study of the *Memories*? First, of course, the book remains what it has always been considered, a colorful and interesting history of a pivotal movement in modern theatre history—subjective perhaps, but what history is not? Recognizing this subjective element, moreover, should free us from serious misreadings. Second, the book gives us a picture of Antoine the man. Once again, it is the man as he wanted to be seen, but if the real human being has been heavily edited, he is still present, and we are constantly aware of his presence. Third, we have Antoine's lively descriptions of his efforts and his acquaintances—perhaps the most delightful part of the book. For all his demurrers about his lack of style, Antoine has a marvelous facility for bringing a person or a scene to life with a phrase. The *Memories* shower the reader with names, but a remarkably large number of them come alive, often with a single bit of description or an anecdote. Finally, even the assembled clippings, the reviews and letters quoted verbatim, are of great value. The *Memories* can boast no unpublished documents, but even the reproduction of previously printed material is valuable for those of us who cannot readily consult the Rondel collections, and if the material is selective and often biased, it was after all Antoine himself who did the selecting, and his choice of illustration is revelatory in itself.

When the arrangement of material in the *Memories* is particularly misleading or the information inaccurate, this is pointed out in the notes. Minor corrections (Antoine, for example, working from clippings, often gives the date of the review instead of the actual opening night for productions outside his own theatre) have not been made, but significant and potentially confusing changes in dates and names are noted. Hopefully, with such corrections, the manuscript can be more readily taken on its own terms.

MARVIN A. CARLSON

ANDRÉ ANTOINE'S

"Memories of the Théâtre-Libre"

Translated by Marvin A. Carlson

PREFACE

I never thought it would be particularly necessary to publish these notes. It seemed to me that this gossip about people and events long past could hardly interest anyone but a few dabblers in the theatre. On various occasions I have been urged to publish it, but time was lacking, and that was not all—for in those moments when I did briefly consider such an enterprise, I dreamed of making this story of the Théâtre-Libre not a dry listing of dates, but rather a faithful recreation, as sincere and also as striking as possible, of the financial martyrdom which is imposed upon those foolhardy souls who attempt to leave the beaten track. This would have been useful to any poor visionary who might some day be rash enough to follow in my footsteps.

But these plans never materialized; and if I had not been particularly strongly urged, I would probably never have gotten around to it. Still, here is a sort of journal all the same—a little disjointed, and made up of notes kept more or less faithfully for seven years. I give it to those who may be interested in it, after having carefully removed all malice and avoided all disagreeable personal remarks. Reprisals? What good would they do? Certainly I was not always right. Moreover, someone who began as our friend or our enemy would often be found to have changed sides as the work developed through its three successive stages—from 1887 to 1895 when, at the Théâtre-Libre, we attacked the tenets of the existing theatre; from 1896 to 1906 when, at the Théâtre Antoine, we won over the general public; and from 1906 to 1914 when, at the Odéon, we made our final struggle against official traditions and administrative routine.

After having re-lived all this, I think that we were all good men at heart, and that neither those who remain, nor those who have departed, emerged lessened in stature from that great era, so fired with passion for literature.

To begin with, a quick glance over our situation in the drama—with the Théâtre-Libre about to appear—will not be without use. In 1887, the French theatre was entirely in the hands of an illustrious trinity; Augier, Dumas, and Sardou had been reigning for twenty years, at the Comédie-Française as well as elsewhere. Perrin, who had just died, was always quick to say: "I need no new authors; one year Dumas, another year Sardou, a third, Augier—that is enough for me."

Certain signs of exhaustion, however, were appearing; Augier had finished his great cycle of *Giboyer's Son, Master Guérin,* and *The Poor Lionesses.* Since *The Fourchambaults,* he had remained silent. Dumas, more active, kept his hand in with *Francillon, The Stranger,* and *Denise;* but his *Road to Thebes,* which had been expected for years, did not appear. Sardou, completely unsuccessful at the Comédie-Française after the great stir of *Daniel Rochat,* had returned to the boulevard. He still had his triumphs—*Dora, Odette, The Bourgeois of Pontarcy*—yet where was the time of *The Benoîton Family, The Blockheads,* and *Our Close Friends*? We were living on Gondinet and Pailleron; Meilhac and Halévy had broken their collaboration, although Meilhac was still setting off a few brilliant displays by himself at the Variétés with *My Cousin* or *Decorated.* The truth was that the end was clearly in sight, and the directors were becoming uneasy.

The poets had, of course, attempted to enter the theatre in the early '70's. But *The Snare,* by Jean Richepin, and *The Hostile Mothers,* by Mendès, were lost in the brilliance of Hugo's triumphant return from exile. His great repertoire, unexploited all during the Empire, barred the way. Banville—although his *Gringoire* was hailed as a masterpiece at the Comédie—had been waiting for ten years for someone to produce his *Socrates and His Wife,* Coppée had but a single one-act play given in the Rue Richelieu, *The Violin-Maker of Cremona;* he remained confined to the Odéon with his *Severo Torelli* and *The Jacobites.* Villiers de l'Isle-Adam, Bergerat, Léon Cladel, and many others were unable to make the grade. Only Henri de Bornier and his *Roland's Daughter* had won any real honor. The fraternal protection of Coquelin the elder for those of his generation brought to the Comédie such writers as Charles Lomon, with his *Jean Dacier,* and Paul Delair, with his *Garin,* but these remained of secondary importance.

At the Odéon, Porel, who succeeded La Rounat thanks to the support of the Daudet salon, paid his debt to them by triumphantly reviving *The Arlésienne,* by presenting *Jack, Numa Roumestan,* the Goncourts' *Henriette Maréchal,* and even a *Renée Mauperin* adapted by Céard. He was, however, already leaning toward Shakespeare and musical adaptations. The Porte-Saint-Martin gave up the old historical dramas. *The Trip Around the World* having made his fortune, Duquesnel restricted himself to the works of Sardou, the only writer who supplied plays for Sarah Bernhardt.

The drama critics had repulsed the first theatrical offensives of the naturalist school, but had little desire to do battle with them again. The most powerful of the critics, Sarcey, with his marvelous understanding of the bourgeois spectator, solidly defended the *status quo.* As soon as he became aware of the presence of Becque, with his *The Vultures* and *The Woman of Paris,* Sarcey kept him out of the public eye, and stoutly resolved to resist a sort of theatre the triumph of which would mean the ruin of everything Sarcey loved and defended. The great critic's flirtations with the young extended only to Feydeau, Gandillot, and Grenet-Dancourt, and to the infamous Vaudeville, of which we shall speak later.

Two men, however, heralded the new naturalistic age: Henry Bauer, an ardent Wagnerian, and energetic champion of Zola, Goncourt, and Becque; and Jules Lemaître, disturbed, perhaps still incredulous, but alert and enough of a dilettante to keep track of the attempts faithfully.

The theatre world—the famous actors and directors—clung to the past with its proven successes and profits. Thus, a stranger situation was never seen: an entire older generation, exhausted, but still standing shoulder to shoulder in comradeship, and, opposed to them, a whole younger generation, chafing under their restraint but helpless to act.

The battle, already won by the naturalists in the novel, by the impressionists in painting, and by the Wagnerians in music, was about to move to the theatre.

This, then, was the battlefield; these, the defenders and the attackers of the fortified position. The time for an assault had come, but who could unite so many scattered elements? Who would give the signal? Chance alone decided. Without having the least suspicion in the world of it, I was going to be the one to unleash forces of which I was quite unaware. It is therefore necessary, before recounting the movements of those who accompanied me into the battle, to search out the mysterious destiny which was going to make me the servant of all.

In later life I have sought to trace back to its source that strange fever which at this moment turned me into a sort of meteor fallen into the midst of theatre life. In the humble world of minor employees where I spent my childhood, neither my origin, nor an upbringing quite devoid of art, had prepared me for such an experience. Can Bergerat be right in saying that my taste for the boards comes from the Parisian streets where I loafed about so much?

My first impressions of the theatre date from Ba-ta-clan, where I was sometimes taken by my mother. I can still see the little green cards which entitled one, for fifty centimes, to a seat and to cherries in brandy. Happy time! Little comedies and operettas (the star of which was a young singer, Lucien Fugère) were given there. In Marais, where we lived, there was also the Théâtre Saint-Antoine, on the Boulevard Richard-Lenoir, a tiny place where Tacova, one of the greats of the 1850's, still gave *Duvert* and *Lauzanne.* But certain presentations at the Beaumarchais made the deepest impression on my youthful mind; I can still clearly see Taillade there, playing the old repertoire of Fréderic Lemaître—astonishing melodramas: *The Ten Steps of Crime, The Lady of Saint-Tropez, Atar-Gull or the Negro's Revenge,* and a *Richard III.* Certainly this great actor was the first to make me dream of the theatre, and I found out later, curiously enough, that he had the same influence on Gémier.

With these memories comes another. A neighbor had a beautiful daughter who played small parts at the Gaîté. She took me one night to sit in the prompter's box for a presentation of *The White Cat*. As I watched, fairyland came to life again, shorn of its infantile seductions. That whole evening I witnessed the unfolding splendors of stage effects and changing scenes. Under my eyes, on a level with the stage floor, the silently opening traps disclosed the stage-hands creating astonishing changes by pulling little rings hooked to the heels of the actors. This glimpse into the inner workings of the theatre did not destroy my illusions; on the contrary, it probably awakened in me a passionate interest in staging.

Except for these two or three chance encounters, I remember no other contact with the theatre; yet I followed the notices, picturing in my imagination productions which I could never attend.

Yet I was fated to see other dramas, real-life tragedies—the war of '70, the siege, the Commune. Escapades which terrified my poor mother took me everywhere—to the ramparts behind the national guard, through the March insurrection, within two steps of the rifle-fire in the Rue Haxo, to the days of May on the Place de la Bastille.

I was the oldest of four children, and as soon as peace was restored, I was sent to work. During my trips as errand-boy for a small businessman, I dawdled interminably before the shop-windows; with the few sous which I had to spend, I devoured such popular publications as the *Good Books,* which, fortunately, offered only substantial and worthwhile things—re-editions of Dumas père, Eugène Sue, or George Sand. What a decisive influence this low-priced literature exerted on my limited bourgeois culture! As yet I felt this only in a great thirst for reading, an enormous eagerness to see and learn.

About this time I was transferred from my unchallenging apprenticeship with the businessman to the Firmin-Didot publishers in the Rue Jacob, a street swarming with publishing firms in the heart of the left bank. From then on, I lived among piles of books. In my office a young man who had left a position at Murger's befriended me. His pockets were always bulging with books and papers, and he wore the romantic beard and hair of all the intellectuals of that time. It was this hardworking and gentle fellow who really opened the horizons of thought and art to me. We would leave the office, threading our way among trucks with supplies from Hetzel and

Quantin, and go to a small bookstore in the Rue Saint-André-des-Arts where my companion got his supply. It was also a delight to go on Thursdays to the Rue Saint-Benoît to buy a copy of *la République des lettres,* the journal Mendès had just founded, which was continuing the publication of *The Bludgeon,* left incomplete by one of the large papers.

Thus, for two or three years, under the guidance of my friend, I became familiar with the Parnassians as well as with the upcoming realist movement. An old reading-room in the Rue Saints-Pères surrendered its dusty treasures to me—all the novels, all the famous plays of the last fifty years. I devoured them all. I am discussing all this at some length because it is a most striking example of how great a role surroundings and chance play in one's destiny.

The Didot firm is quite near the Ecole des Beaux-Arts. As I kept all my money for papers and books, I naturally did not eat, so every day between noon and one I spent my free time drifting along the quays, snooping into the booksellers' stalls. From time to time, the gate of the Beaux-Arts stood open for some exposition—that of Manet, recently dead; a retrospective view of Henri Regnault, killed at Buzenval; or the competition for the *Prix de Rome.* This view of the healthy and vigorous work of the painter of *Père Lathuile* impressed me deeply. The battles which were fought over the *Olympia* introduced me to Zola, who was an indefatigable warrior in them. Henri Regnault gave me a passionate curiosity about the Orient; Formentin, discovered in his turn, led me several years later to volunteer for service in the south of Tunisia. Finally, a small room of former *Prix de Rome* winners led me, by virtue of the classic subjects unalterably imposed upon the contestants, into mythology and Greek and Roman history. During this time, I ardently explored the Louvre, the Luxembourg, all the museums of Paris. A final happenstance then put into my hands the guiding thread indispensable for finding my way through this labyrinth; I happened one day into a course by Taine on the History of Art, and did not miss another lecture. Then I turned to the libraries—the Nationale, the Mazarine, and especially Sainte-Geneviève, which was open in the evenings. It was the sort of culture that most young men of my age had left behind them in school, and my mind, becoming somewhat more orderly, began to arrange it in a meaningful fashion.

Earning my living increased my freedom somewhat, and I was able to go to the theatre. Hugo returned from exile in an apotheosis; the Odéon revived *Ruy Blas* with Sarah Bernhardt, Mélingue, Geffroy, and Lafontaine, and *Hernani* was put into rehearsal at the Comédie-Française. It was the time of the debuts of Mounet-Sully in *Andromache* and *Marion Delorme*. An incomparable troupe—Bressant, Mme. Plessis, Madeleine Brohan, Mme. Favart, Got, Delaunay, Coquelin the elder, Thiron—introduced me to the great classics. Since I went to the theatre every evening, this expense would have quickly exceeded my income if I had not become an assistant to one of the leaders of the claque. He welcomed me for a few sous, on condition of my participating "in the service." When I was first appointed to the Odéon, I even had the pleasure of meeting old Boutin, in his velvet cap, who was still there, a bit flabbergasted at re-encountering one of his former faithfuls now risen to the position of director.

But before long I wanted to get even closer to the great actors who fired me with enthusiasm, and—working under old Masquillier, the director of the extras at the Comédie—for several years I appeared in the whole repertoire, eyes wide open, ears stretched out toward everything that happened in the great house. Nor did I neglect the Gymnase, the Vaudeville, the Porte-Saint-Martin, or the Ambigu. Thus my vocation as an actor mysteriously developed. I got into the habit of learning by heart the scenes played by the famous actors, whom I followed about like their own shadows.

About that same time I met a professor Marius Laisné in a diction course at the elementary school in the Rue de Vaugirard. He was running a small school of oratory in the Rue de Seine, and I became a regular supporter of it. It was there, piqued by the study of the classics (a study which many people have ignored), that I developed my inclination for the theatre at last to the point that, fifteen years later, I was able to prompt my artists at the Odéon in all the great roles of the repertoire.

I therefore presented myself, without success of course, for the admission examination at the Conservatory. Then, as now, it was wishful thinking to hope to pass that threshold without individual recommendation. After this set-back, since I had a good deal of common sense and a certain aversion to spending my time in fruitless endeavors, I renounced a career which seemed impractical to enter. Moreover, I was then called up for military service; its five years were an eternity, the end of which I did not even think about. But my hard and studious youth had endowed me with a very strong individuality; my poverty and the passion for learning had given me a moral health and an equilibrium which were both rare. The physical life of the regiment was going to finish making a man of me.

Upon my return from the regiment in 1883, after a wonderful and stimulating period in southern Tunisia, I resumed my life as an employee. I could not suspect that soon, when I was twenty-eight, some apparently insignificant happenings were going to upset my life completely.

Three years later, about 1886, I was still at the Gas Company, leading the toilsome and monotonous life of one employed at 150 francs a month. This was not much to live on, so a supplementary job at the Palais de Justice filled out my meager income. Ah, me! How many official documents I scribbled. They must still have whole closets full of them there. This, with the Gas Company, made a working day of thirteen or fourteen hours. I had become an excellent employee—no stray impulses, not the slightest dream of adventure.

And then came the grain of sand. One of my office mates was a member of a group of amateurs who, under the name the *Cercle Gaulois,* were giving little dramatic presentations for their relatives and friends every month. There has always been a keen interest in amateur theatre in Paris, but at this time societies like this were found in profusion; people acted then as they dance today. Curiosity led me to attend one of these modest evenings, held in a little room in the Passage de l'Elysée-des-Beaux-Arts, at the foot of a stairway from the Rue des Abbesses. It was very pleasant—young folks, employees, workers, gathering after their daily work to spend their time decently and profitably. In this nook I rediscovered the lost dreams of my youth; but before long I began to feel that these people were wasting their time.

I undertook to renovate the repertoire (based on *The Canoness,* by Scribe, and similar pieces of completely lifeless nonsense) by introducing more modern works—*The Marquis of Villemer, The Ideas of Madame Aubray, Gringoire.* I became most interested in the progress of our organization without, it must be said, neglecting my other work. As a result, I was often forced to slave all night over my official documents, in order to leave my evening free. A neighboring organization—the *Cercle Pigalle*—also gave dramatic productions, but they had more money than we, being composed of paymasters and young businessmen. Each winter they presented, with great festivity, a revue composed by some member of the society. Even Sarcey did not disdain to visit these and to compliment the amateurs politely in his column in the *Temps.* Their superiority over us, the poor neighbors, plagued me enormously; I planned to surpass them, persuading my comrades that if we diverted ourselves by presenting plays, other young people must also relax by writing plays. It was only a matter of finding them.

My plan was adopted, and everyone set out to look. Yet, kept all day long at the Gas Company, never seeing a soul, how was I to reach these future playwrights? A friend acquainted with my high ambitions discovered the first rare bird. It was Arthur Byl, who soon sent me a rather formless one-act play. It was naive and violent, but still it was something unpublished. He proved willing to entrust his cub to us for our next program. A few days later, Byl introduced me to Jules Vidal, an important and already well-established man, having published a book and become a member of the famous Goncourt circle at Auteuil. Vidal spoke of introducing us to Paul Alexis, one of the Five of the *Médan Evenings.* The prospect of moving into such circles made my head swim. As Vidal had foreseen, the contact with Alexis was easily made, and Zola's friend gave us an unpublished one-act play which had been recovered from the papers of Duranty. With Byl's play, and the masterpiece by Vidal, it made a complete program. But shortly thereafter, Alexis staggered me with the news that he had spoken of our plans with Léon Hennique, another member of the *Médan* group, who had just had a play, taken from a novel by Zola, refused at the Odéon. Hennique seemed disposed to entrust it to us. I realized instantly that the name of Zola on our program would guarantee us the attention of Sarcey. Hennique sent me his manuscript of *Jacques Damour,* and our program was launched. Alexis, in his daily columns in the *Cri du Peuple,* called attention to the plans of our little group. Thus, we had a paper committed to us; our old rival the *Cercle Pigalle* was certainly going to be outstripped.

Yet, Zola's name was already causing some misgivings in our society. Certain of the members were disturbed by the notoriety I was gaining. Finally, the club's name and meeting place were both refused me for such a presentation. I was allowed to rent the room, but only on the condition that I do nothing to disturb the somnolent quiet of the house. This was serious. Deprived of the resources of our organization, which I had counted on to meet the expenses of the evening, I had to assume these expenses personally, and of course I did not have a sou at my disposal.

All the details of the birth of the Théâtre-Libre will be seen in the notes which I began to take at this time. I have given all this prefatory material only to make it clear that no one foresaw at that time where we were going. As for me, I did not have the slightest plan of becoming a professional actor or director, and I should have laughed indeed if anyone had predicted to me that we were going to revolutionize dramatic art.

JANUARY-JUNE, 1887

JANUARY 16, 1887—This evening after dinner Jules Vidal took me to meet an acquaintance of his from the Goncourt garret—Paul Alexis—to whom he has spoken about our plans for producing new plays. Zola's friend lives at the very top of the Butte; there is an incomparable view of Paris from his study. He is a large pleasant fellow with clear eyes under the eyeglasses his nearsightedness requires, large falling mustaches, an affable manner, and a winning smile. Although I was at first greatly intimidated at being near a man intimate with Zola, he very soon put me at ease. Alexis did not have a play, but was excited by our idea and recalled a short play in the *guignol* tradition among the papers of Duranty, for whom he is executor. He no longer has this *Mlle. Pomme,* however, having given it to a little society he is president of—a half-literary, half-artistic group which meets in a garret in Montmartre. Now these young people have already begun to rehearse the play for one of their evenings, but they have no objection to visitors, and Alexis has offered to take us there soon.

JANUARY 24, 1887—Paul Alexis has introduced me to *La Butte,* that group of artists of which he is president. They meet in a garret at Jean Noro's (a student of Courbet) in the Rue Ravignan each Saturday evening to recite poetry, read articles, and discuss politics and literature. The place is built of wood, and strongly resembles a Siberian *isba.* The young people welcomed us with great cordiality, but I immediately sensed that many of them were reluctant to get involved in an experiment which Zola's name had marked with the taint of naturalism. The symbolist clique especially felt this way, yet I sensed that there were iconoclasts among them who supported me. At last it was agreed that Duranty's play would appear on our program, and that three members of *La Butte,* under the pseudonyms of Pausader, Cosmydor, and Lucque, would lend us their assistance. I have little confidence in the talent of these improvised actors, but we must move on all the same.

JANUARY 29, 1887—*The Ideas of Madame Aubray,* our little presentation this month at the *Cercle Gaulois,* seems promising, and Paul Alexis (who writes a sort of theatrical review in slang in the *Cri du Peuple* signed Trublot) announced our performance today with a most pleasant commentary.[1] How strange it is to see my name printed in a newspaper for the first time!

FEBRUARY 8, 1887—Alexis invited me to the unveiling of a monument that Duranty's friends were having set up at his grave in Père-Lachaise.[2] A large crowd was present, and I got my first look at Henry Céard who, as secretary of the Monument Committee, made the presentation to the family. He is a tall fellow with a monocle, already graying a bit, and was dressed in a hooded cape which made him look even taller. He read his address with polish and confidence. But what interested me most was Zola, who also came, and a charming woman of most radiant beauty whom I met, named Séverine. After the ceremony, while the others returned to the entrance of the cemetery, I lagged behind to watch Zola, who remained for a long time in contemplation before the immense view of Paris spread out at his feet in the fading light.

FEBRUARY 17, 1887—Last evening the actors at the Théâtre des Nations gave a dress rehearsal (for a few close friends) of *The Belly of Paris,* adapted by Busnach from Zola's novel.[3] I could see no

---

1*The Ideas of Madame Aubray* was presented by the *Cercle* on February 28 and March 2. Antoine's entry is rather confusing. What Alexis announced was not *Madame Aubray,* but Antoine's forthcoming evening of original scripts.

2This ceremony actually took place on April 8, after Antoine's first presentation. Antoine had therefore certainly met Zola and probably met Céard (*see* March 29, 1887) before this date.

3The theatre on the date of Zola's play was called the Théâtre de Paris. It had been called the Théâtre des Nations only from February, 1885, until October, 1886.

trace of the book except in the setting, which was quite vivid and realistic; as for the rest, it was nothing more than a rather heavy melodrama. Mme. Marie Laurent enjoyed a great success, and Taillade especially was admirable throughout in the melancholy and grandeur of Florent. There was a beautiful setting showing the Champs-Elysées in the evening, with the carriages of the market-gardeners going down toward the Halles.

MARCH 5, 1887—Now that we have finally settled on our program, with *Mlle. Pomme, A Sub-prefect, The Cockade,* and *Jacques Damour,* other difficulties are arising. The *Cercle Gaulois,* which was to present this program, is balking. The majority of the members, led by those who were not cast in the production, have decided that it is not in line with the stated aims of our little organization. The decision was announced to me by our president, old Krauss, the best and most civil of men, a retired officer and septuagenarian. It was he who, seized with a boundless passion for the theatre in later life, built the little wooden auditorium in the Elysée-des-Beaux-Arts with his own hands. Everything there is his own work—the little stage, the settings, and the smallest of properties. This task took several years, after which he founded the *Cercle* and gathered amateurs to perform in his theatre. At my instigation, he had, rather reluctantly, been forced to abandon his beloved repertoire of Scribe, Théaulon, and Bayard, but the new direction in which I was leading the organization led him to revolt. He told me that our program should be given under another name, that he could only rent the theatre to me, without taking any sort of responsibility, and that the rehearsals could not be held there, as this would disturb the peaceful routine of the *Cercle.* This sudden blow rather staggered me, and several members asked rather maliciously what I was going to do.

MARCH 6, 1887—The defection of the *Cercle* is a terrible blow, for I had naturally assumed that our production would be given on the society's budget; now, on the contrary, I must find the hundred francs for the rental of the theatre myself, along with whatever else is necessary for the production. I have solved the rather serious problem of rehearsals, which must be held in the evening since we are all occupied during the day. No rooms were available for rental, and even if they were, where would we get the money? As a last resort, I came upon a tiny billiard room in the rear of a barrel-vault in a little tavern which is located in the Rue des Abbesses, next to the Elysée-des-Beaux-Arts. The proprietor has agreed to light it for our rehearsals each evening with a modest gas burner from 8:30 to midnight, on the condition that each of us buy a drink. Since I cannot expect my companions to pay for this, it still means an expense of fifty sous to three francs every evening, and with my finances in their present state, I can hardly see where I am going to get it.

MARCH 6, 1887—Now that our plays are decided upon, and rehearsals started, there still remains the problem of getting a program printed. A small lithography shop in the Rue de Châteaudun has made me a rather good offer—eight francs per hundred. Last evening Byl met me after work and we had an absinthe at the Café du Delta, still looking for a title with which to baptize our venture. I was convinced that if we were to avoid seeming merely amateurish, and yet to affirm the amateur side of our undertaking, we must use no designation which might suggest a regular theatre. For several days I have been looking for an epigraph rather than a name. There was one I had borrowed from Hugo — "The theatre set free" — which sounded very good, but did not seem quite right to us, a bit too romantic, perhaps. Then, as we were mulling over the problem, Byl, who was stirring his pernod, suddenly cried: "Well, then, the Théâtre-Libre," and I felt immediately that this was exactly what we were looking for.[4]

MARCH 10, 1887—At last we have begun our rehearsals in the tavern, and by economizing on my dinner, I was able to meet the expenses of the evening. Emile Paz, a good friend from the *Cercle* and a fellow theatre-lover, has discreetly helped me as much as he could. Indeed, our new arrangements would be quite satisfactory if

---

[4]In a letter to Fouquier dated April 3, 1887, Antoine gives credit to Alexis for christening the Théâtre-Libre. This contemporary letter is surely more to be trusted.

it were not for an enormous billiard table—truly the largest I have ever seen—which fills the center of our rehearsal room. It is a most unusual challenge to set the scene (if what we do can be so described) in the narrow free space between the sides of this table and the walls, but everyone is working devotedly and we are making progress all the same.

MARCH 11, 1887—I just now screwed up my courage, and at five o'clock when I left the Gas Company I went to the *Figaro,* where I saw Jules Prével, the theatre reviewer. I found him to be a small gentleman, very fashionable, but thin and gray, with a rather grumpy air. He received me upstairs in the waiting room, and was clearly astonished by my poor and shabby employee's garb, so out of place in these uptown Parisian surroundings.

Stammering in my emotion, I told him about our project, and our dream of attracting a little attention in the press as our rival, the *Cercle Pigalle,* did. He seemed to feel a little of my enthusiasm, and called my attention to the fact that our entertainments were of interest only to ourselves and that a paper like the *Figaro* could not tell its readers about them despite the names on our program. Yet, flustered and beset as I was by the contentious turn this interview was taking, I must have been eloquent, for the good man grumbled, "Well, we'll see about it," and he did take one of my programs as he showed me out.

MARCH 12, 1887—Victory! When I opened the *Figaro* this morning, I found the following announcement in it—more complete and more benevolently explicit than I would ever have dared to hope:

A special presentation of four new and quite unusual unpublished one-act plays will be given in the near future, behind closed doors, for critics and men of letters. The evening will be free of charge and by invitation, and is of unusual interest, due to the names on its program—Emile Zola, Léon Hennique, Paul Alexis, and the late lamented novelist, Duranty.

The four new plays will be:

Jacques Damour, a drama in one act by M. Léon Hennique, based on a novel by M. Zola which appeared in the *Figaro.*

Mlle. Pomme, a farce in one act by Duranty and M. Paul Alexis.

The Sub-prefect, a tragedy in one act by M. Arthur Byl.

The Cockade, a comedy in one act by M. Jules Vidal.

The plays are being energetically rehearsed, and they will be performed as soon as they are perfected, probably before the end of the month.

The actors are members of the *Cercle Pigalle,* the *Cercle Gaulois,* and the *Cercle de la Butte,* and performers from various theatres.

If this experiment succeeds—and the organizer M. Antoine, a young leading man, is taking great pains to succeed —then it will surely be followed by others, and young writers will gain a wonderful outlet for their work, and be able to present their plays in living form to the directors, instead of on a sterile manuscript.

MARCH 13, 1887—Prével's notice has gone the round of the papers; now *Paris,* the *Evénement,* the *Soleil,* the *Justice,* the *Liberté,* the *Voltaire,* the *Gil Blas,* and the *Temps* have announced our production, and we are preparing for the 30th. We cannot present it any earlier, for I must have my salary from the Gas Company in order to give old Krauss his hundred francs.

MARCH 20, 1887—It seems to me that we should have a bit of a prologue as a curtain-raiser next Wednesday, but to whom should I appeal?

Byl has offered to put together a few lines suited to the occasion. They will be given by Burguet, a member of the *Cercle Pigalle,* a student at the Conservatory, and the most secure and reliable among us.

MARCH 25, 1887—Arthur Byl has brought me his prologue:

16 ·

LES OURS
Prologue Scientifique
Recommandé par un ami,
Je viens de visiter les cages.
Les ours sommeillent à demi
Courbés sur la blancheur des pages.

Le griffonnage affreux des mots,
Muselière calligraphique
Emprisonnant les animaux,
Rendait l'acte moins héroïque.

Monsieur Zola, l'un des gardiens,
Des quatre m'a conté l'histoire;
Il m'a cité les ingrédients
Apéritifs qu'on leur fait boire.

D'après le maître de céan,
Ils viennent du "naturalisme,"
Au delà du vaste océan
Atlantique de crétinisme.

Oh! c'est un pays très lointain.
Les indigènes y cultivent
Surtout le document humain;
On prétend même qu'ils en vivent.

Mais, j'abuse de toi, public;
J'ai des choses à dire encore.
Pour causer un peu du verdict,
Abandonnons la métaphore.

Demain, dès que poindra le jour,
Toute la presse quotidienne
Enregistrera-t-elle un four
En sa chronique parisienne

Ou bien un succès colossal
A faire pâlir Valabrègue,
Fétiche du Palais-Royal,
Et Grenet-Dancourt son collègue?[5]

ARTHUR BYL

It is not inspired, but it will more or less suit the purpose even so.

MARCH 26, 1887—We are now ready, and the invitations have been delivered. Paz helped me with this, in order to get out as many as possible, since the cost of postage would have been frightful. Now I am quite concerned about Hennique. I never dared ask him to come and see his play performed around a billiard table, and yet, we must let him see it. We agreed with our friend Alexis, a delightful person as youthful as we, that I should ask old Krauss to lend us the stage tomorrow evening so that Alexis can bring his friend.

MARCH 27, 1887—I had a lot of trouble this morning finding the furniture and properties, since I scarcely had the means to rent them. I spoke to my mother about it, and she allowed me to take

---

[5]The verse is certainly, as Antoine notes, "not inspired." The following translation attempts to maintain something of the peculiar imagery and unusual turns of the original:

THE BEARS
A Scientific Prologue

A friend just sent me to the zoo
And as I strolled among the cages,
Four drowsy bears came into view
Bent over closely-written pages.

No danger lay in pausing there,
The old ferocity was gone.
For scribbling they had left their lair,
Put calligraphic muzzles on.

Monsieur Zola, guarding the fence,
Told each bear's history in brief,
And listed the ingredients
Each took in his aperitif;

Then, to our questions he replies:
Their native land of "Naturalism"
Across a vast Atlantic lies—
The boundless sea of Cretinism.

Strange harvests grow across that sea,
For there are found on every stem
Documents of humanity;
'Tis even said they live on them.

But, friends, your patience I abuse,
And want to speak of one thing more,
So let us turn to the reviews,
Abandoning my metaphor.

Tomorrow at the break of day
When the news dealers open shop,
And all the papers have their say,
Will they pronounce our play a flop

Or rather a colossal hit
So that, at the Palais-Royal
Valabrègue will blanch at it,
As will Grenet-Dancourt, his pal?

the furniture from her dining room—chairs and a table—for the room behind the shop in *Jacques Damour*. I did not want to ask permission to leave the office early, since the minor commotion in the press had already made the assistant manager of my department suspicious of me, so it was not until five that I could rent a handcart and pull our furniture all the way down the Boulevard Rochechouart to the Rue du Delta, then to the Elysée-des-Beaux-Arts. Old Krauss was astonished by the splendor of such a setting.

Then the rehearsal on stage. Old Krauss, won over in spite of himself by our enthusiasm, worked eagerly, once he was assured that no damage would be done. He did all the stagehand duties alone, in a costume of blue denim with his red Rosette pinned on it.

Alexis brought Hennique, who seemed quite stunned by it all, for at the end he said to Alexis: "If they are rehearsing again tomorrow, we will bring Zola. He must see this."

MARCH 28, 1887—The rehearsals go on. Zola came with his wife, the editor Charpentier, and two friends.

When we finished *Jacques Damour,* Hennique led the master onto the stage, and Zola backed me into a corner under a gas burner. My nerves gave way as his eyes ran over me. A look of astonishment was on his face when at length he abruptly asked me: "Just what are you?" He let me stammer in confusion under his searching gaze before he continued: "It's very good, very good indeed. Hennique, isn't it very good? We'll be back tomorrow."

MARCH 29, 1887—When I arrived for the last rehearsal, I learned from Alexis that Zola, who was enchanted yesterday evening, had come back with more friends—Duret, Céard, Chincholle of the *Figaro,* and even Alphonse Daudet. After the curtain fell, Daudet was most genial to me and unsparing in his praise. We all left the little auditorium together and went down the Elysée-des-Beaux-Arts; Daudet, who is a bit lame, leaned on my arm. At a bend in the little street he stopped before a house with grilled windows and said: "Antoine, I see ghosts in your street tonight; there is the house where I knew the woman who became my *Sapho.*"

• 19

MARCH 30, 1887—The great evening. I drew my salary at the Gas Company before five, and so I am sure to be able to pay old Krauss his hundred francs. Aside from that, I have no idea whatever where we are headed or how all this will turn out.

Chincholle, who came up last night with Zola and Alphonse Daudet, had an article in the *Figaro* this morning, in which he speaks of last night's rehearsal in terms which will surely stimulate curiosity.

MARCH 31, 1887—Last night's performance turned out magnificently, although I was quite shaken by the beginning. Burguet appeared saying that he had lost his copy of Byl's prologue. Then, when the curtain went up, he saw that my brother was not in the prompter's box, as he was supposed to be, and he stood downstage, paralyzed by fright. I was in the wings, talking with Zola, with one ear cocked toward the stage. I became livid upon hearing Burguet stop so abruptly, and I said to Zola: "We're off to a good start."

Mlle. Pomme went by unnoticed.

There was some response to Vidal's play, but Byl's one-act, *A Sub-prefect,* scandalized many in the audience, and was hissed.

In sum, the evening was lost before we began *Jacques Damour.* I was too nervous to know what happened exactly, but I have a definite impression that we created an enormous effect.

Very few critics came, despite our support from the *Figaro.* In the audience were Emile Zola, Daudet, Hennique, Chincholle, La Pommeraye, Denayrouze of the *République française,* and Aubry-Vezan of the *Petite République;* I think that was all. The journalists were all at the Bouffés, at the premiere of a comic opera, *The Gamin of Paris* by Gaston Serpette.

APRIL 2, 1887—I opened the *Figaro* this morning to find, at the top of the page, an article by Henry Fouquier which surprised me very much.

After a picturesque description of his trip up the Elysée-des-Beaux-Arts, Fouquier described our performance, saying that as he read the list of authors, it suddenly struck him that there was real literary interest and life in this obscure little theatre lost in the wilds of Montmartre. And so he came, leaving until another day an operetta which he knew in advance had been mixed by a master's hand out of tried ingredients, because, he said, we need new things. He went on to say that the more trustworthy critics all recognize this and that the more noted and established dramatists are seeking the same new approach which intrigues and stimulates us.

He declared that he felt in *Jacques Damour* an indescribable grandeur which made a profound impression on an audience who were prepared to forgive a work anything provided only that it touch their hearts.

Here are the concluding lines of the article. I find them most disturbing:

"I only wished to note a curiosity of this Paris of ours, so remarkable and inexhaustible in surprises, where one may discover behind any door left ajar or any half-opened window one of these mysterious fires, lighted by working man or madman, which in time may spread into a new dawn, or a devastating conflagration."

La Pommeraye says in his paper: "Tears welled up in every eye; no one held back. And after having wept, we all cheered."

In the *République française,* Denayrouze says this about the play adapted by Hennique from Zola's novel:

"The effect was enormous, and not only on the uninitiate. I am sure I saw an unusual gleam behind the eyeglasses of Henry Fouquier, Alphonse Daudet, and La Pommeraye. As for myself, I must aver that I was deeply moved by this little play. If the tyrannical M. Goblet did not still reign over France, I would beseech M. Porel to couple it with the next short play he plans to present at the Odéon. But since the play has the taint of Zola on it, we might as well ask the director of the second Thèâtre-Français to put dynamite under his official chair.

"Even so, if the naturalist theatre produces many plays like this one, it can rest easy about its future."

APRIL 3, 1887—My greatest disappointment was the absence of

Sarcey, due, I was sure, to some trick of our rival, the *Cercle Pigalle*.

I wrote to the critic of the *Temps* reproaching him for not encouraging an experiment done almost solely for him, and he was gracious enough to send a polite note in return to vindicate himself—truly a charming and indulgent gesture. He says that he was called away that day for a conference in Lille, and so that I could have no doubt of it, he pinned his railway ticket in the corner of the letter. He closed with the promise that if we give another performance, he will not fail to come.

APRIL 4, 1887—We have certainly succeeded. Porel, who refused *Jacques Damour* before, has told Hennique that he will accept the play for the Odéon.

In looking back over the results of our production, I was quite overwhelmed. The performances which my companions and I first planned to be simple entertainments given by the *Cercle Gaulois* have apparently far exceeded our expectations at the very first trial.

Byl and Vidal, among those most impressed, met me today as I left work and insisted that we continue. Paul Alexis feels the same way, and I feel pressure from all sides for a new effort—but with whom, and for what? Moreover, such productions are expensive, and it will be a long time before I can make up the three or four hundred francs that this one has cost me.

APRIL 5, 1887—I arose this morning with my mind made up. Our great success, the reception of *Jacques Damour* at the Odéon, Fouquier's article—everything leads to an inescapable conclusion. I can no longer hesitate; a second production must be given. The question of money, however, continues to haunt me. I talked it over last evening with Emile Paz, who has a very practical turn for a fellow his age, and he suggested getting up a sort of small collection among ourselves by joint contribution, the total of which, combined with my salary at the Gas Company, should just about cover the expenses of another production. He seemed so anxious to participate in this that I'm sure we can rely on him. We have therefore decided to give a second production before summer, and I told him that I would set right to work to find a bill which I hope will be of unusual interest.

April 6, 1887—When Byl and Vidal heard of my plans to continue, both came to offer me a second play for the next production. When I protested that I didn't think it was possible to give another of their plays right away, things became quite unpleasant. In vain I pointed out that we had been able to attract a few important critics to our first presentation, and that we could not attract them again unless we offered them something new and different. My first two authors quickly shifted from displeasure to hostility; but I feel that I have paid my debt to them, and I gave them to understand that I intend to remain the master of my venture.

April 9, 1887—I found at my house the manuscript of a short play, a gripping one-act in the "underworld" style of Henry Monnier, written in a slang which combines comic and tragic elements. This will be excellent for a second bill, since I foresee it giving just the right effect of novelty and unexpectedness.

April 10, 1887—One of the papers has printed a protest from Byl and Vidal against my second production. It asserts that they have the true Théâtre-Libre and that it will give its next presentation under their direction in the little Théâtre Montmartre. This is annoying, but I will not let myself become irritated; they really mean no harm, but simply do not understand what we are doing.

April 10, 1887—I am convinced that the program of our second production should bear the name of a noted author capable of attracting the curiosity and attention of the press; otherwise, we will soon disappear from sight. It seems to me that the name of Emile Bergerat would be perfect. His furious campaigns and resounding protests against the existing theatre make him admirably suited to support this endeavor of the Théâtre-Libre. Moreover, Bergerat's influence and his high position at the *Figaro* will surely command the attention of his fellow journalists. I have written to him asking for an appointment, preferably some evening after dinner, since my job at the Gas Company keeps me occupied all during the day.

APRIL 11, 1887—Last night I went to Emile Bergerat's home in the Rue Galvani at les Ternes.[6] Awed at the prospect of meeting him, I decided to have my brother accompany me. We arrived promptly at eight in the pleasant dining room where Caliban[7] was just finishing dinner with his two small children and Mrs. Bergerat.

He immediately welcomed us with a good-natured cordiality, and I was a bit amused to see that he nourished such a passion for the theatre that he greeted me as a real director. Henry Fouquier's article had already acquainted him with our project, and as soon as I disclosed my plans, he became most enthusiastic.

"Of course," he exclaimed, "I have a play for you!—one in three acts which the Français refused, after having put me off repeatedly. If you can speak verse, the role designed for Got will suit you perfectly."

And he immediately went to look for a manuscript in his study— a little summer-house at the back of a small garden. We were served tea, and he launched into the reading of his *Bergamasque Night* with such imagination and vigor that I confess I missed many of the details, being so amused by his lively features, which lit up with childish gaiety as he emphasized the multitudinous rhymes. Near midnight my brother and I found ourselves wandering in the suburb of Ternes, glowing with enthusiasm over such a welcome and such a success.

APRIL 12, 1887—The head clerk at the Gas Company glares at me constantly and is watching my work much more closely. Henry Fouquier's article has passed through everyone's hands here, and caused quite a stir. I think I would do well to be on my guard.

APRIL 20, 1887—We simply could not return to our billiard room

---

[6]Here again Antoine is mistaken in his chronology. His request for an interview (which Bergerat quotes in his *Souvenirs d'un Enfant de Paris*) is dated April 11, but the interview here described did not take place until April 24 (*vide Antoine's Lettres à Pauline*, letter C). The rehearsals which Antoine describes as taking place in April must, therefore, be placed later.
[7]Bergerat's pen name.

in the Rue des Abbesses for the rehearsals of Bergerat's play. That sort of thing was good enough for the Bohemian improvising we had to do for our debut, but Bergerat, who is accustomed to regular theatres, would be terrified by it.

While we were desperately searching, my devoted and enthusiastic friend Barny offered to ask the concierge of the house where she lives on the Rue Bréda if we could rehearse each evening in a little vacant ground-floor apartment facing the court. She will bring some lights down there and we can rehearse undisturbed, on the condition that we are quiet enough not to disturb the rest of the tenants, who retire early.

APRIL 20, 1887—I was a little uneasy about telling Bergerat of the arrangements we made with Barny for the rehearsals of *The Bergamasque Night;* but the excellent man was, on the contrary, enormously amused by all the oddities of this adventure. He never misses a meeting, and, seated on an old trunk, which is the only chair in the unoccupied apartment, he presides over all our rehearsals.

MAY 10, 1887—Yesterday, Paul Alexis kindly gave me a ticket to the Vaudeville for the premiere of *Renée,* the play Zola adapted from his novel *The Quarry.*[8] I was happy to be present at the performance, perched in the top balcony, since it was hailed as an important manifestation of naturalism.

Deslandes, the director, a rather old-fashioned but well-informed Parisian, offered Zola his theatre and gave him a free hand in all matters relating to the play. Excitement ran high; *Renée* has a long history of unpleasant experiences with directors, and has been called a violent, audacious, and iconoclastic work. Thus, from the rise of the curtain, an atmosphere of the battlefield reigned in the theatre. And sure enough, the very public which allows *Phédre* soon became indignant and protested against the same subject in a modern setting! It must be admitted that the leading lady, Mlle. Brandès, although an individualistic and original performer, was too much accustomed

---

[8]According to a letter written at the time, Antoine's invitation to this premiere came from Hennique, not Alexis. The date of the premiere was actually April 16.

to the romantic theatre of Dumas and Sardou, and got quite out of her depth in the major scenes. The hostility of the audience confused her, and she contributed to the play's lack of success despite the courageous resistance of certain of the spectators, whose efforts I seconded from above with great zeal!

MAY 11, 1887—I saw Alexis this evening, and he tells me that Zola is not at all depressed by the unfavorable and ill-tempered reviews. His only regret is that he was a bit dispirited when he later attended the supper which had been arranged at Paillard's, across from the theatre, with Goncourt and the Daudets. His friends stole away from this gathering, awkward and embarrassed by the failure.

I made a new friend at the performance. Perched as I was in a bad seat in the last balcony, I was quite disagreeably surprised to find, upon my return from the intermission, that my place had been taken by an unknown person who refused to give it back. The same thing was happening several steps away, where a young man with an unusually yellow complexion and a piercing voice was storming at a gentleman who had taken *his* place. Seeing me in the same situation, the stranger said to me: "Let us go downstairs together, sir. I am secretary to a police commissioner, and I promise you that we'll get our seats back." Sure enough, the two intruders were turned out, and as I talked further with my young benefactor, I found that he was none other than Oscar Méténier, who has just begun making a reputation with a book of original short stories, *The Flesh*. He is, moreover, the author of that one-act play, *In the Family*, which is now at my house, and I told him that rehearsals were just beginning, prior to its presentation at the Théâtre-Libre.

MAY 20, 1887—This evening as we were leaving our rehearsal at Barny's house in the Rue Bréda, Bergerat graciously invited us to some refreshment at the nearby Café de la Nouvelle Athènes in the Place Pigalle. Just about midnight, the waiter who was serving us told us that the Opéra-Comique was burning.[9] People who were

---

[9]Antoine anticipates this disaster, which actually occurred on May 25. The theatre reopened October 15 in the former home of the Théâtre-Lycée.

coming up from downtown Paris had the most fearful stories; the theatre was on fire from top to bottom. Still, we were reluctant to go down. Morning was approaching, and I had to be at my office early. Bergerat, too, flinched at the prospect of an almost sleepless night, since he still had to go all the way home to les Ternes.

MAY 26, 1887—Since we were planning to rehearse *The Bergamasque Night* all the way through, Bergerat brought Coquelin the younger, wanting to get his opinions on these amateur interpreters. Coquelin was most polite and gave us some very practical advice and suggestions; but, when he went over my role with me, he seemed to attach what I considered a quite exaggerated importance to the preparation of what he called "effects." I think that this device of interrupting the play to wink at the audience saying "Just watch how clever this is" is really quite the contrary of what I am trying to do.

MAY 27, 1887—Whether I planned it that way or not, the name "The Théâtre-Libre," which the first program carried to emphasize our project's modest nature, has become the name of a theatre, and in spite of myself, I have become the director of this Théâtre-Libre.

For our second production, we decided to emphasize that this is no public playhouse, but a special private society, by sending out announcements folded in the form of wedding invitations, with this text:

> *The Théâtre-Libre, 37 Passage de l'Elysée-des-Beaux-Arts.* M. Emile Bergerat, M. Oscar Méténier, and the founders of the Théâtre-Libre request the honor of your presence at the performance of two dramatic experiments:
>
> 1st A realistic play in one act and in prose, entitled *In the Family,*
>
> 2nd A tragi-comedy (in the old style), three acts in verse, entitled *The Bergamasque Night.*
>
> And they hope that these two experiments, one a poetic comedy and the other a naturalistic drama, will distract you for an hour or two from the cares of everyday life. Performance May 30, 1887.

The anonymous "founders of the Théâtre-Libre," among whom I include myself, refers to the few participants in the little subscription which Paz organized.

MAY 31, 1887—This time the press turned out in full force. I am told that the audience was marvelous, but I was personally so absorbed in the performance, which went very well, that I was aware of nothing else.

To begin with, Bergerat, whose influence I was depending on, brought the full drama staff from the *Figaro* as well as many Parnassian friends—Jean Richepin, François Coppée, Catulle Mendès, and Paul Arène. Lockroy himself, just made a minister, was there with his wife and George Hugo. I am also told that Porel, director of the Odéon, Got, Coquelin the younger, Vitu, Sarcey, La Pommeraye, Edmond Deschaunes, Georges Duval, Stoullig, Ollendorff, Carjet, the painter Duez, and the musicians Chabrier and Audran were present, seated side by side on our rough wooden benches.

The place was far too small for such a gathering, and since we had no foyer, all of these brilliant Parisians stood outside in the open air, on the staircase leading from the Elysée-des-Beaux-Arts to the Rue des Abbesses. I am told that Got, witnessing by candlelight the play by Bergerat that he had not been able to do at the Français, told his neighbors: "The Théâtre Illustre is reborn here."

JUNE 1, 1887—We have gained the respect of the critic of the *Figaro;* Auguste Vitu regards our efforts most kindly. The critics seem generally agreed that Méténier's play was the more novel; Mévisto's beautiful delivery of the speech describing the execution created a considerable effect.

Sarcey's review in *la France* has high praise for the actors and for what he calls their extraordinary perfection in details; but he concludes by saying that if *In the Family* is the theatre of the future, he sincerely hopes that he will be gone before it comes. He maliciously avoids saying a word about *The Bergamasque Night,* since he and Bergerat have a long-standing feud.

JUNE 6, 1887—Jules Lemaître, in his article in the *Débats,* is most favorable toward Bergerat. He also speaks at some length of a new play by Tolstoi, called *The Power of Darkness,* which has just appeared in translation and which sounds to me as if it would be admirably suited to our theatre.

Henry de La Pommeraye, who used the production of *Jacques Damour* as a pretext for another essay on his theory of sympathetic characters, disapproves of Méténier because the thugs and cutthroats of *In the Family,* etched as with aqua-fortis, lack the grace and softness of a chromolithograph.

JUNE 8, 1887—The repercussions of our first production have made it evident that the Théâtre-Libre must become a solid and permanent organization. Next winter I am going to devote myself to putting on eight or ten productions at the rate of one a month. Honorary members, lovers of the theatre, will give contributions to defray expenses. The most pressing matter is the drawing up of a program. I said as much to Méténier, whom I met this evening at the Chat Noir, and when I mentioned to him that Jules Lemaître's recent article had interested me in *The Power of Darkness,* but that I was not satisfied with the translation, he suggested that we make a new one. When I pointed out that he was completely unfamiliar with the language, he told me of one of his friends, Pavlovsky, a correspondent of the *Novoë Vrémia,* who could help him with the task.

JUNE 10, 1887—The details of the fire at the Opéra-Comique are frightful. The official number of dead is five hundred, but everyone is sure that when the debris is cleared it will be much higher. Yesterday I managed to get near the smoking ruins; it is unimaginable. The current slump in theatre attendance will surely get worse; public apprehension and uneasiness will show in the receipts.

JUNE 10, 1887—This evening Salis drew me aside at the Chat Noir, where we are accustomed to going at the end of the evening. The talk going around these days about Méténier's play has given him an idea. He has just moved into a house in the Rue Victor-Massé which has a salon beneath the two ground-floor rooms which he could transform into a theatre. There he would like to give performances of short one-acts and monologues by artists of the house. He suggested that I inaugurate this venture with Mévisto, Barny, and Luce Colas, by giving Méténier's *In the Family.* He would give us 100 francs a day—a handsome figure indeed— and I would have accepted had I not recognized that this would inevitably lead to the disorganization of our little society, for, since we all work each day, we have no time to get together to prepare our productions except in the evenings.

JUNE 13, 1887—I received a note from Catulle Mendès who, at my request, invited me to his home, Villa Dupont, this morning.[10] I was shown up to the second floor of a small town house, to a study with lovely autograph material by Hugo hung on the walls.

I heard water splashing behind the draped doorway of a neighboring room, and then a man wrapped in a dressing gown appeared, addressing me in an already cordial and familiar tone: "Good morning, my dear friend. Pray wait a moment until I am dressed and we can chat over breakfast."

As he finished dressing, I told Mendès the whole brief history of the Théâtre-Libre. At first he showed little interest, but gradually I began to sense in him the same unfulfilled passion for the theatre that I had felt in his brother-in-law Bergerat. He was clearly fascinated by the prospect of being presented anywhere, even on so ephemeral a stage as ours. In vain he was called for breakfast; he talked on, saying that he had nothing at hand, but that it would be possible to put together an act between now and the re-opening. Then he began leafing through a collection of the *Gil Blas,* saying: "Wait, just look through this series of tales, especially *Tabarin's Wife.* I think I could make a rather fine thing from that." The summonses

---

[10] Once again, Antoine has apparently confused a request for an interview with the interview itself. In his *Lettres à Pauline,* letter CXII, he reveals that he saw Mendès and Got (*vide* June 15) the same day, Sunday, July 3. June 13 would be impossible in any case, since Antoine was still working at the Gas Company and could not have spent an entire week-day with Mendès, such as he describes.

to breakfast continued from downstairs, but we did not go down until I had read the story and was beginning to have an idea of the quaint and stylishly literary play which he promised to write before autumn.

Below, we met Métivet, the young designer, who had brought some of his sketches for a projected book. During a breakfast of tastefully prepared delicacies, I got my first taste of Mendès' splendid conversation.

Somewhat later, after coffee, I started to take my leave, but Mendès said: "Just wait a moment, my dear friend, and we'll go back together. I have business in Paris." And so we trotted off to the Opéra, with me smoking one of his enormous cigars, and him still talking. After a short stop at the *Gil Blas,* where everyone greeted him with great respect, Mendès took me by Tortoni to call on a friend who, he said, was expecting him. He continued to resist all attempts at withdrawal so warmly that at seven o'clock we were sitting down together for dinner at the Maison Dorée with the appetites of people who had fasted for days. After raising a fuss over the imperfect cooking of a leg of mutton, Mendès insisted that I join him in an unbelievably large number of bottles and small glasses of various drinks. Toward nine o'clock in the evening, I was still with him, in a box at the Folies-Bergère, and when the performance was over, we drifted into the Pousset bar in Montmartre to eat again. Finally, at three a.m., he allowed me to depart, and then only because they had put us out and the waiters were falling asleep in the deserted bar.

JUNE 15, 1887—Since I know that Got made a special effort to come to *The Bergamasque Night,* I wrote to thank him. An exchange of letters and a visit were the result. I called on him at his little house in the village of Boulainvilliers, where he received me one morning in a dressing-gown, with a warmth that made me quite proud.

He asked many questions about our plans for the Théâtre-Libre, and I confided all my projects as well as the problems I anticipate. The success that I expect forces me to go on, but since I am, after all, a penniless working man, I cannot give up the job which pays for my living. This sensible resolve not to burn my bridges behind me seemed very wise to him, especially, as he said, since I was nearing the age of thirty, already too old to embark on a career in acting. He feels that our pleasant little society can amuse the Parisians and give us a taste of amateur celebrity which will satisfy our passion for the theatre. His suggestion is that we continue our association on the resources of our subscriptions, and if the work becomes to heavy in addition to our regular jobs, we should simply copy the organization of the Comédie-Française, each one in turn taking over the duties of the week, and thus sharing the work and the responsibilities.

JUNE 20, 1887—The success of *The Bergamasque Night* and the patronage of Mendès have so improved my position that I now feel ready to address myself to Banville.

I requested and received a noon appointment (as always, I had to consider my hours at the Gas Company), and I arrived at the home of the author of *Gringoire,* in the Rue de l'Eperon, just as he was sitting down to lunch. I was asked to wait in a small circular hall, a study lined with books, and shortly after, the old poet appeared, drawing a napkin out of his vest, and with his famous black beret on his head. He will always be associated in my memory with the scent of the cheese (livarot, beyond a doubt) which he must have been eating. I was all the more aware of it since, having had to dash all the way over to the Saint-Germain district during my lunch hour, I had not eaten a bite. I immediately recognized the familiar profile of the poet, so often reproduced in portraits. He listened politely to me, amused by my passion and my naive self-assurance.

Finally he spoke: "Do you know how to speak verse? It is not easy, and nobody does it any more. Except for Coquelin, no one at the Comédie still has the knack."

I told him that I had decided to come to him because his case is one of the most significant examples of the ills of the contemporary theatre; the reactionary forces are so strong at the Français and elsewhere that after the success of his *Gringoire,* a play still in the repertoire of the Comédie, he had been forced to wait fifteen years for the production of *Socrates and His Wife.*

A short silence followed, during which I felt him inspecting me from head to toe, and then he asked me whether I had performed in any of his plays. Since I had memorized *Gringoire,* he had me recite passages from it, especially "The Ballad of the Poor."

I poured out my soul to him, and then stood breathless, my heart racing. "Very well, young man; it is agreed. I am leaving for la Nièvre, but I will work for you during my vacation. I have an idea for a Pierrot play which will just answer your purpose. You can announce *The Kiss,* and I'll have the manuscript to you in autumn." I ran breathlessly all the way back to my office in the Rue de Dunkerque in order to be there by one o'clock, but never had a single regret about missing my lunch.

JUNE 25, 1887—The more I consider our plans for next season, the more it seems to me that the best formula is to arrange programs in the pattern of our first ones, coupling the work of an established author with that of a beginner, who will thus benefit from the interest awakened by his illustrious partner.

It is clear that Bergerat's reputation was a great help to Méténier, who could never have attracted so brilliant an audience to hear *In the Family.* Thus, even while I set to work finding well-known authors, I asked Sarcey to bring to my attention any plays among those sent to him which seem to suit our program. He was good enough to give my letter the enormous publicity of his column.

JUNE 28, 1887—Peace has been made with Byl and Vidal. Their attempt at secession and competition collapsed in the face of my activity, but I shall not forget this first lesson.

I think it only right that they be given some compensation for the undeniable part they played in our first program, not only because each furnished a play, but because Vidal, by introducing me to Alexis, opened the way to Zola, and Byl christened the Théâtre-Libre. We have therefore agreed that for the next season (1887-

1888) they will make me an adaptation of the Goncourt novel, *Sister Philomène*. Vidal is responsible for obtaining the master's authorization, and if necessary, I will have Alphonse Daudet ask as well.

Rumor has it that Edmond de Goncourt is now writing a play in ten scenes adapted from *Germinie Lacerteux,* which is certain to be of artistic importance if the theories stated in the preface to *Chérie* can be trusted. Since *Germinie* will surely be accepted at the Odéon, I am all the more happy to have *Sister Philomène.* If our little corner is to be considered as one of the laboratories of today's realistic movement, we cannot allow ourselves to be outdone by a regular theatre, especially an official and subsidized one.

JULY-DECEMBER, 1887

July 1, 1887—Since my program is almost decided, I have told Paz that we should now publish it in a small pamphlet to be distributed to those who are likely to subscribe to our future performances.

Some dependable source of income is our most pressing need at present; the performance of May 30 left me with almost nothing, and we are lost if the Théâtre-Libre cannot find steady support now, with the clamor that surrounds it. The expense of the brochures, which will come to perhaps two or three hundred francs, is a serious problem; but Paz, with his shrewd business sense—and I think maybe by standing surety for it as well—has found a printer, Ethiou-Pérou, who will give us the credit we need.

July 4, 1887—This evening in his column Sarcey gives my address, 42 Rue de Dunkerque, saying that he is inundated by letters from all corners of France asking him where to send manuscripts for me. He ends by saying: "Somebody will have a lot of fun dealing with all of them; I laugh in my white beard to think of it."

July 5, 1887—I ran, between noon and one o'clock as always, to the Rue de Châteaudun, to see a M. Ancey de Curnieu who had sent me a short note offering me a play. Here too my unusual hour of arrival surprised the gentleman at his lunch. I was shown into a rather rich salon where I met a tall young man who was, if possible, even more timid than myself. He gave me a short play, *M. Lamblin,* which I brought away with a strong feeling of curiosity.

July 6, 1887—When I told Bergerat that Porel, in a note as pleasant as it was unexpected, had asked me to come and see him, Bergerat replied: "I don't want you to go there alone; you'll let yourself be taken in. When has he invited you?" So we agreed that at five he would accompany me as far as the Café Voltaire, which is across from the Odéon.

It was the first time that I had ever entered the stage door of that old theatre which had been the center of my youth. From the stairway, one's glance first falls on the windowed den of the management's famous servant, Emile, its walls hung with autographed photographs of the actors of the house. The suspicious Emile gave me a grim look, but nevertheless showed me into the great comfortably furnished corner room where Porel welcomed me with a great good nature and a patronizing openness. He showed me to a very small and low chair near him, so that he could maintain an indisputable dominance from the height of his armchair. It was admirable blocking.

"My dear sir," he began. "You seem to be an artist. I have seen one or two of your productions; they were quite entertaining, in a Bohemian sort of way, but hardly of great importance. You have no illusions about that, eh? It is a studio theatre for a small group of Parisians.* Before six months have passed, these people will grow tired of it and desert you. You should therefore profit by this windfall while you can. Since you have dreamt of becoming an actor, seize this opportunity to find a position for yourself. You seem to have talent and there may be a future for you in the theatre. You have a real aptitude for it, but you do not yet know your trade; come learn it with me. At your age, one is content with little. I will give you 500 francs a month and you will make your debut in a revival of Augier's *The Contagion*. Got created the principal role, and it will suit you perfectly."

I was momentarily stunned by the offer; it was the oldest dream of my youth realized as if by magic. But some instinct made me hesitate: "You are right. This would be an unlooked-for opportunity for me. I certainly have no illusions about the future, but I have already made commitments and laid out a program. I must complete all that first. If you feel the same way next year, I will probably be most happy to speak with you again."

---

*The words of Sarcey in a recent column [Antoine's note].

At the café across the street, Bergerat, his eyes narrowed and his sharp nose thrust out, had me repeat the entire interview for him. Shaking with laughter, he observed: "Just as I thought! Ah! The rascal! If you had listened to him, old fellow, you would have fallen right into his trap, just as I expected. You would have been done for, strangled."

JULY 7, 1887—A beautifully wrapped package was delivered to me yesterday, containing the two thousand copies of my little pamphlet. I am convinced that if this printed matter were sent out as it is, it would be lost in the flood of handbills, so I have set myself to writing long and detailed letters to accompany each pamphlet, differing according to the recipient. This will avoid the impression of a circular. I am sending them to everyone who subscribed to Lamoureux' recent presentation of *Lohengrin* at the Eden.

JULY 10, 1887—I spend every night writing covering letters. Although hard work is nothing new for me, it is an enormous task, since each letter is composed to suit the personality of the addressee and is a full four pages long. Nearly thirteen hundred of them are necessary.

Moreover, I cannot raise the money to pay the postage on these announcements, so when they are written, I must deliver them myself. All this is done at night, since my work and my punctuality are closely watched at the office during the day. My superiors have grown more rigorous—irritated, I am sure, by the stir I am making in the press.

JULY 24, 1887—Tonight I finished the delivery of the thirteen hundred announcements of our program and their accompanying letters. I had to begin my rounds about ten in the evening, in order to be finished by five or six in the morning. Since I must be at the office at nine, I am literally asleep on my feet. When I delivered the last envelope this morning, at Clemenceau's house in the Avenue Montaigne, I was so groggy from lack of sleep that it took me a full five minutes of searching in the early dawn to find the letter-box, which was under the ivy of the little entrance-gate.

JULY 25, 1887—Today I committed a mad act, the consequences of which are quite beyond my power to predict. About nine-thirty this morning, without the slightest consideration, I abruptly resigned from my job at the Gas Company. This done, I took my hat from the cloakroom and walked out, leaving my envelope with the concierge, who was astonished to see me leave without the required permit. I had suddenly realized that it was infantile to try combing Paris for subscribers while remaining locked up all day in an office. I'll need all the time and energy I have, and more, if I am to be ready by this coming September.

By that time, I must have found a suitably equipped place for our rehearsals and established a solid organization which can be taken seriously and which is equipped with the means to accomplish what is expected of us.

AUGUST 1, 1887—Sarcey printed my program and its accompanying letter this evening, along with a most benevolent commentary. I am quite proud of the list of plays, which almost every paper printed:

Sister Philomène, a two-act prose play, adapted by Jules Vidal and Arthur Byl from the novel by Edmond and Jules de Goncourt;

All for Honor, a one-act prose play, adapted by Henry Céard from Emile Zola's novel, *Captain Burle;*

Esther Brandès, a three-act prose play by Léon Hennique;

The Butchers, a one-act verse drama by Fernand Icres;

Cleopatra, a five-act prose play by Mme. Henry Gréville;

The Serenade, a three-act comedy in prose by Jean Jullien;

The Escape, a one-act prose play by Villiers de l'Isle-Adam;

Tarbarin's Wife, a one-act tragicomedy in prose by Catulle Mendès;

The End of Lucie Pellegrin, a one-act prose play by Paul Alexis;

My Poor Ernest! a prose comedy in one act by Henry Céard;

The Power of Darkness (from the Russian stage), a drama by Count Tolstoi especially translated for the Théâtre-Libre by M. Pavlovski, and adapted for the French stage by Oscar Méténier;

The Fall of the House of Usher, an adaptation by Oscar Méténier and Arthur Byl of a tale of fantasy by Edgar Poe.

Théodore de Banville and François Coppée have each promised the Théâtre-Libre an unpublished play for this season. The titles are not yet determined.

Finally, Paul Bonnetain, Lucien Descaves, Ajalbert, and Oscar Méténier will each present a one-act play.

The 1887-1888 season will be filled out by a comedy in three acts by Diderot (a play the critics have often wanted to see staged),[11] and an end-of-year Revue, produced by the collaboration of all the authors of the Théâtre-Libre.

May we also mention the important backlog of plays which assure us a second season? Posthumous works of Victor Hugo and Jules Vallès were considered for presentation this year, but these plays were put aside to leave more room for young authors.

Bergerat, Jean Richepin, and others are also disposed to lend their assistance to the Théâtre-Libre, if it proves necessary.

AUGUST 7, 1887—Henri Lavedan, a young man who has already published several highly-praised books, wishes to offer me something for the Théâtre-Libre. I met him and his collaborator, Gustave Guiches, at Perroncel's, a fashionable restaurant across from the Gare Saint-Lazare.

In a small room there, the two writers read me two short scenes

---

[11] The play was Diderot's *Is He Good, Is He Evil?* but Antoine did not succeed in presenting it until he became director of the Odéon.

which they call *Quarter Hours*—brief sketches of singular pungency and depth.

AUGUST 12, 1887—I have not received a single response from my thirteen hundred letters! Five or six times a day, my heart beating wildly, I ask my concierge in the Rue de Dunkerque if there is anything for me. Paz, who is most kind and who gives me much encouragement, has guessed the reduced circumstances in which I have struggled since I left my job, and therefore often asks me to dine at his parents' home in the Rue Le Peletier. A little while ago he triumphantly brought me our first subscription, from a businessman friend of his.

AUGUST 13, 1887—In my terrible confusion at this frightful silence after so many walks and letters, I have often thought of the hospitality the *Figaro* has shown us. I have therefore written to Albert Wolff, the paper's most influential columnist, to call his attention to my project, and to say that I have dared to knock at his door because I have much more to offer than vague promises. The reverberations of the first two performances of the Théâtre-Libre, as his own paper witnessed, ought to serve him as proof of the potential literary interest of our experiment.

The noted newsman wields great power; if he condescends to commend our venture in one of his "Letters from Paris," all will be saved.

AUGUST 15, 1887—This morning I received this letter from Albert Wolff:

Saint-Germain-en-Laye

Monsieur,

I found your letter most interesting, but you have far too great an idea of the influence which I might have on the fate of the Théâtre-Libre.

You need 7000 or 8000 francs, and you assume that nothing could be easier than obtaining them.

" . . . Get 20,000 francs," says a married woman to

Thiboust, "and we shall fly the country."

"I would be delighted to get 20,000 francs," answers the vaudevillist. "Tell me where!"

You seem to think that ten lines from me will make this 8000 francs jump out of the tills.

I must first inform you that the matter of the Théâtre-Libre is outside my province, that we have Vitu at the *Figaro* for that.

Then I might add that the average man is not really much interested in your praiseworthy experiment. Théâtre-Libre or no, what's that to him? He will remain deaf to your problems, and he won't give you a sou.

If 7000 or 8000 francs can keep the Théâtre-Libre alive, Sarcey, Vitu, and the rest of the critics can find them more easily than I. It would be a matter of finding seventy or eighty persons among us—directors, prominent authors, critics, perhaps even a few journalists—who would each be willing to donate 100 francs. If such a movement were launched for the Théâtre-Libre, all would be well, but I can not and would not want to launch it, even if the time were favorable, which it is not. Everyone else has left Paris, and I am leaving to join them. So come and see me about the 15th of September, and we can speak more to the point.

Yours most sincerely,
Albert Wolff.

September 15! By that date I must already be under way, organized and ready to give the opening performance of the season!

AUGUST 15, 1887—I told Bergerat of my disappointment with Albert Wolff. "Imbecile!" he said. "If you had only asked me about this, I could have taken care of it. Why must you go address yourself to these pundits?" I could not tell this noble and devoted man that I would have been ashamed to impose on him when he has already done too much for us.

And sure enough, in his turn on the paper yesterday, he worked a witty and informative lead article into the *Figaro* headed "The

Little Odéon," in which he gave the public all the necessary information. With the support of so influential a journal, I feel my hopes reviving.

AUGUST 20, 1887—Bergerat's article brought me a letter from a marquis, giving me an appointment at his home on the Avenue Kléber. I went with my heart in my throat to see this man in his beautiful town-house, and after the most polite and infinitely flattering phrases, he offered me a comic opera of his own making, the music of which was by an amateur among his friends!

SEPTEMBER, 1887— Porel has kept his promise to Hennique. It was rather a noble gesture, for he must be irritated by the Théâtre-Libre; and the success of *Jacques Damour*,[12] after all, forced him to give a play which he had previously refused. Hennique invited me to the dress rehearsal and, as I feared, the play did not recapture the great emotion which it aroused at our theatre. They have made the mistake of giving the role of that poor devil, emaciated by hunger and grief, to Paul Mounet, a magnificent athlete; as a result, his pained resignation was unconvincing. Realism can only assert itself if from now on we follow a different interpretation from the current practice in the theatre—one of simplicity, naturalness, and restrained emotion.

SEPTEMBER 1, 1887—I can no longer imagine how Paz and I did it, but we are now set up at 96 Rue Blanche, in a large studio, with a private stairway at the back of the court-yard and a pleasant smoking-room. Moreover, we have all begun work there, two dozen subscribers have been signed up, the gas and rent have been paid, and Paz, who is positively wonderful, has talked an upholsterer into delivering some couches, three dozen chairs, and some curtains on credit. We have registered offices, and are the object of the ingenuous admiration of the authors and other young people who are already coming up regularly every evening to chat and to inquire about the beginning of rehearsals.

12Presented at the Odéon September 22.

I no longer have a cent or a home; for the time being, I will sleep on a small cot which is folded up during the day and passes for a property.

SEPTEMBER 5, 1887—Rodolphe Darzens, a poet who has become the fencing master and archivist of the Théâtre-Libre, has obtained from Villiers de l'Isle-Adam a one-act prose play, *The Escape,* which we are rehearsing with *Sister Philomène* each evening in the Rue Blanche.

Villiers, magnificently Bohemian with his long locks and strange eyes, under the pretext of instructing his actor, seizes any opportunity to play the convict who is the hero of his drama, and his portrayal is so gripping that, for the pleasure of the thing, I often let him go all the way to the end.

SEPTEMBER 6, 1887—This morning I had the pleasure of finding our program of 1887-1888 in the *Figaro,* next to that of all the other Parisian theatres, with a fine article by René de Cuers.

OCTOBER 2, 1887—I have been called up for a training period of twenty-eight days—a setback I hardly needed. I would certainly ask for a postponement if this meant leaving Paris, but since I am ordinarily able to serve my time near home and our rehearsals in the Rue Blanche can only be held in the evenings anyway, I will try to avoid giving inconvenience to anyone.

OCTOBER 3, 1887—Ancey tells me that after one of our first productions he, knowing that I was employed by the Gas Company, went to get my address from the door-keeper there. The latter answered: "Which Antoine? Ah, the one who turned out badly and went into the theatre? Here is his address."

OCTOBER 5, 1887—We are opening the season with 3700 francs in subscriptions, but the first two productions and the preparation of the location in the Rue Blanche have put me a thousand francs in debt. There is not enough to go much further; however, we are rehearsing *The Escape* and *Sister Philomène* feverishly, and after they are given, we shall see.

Baston, a friend from the *Cercle Gaulois* who has become my stage manager, is as enthusiastic as I am, and has taken upon himself the tasks of painting and carpentry as well as whatever else is needed. He is now making twelve hospital beds (required for the Goncourt play) from calico, for even if old Krauss rents us his auditorium and his pseudo-settings, we must still furnish whatever else we need in the way of furniture and properties.

OCTOBER 12, 1887—Yesterday we presented *Sister Philomène* as our first production of the season; the house was splendid and wildly enthusiastic. The evening was almost universally considered a great success, although a few critics found it rather gloomy as a whole and called for some cheerful plays. In the first scene, in the hospital, there was a "God!" which created a bit of a stir, but no one complained about it, since I ran it into the sentence without dwelling on it. M. de Goncourt was delighted to see his audacity so readily accepted.

OCTOBER 13, 1887—After the first act of *Sister Philomène,* M. de Goncourt appeared on stage to introduce me to a giant of a man, smiling and cordial, who bore a remarkable resemblance to Dumas *père*. It was Henry Bauer, the noted critic of the *Echo de Paris,* and I felt him to be much in sympathy with our ideas.

OCTOBER 15, 1887—Old Krauss has informed me that the members of the *Cercle Gaulois* are refusing to allow us to use their theatre any longer for our productions. They feel that these evenings seem likely to stir up too much controversy, which in turn will disturb their tranquillity. For his own part, old Krauss soberly confided that during the applause and wild enthusiasm of the spectators the other evening, he had been concerned over the strength of his little theatre. So, in short, the place I had counted on for the entire winter has been taken from me, and with the limited means at my disposal, this is a serious setback.

OCTOBER 16, 1887—Following our expulsion, we held a council yesterday evening in the Rue Blanche. I told Jean Jullien, Méténier, Hennique, and the others who were there that I would begin searching for a new home, but a silent irritation appeared on the faces around me, and a few even expressed their disturbance and anger at the prospect of seeing their plays delayed. I must stand fast and bring things off if I am to remain in charge. Mendès, who comes every evening, is the most buoyant, although the next play, *Tabarin's Wife,* is his. Gaily ready for all adventures, he demonstrates a trust and a confident friendship which both sustains me and inspires some of the same in the others.

OCTOBER 17, 1887—Mendès and I just went down to the far end of the Avenue de Clichy, near the Fourche-Saint-Ouen, to visit a sort of low-class concert hall which the people of the district call "The Spitting Doll," where, the great poet tells me, he would not at all mind seeing his play given.

But this evening, when we put this proposal before the members at the Rue Blanche, there were such disgusted looks on the faces of several that I promised them to try to find a better lodging for the Théâtre-Libre, if I can.

OCTOBER 18, 1887—Baston and I went to call on a director in the neighborhood—Pascal Delagarde, formerly an actor in this suburb, but now become director of the Théâtre Montmartre and the Théâtre des Bouffés-du-Nord.

We were received by this important colleague just as he had finished dining. His scorn was such that he did not even offer us a chair, and we were turned out crestfallen and humiliated into a narrow and dingy stairway after a waspish, scarcely civil refusal.

Then I thought of the Beaumarchais, near the Bastille, and we hurried over there. But standing before that death-like facade—for the theatre has long been closed—we decided to continue our rounds of Paris tomorrow, thinking vaguely of theatres on the left bank.

OCTOBER 19, 1887—This morning, with Baston, I resumed the

search for a theatre, and since my companion reminded me that the three houses on the left bank are under a single director, we went directly to the Rue de la Gaîté in Montparnasse, where, standing before a pleasant, recently constructed house, I resolved to make every effort to make myself welcome there. Any apprehensions I had about the remoteness of these outlying districts vanished before the hope of giving our presentations on a real stage with real settings.

The door-keeper took us to a bar across from the theatre where Hartmann, the director, was taking a glass with his stage-hands. We first had to join him at the bar for a drink, and I had not even finished explaining my proposal to this worthy man when he cried: "Why of course; I could ask for nothing better. I have heard of your venture. What you are attempting is very good, very diverting. Since I close every Thursday to change the program in my theatres anyway, my auditorium is then yours, on your own conditions."

The old theatre man, already glowing with enthusiasm, described beautiful settings in his warehouses which his melodramas never used, and spoke of a forest drop by Cicéri from the old imperial theatre of the castle of Saint-Cloud.

This was really a good morning's work. If we ever accomplish anything worthwhile, this worthy man will have had a great share in it, and we should never forget him.

I announced triumphantly this evening that from now on we are going to produce in Montparnasse. In vain I described the theatre— a real one, with stage, settings, and lighting—I met shrugs and averted eyes on all sides; in short, there was no enthusiasm at all. But I was not particularly upset by this, for I realized that now, thanks to Hartmann, we would have facilities for productions beyond the imagination of these authors. There were harsh recriminations, but I replied that those who were not happy could take their works elsewhere. Mendès, with his air of confidence, was the only one to lessen my inner distress at the frailty and lack of faith of almost all the others, so willing to desert.

Henry Fouquier came toward the end of the evening as usual, and in a bit of conversation with Mendès and myself, said to his colleague: "It is delightful to see such self-confidence, but an old Parisian like myself can guarantee you that you will never be able to bring audiences across the river for new plays." And this is certainly not reassuring.

OCTOBER 20, 1887—I jot down this description of the Elysée-des-Beaux-Arts, where we gave our first productions. It is from the fine article which Jules Lemaître wrote about us in the *Débats*:

> The address on the letter of invitation was 37, Passage de l'Elysée-des-Beaux-Arts, Place Pigalle. Thus, last Tuesday about 8:30 in the evening you may have seen dark shapes threading their way among the booths at the Montmartre fair, and winding hesitantly among the puddles of water on the pavement around the Place Pigalle, peering at the signs on the street-corners through their glasses— no such street, no such theatre. At last we passed the light of a wine merchant and went on up a steep, tortuous, dimly lighted street. A line of coaches slowly mounted, and we followed them. On either side were tumbledown hovels and dirty walls, at the far end a dim staircase. We looked like the three kings, in overcoats, in search of a hidden and glorious manger. Did we find the stable where that senile and doting old man, the drama, is to be reborn? I still don't know. What I do know is that we passed a most entertaining evening at the Théâtre-Libre.

> The auditorium is very small, rather amateurishly daubed with paint, and resembling the concert halls found in the chief towns of some districts. One could shake hands with the actors across the footlights, and stretch out one's legs over the prompter's box. The stage is so small that only the simplest scenery can be set up on it, and so near the audience that scenic illusion is impossible. If such illusion were born in us, it was because we created it ourselves, as the good spectators did in the time of Shakespeare, seeing what the writer asked them to see, or in the

time of Molière, when the illusion was not broken at all by the coming and going of the candle-snuffer.

The great critic concludes by saying that "the naturalness of these amateurs sets them apart from the playing of many professional actors."

OCTOBER 22, 1887—Villiers' terrible irony disturbs me; in his extraordinary stories, the old poet betrays a deep vein of bitter querulousness which is quite shocking. I often accompany him down the Rue Blanche in the evenings. He has little affection for his Parnassian friends—Coppée, Mendès, and the others—but I forgive him for this, knowing from Darzens the torments of his mysterious life, spent in heart-rending poverty.

We generally leave Pousset's, then linger a bit longer, in whatever small cafés remain open, over glasses of chartreuse. As we climb back up toward Montmartre—for he lives somewhere on the Butte, although no one knows just where—Villiers tells me of plans for short stories and plays, often stopping under the illumination of a gas light to act out the high points for me.

One evening, when I asked him about Rouvière, whom I had never seen, but of whom the Parnassians said astonishing things, he stopped in the street to give Hamlet's soliloquy for me with the intonations and facial expressions of the great departed actor, his long hair sweeping over his majestic features.

OCTOBER 27, 1887—I never know whether Villiers de l'Isle-Adam is serious or joking. Having been rather ill-treated by Sarcey concerning our production of his play, *The Escape,* Villiers has written a vigorous reply to the master of the *Temps,* with some amusing thrusts which deserve to be recorded:

> To tell the truth, I was hoping that M. Sarcey himself, upon re-reading his work today, would recognize the enormity of his error and rectify it. As a rule, I give him eight days for this. A word would suffice. Yet I have glanced over his latest column, and although he is still talking about the Théâtre-Libre, what I am waiting for is not

there. Yet I have evidence before me which proves that the noted critic does sometimes retract the slips and errors which escape him.

For example, here are three consecutive numbers of the paper the *Gaulois,* dated the 23, 24, and 25 of June, 1870. In the course of an article entitled "The Patricians," M. Francisque Sarcey (an ex-patrician himself, having often signed his name "Sarcey de Sutières," since he was born in that area about 1827) stated that someone should "in all sincerity" point out the errors of the Count de Nieuwerkerke, then featured at the Beaux-Arts. The Count sent two of his friends to call on M. Sarcey, who was nowhere to be found. Then spontaneously, and of his own accord, M. Sarcey published in the same paper, the very next day, an article entitled "An Error," declaring that his trust had been abused, that he had been badly mistaken, beating his breast, etc., the whole thing couched in a light tone of *errare humanum est* such as clever folk often employ when forced to change their tune. M. de Nieuwerkerke, however, was not satisfied, and sent two other friends, the generals Bourbaki and Douai, who found M. Sarcey at home. This visit led the very next day, June 25, to the following note being placed in the *Gaulois* and subsequently in all the other papers:

"I am truly distressed at having employed, in respect to M. the Count of Nieuwerkerke, expressions at variance with the esteem in which I hold him. Among the many opinions which I have expressed, there were a number which should not have been expressed at all, for one should not attack others (ah, how true that is), at least not heedlessly and without having coldly weighed the possible consequences of such an act, 'considering that the man might have friends in high places who are our friends as well.'

(signed) Francisque Sarcey."

• 49

The "quibbling and highly mannered" style used here might lead one to assume that the note was motivated solely by some sort of distress, or even panic. No, such an assumption would be mistaken. I ought to and want to believe that M. Sarcey was sincere, as he was on the preceding day. In one or two previous encounters, he conducted himself in a quite proper fashion. If his imposing presence makes him a little weak at swordplay, still he knows how to handle a pistol. Indeed, I have heard it said that, having received a hole in his hat during a duel with the latter weapon, the great critic paraded slowly and solemnly all over Paris for almost six months, in the most bourgeois manner, this glorious hat upon his head—a caprice which he finally had to give up, doubtless because of the head-colds which this perpetual current of air maintained in his skull. His steadfastness cannot therefore be questioned in the Nieuwerkerke affair.

OCTOBER 31, 1887—The dedication of the published version of *Tabarin's Wife*:

Monsieur,

The stage where you and your young companions present plays is both the consolation of old romantics and the hope of young naturalists. You seek out and welcome the new, the unusual, the daring. That which "is not suited for the stage" appears on your stage, and is applauded. In several evenings you have done more for dramatic art than many other directors have done in several years; the renaissance of true drama, true comedy, and farce may well be dated from the inauguration of your free stage. You have made only one mistake—that of asking me for *Tabarin's Wife*. I am afraid that the brutal brusqueness of the ludicrous, yet tragic scenario can only strain the indulgence of both critics and public. Yet such as it is, and however it may be received, allow me to dedicate this play to you as a witness of my enthusiastic approval.

October 31, 1887.   Catulle Mendès.

NOVEMBER 2, 1887—I dined this evening with Théodore de Banville in his home in the Rue de l'Eperon. He introduced me to Jean Richepin—my first meeting with him—and to his son-in-law, the painter Georges Rochegrosse, with whom I spoke about costumes for *The Kiss*. Paul Vidal, a young musician, has written a delightfully fluid score for Banville's play, and he performed it for us on the piano. I was worried about who could play the music, but he reassured me, saying that his fellow students in the Crosti class at the Conservatory will come to interpret the little score. As for the solo, Mlle. Bréval, a young student of one of Vidal's friends, has an admirable voice which she would be delighted to place at our disposal.

NOVEMBER 4, 1887—Méténier tells me that he has obtained a promise from Mlle. Marie Laurent to come to play Matriona for us in *The Power of Darkness*. I find this difficult to believe, however, for I am only too aware that the professional actors bear little affection for us, either because they pity our inexperience, or because they are actually disturbed by the interest the Théâtre-Libre has stimulated.[13]

*   *   *

NOVEMBER 12, 1887—This evening after the rehearsal of *Tabarin's Wife* we supped at Lavenue's. A success seems assured and the evening was quite merry. Mendès, the most stimulating of companions, was dazzling, and led us to drink so much that almost everyone became tipsy—even Rosny, who became obsessed with the idea of obtaining the measurements of the skulls of all present so that he could classify them anthropologically.

---

[13]Mlle. Barny eventually played this part.

NOVEMBER 13, 1887—We gave our first production at Montparnasse —a success, despite a few annoying incidents. Hennique's fine *Esther Brandès,* a powerful and restrained study, was greeted with distrust, but *Tabarin's Wife,* by Mendès, was emphatically supported by a large contingent of poets, which saved the evening.

NOVEMBER 14, 1887—A complication has arisen which threatens to undo everything we have accomplished. Emile Paz, untrained in the duties of house manager, was in charge of welcoming our guests. It being his first time in this position and in this theatre, he was caught off guard by the flood of arrivals, and he had the doors closed to give himself time to get organized. The people arriving from downtown then ran afoul of the local police, who, being accustomed to the unruly crowds of this area, made absolutely no distinctions, and all sorts of incidents were the result. People like Meilhac were roughed up, and the irritated public swamped the box office. A fine way to treat all these fashionable society people after they climbed all the way up here to give proof of their good wishes! The next day, all the reviewers protested, and some, like Gramont of the *Intransigeant,* requested us in the future to keep our invitations to ourselves!

NOVEMBER 15, 1887—Last evening I dined for the first time at Alphonse Daudet's home in the Rue de Bellechasse, with all the young literary figures of the hour.[14] I was horribly embarrassed at finding the small salon already filled with people when I arrived. I bumped into all the chairs in crossing the room, and my voice broke as I spoke to Mme. Daudet.

---

[14]According to Goncourt, Antoine first dined at Daudet's on April 6, 1888. Antoine's expressed future plans at that date are worth repeating:

He wants two more full years devoted to presentations like those he is presently giving, two years in which he will learn the fundamentals of his trade and the elements of theatre direction. After this, he hopes to gain a subsidized theatre from the government; then, with 600 subscribers or a revenue of 60,000 francs, and with a capital of a hundred thousand francs, a house free from rental, and a group of actors discovered by him and reasonably paid, he plans to become the director of a theatre where one hundred and twenty plays a year would be given. They would pour out onto these boards anything slightly dramatic found in the portfolios of the young. For, whatever might be the success of a play, his idea is that it would be given only fifteen days, at the end of which time, the author would be free to take it to another theatre.

Although the master, much amused at my timidity, politely put me at ease, I spent the dinner listening to the others. Goncourt and Daudet did most of the talking, only occasionally aided by the elder Rosny. The others remained silent out of respect, never opening their lips except when challenged by Daudet, who was very adept at leading the conversation. I was seated near a young man with whom I slipped away as soon as possible, and we walked back down the streets toward home together, after stopping in a bar across from the Gare de Sceaux.

He is Lucien Descaves, an employee in the civil service, whose first works have just begun to come out, and who has promised me something for the Théâtre-Libre. A small man whose rather grumpy features are offset by his sparkling eyes, he manifested a straight-forwardness and stability which drew me toward him at once.

NOVEMBER 20, 1887—Jean Jullien is a bit older than most of us. A large and hefty fellow, he already has the graying beard of the elderly student; and despite his ironic smile, he is rather timid. He has traveled a good deal in the Algerian Sahara. I sometimes go to dine with him at the famous Laveur pension in the Latin Quarter, where nothing has changed since the time when Gambetta, Floquet, and most of the rest of our present parliamentarians had recourse to the legendary credit of the house. Any student from a respectable family can live on credit at the Laveur pension and pay for it when his studies are finished and he has found a position. The place is teeming with young men, and visitors are shown the tables of famous men who lived there, many of whom have carved their names in the wood with the point of a knife.

NOVEMBER 21, 1887—We already have enemies, and I cannot imagine why. They dwell on the minor incidents at the box office before our last performance, and on the remoteness of our theatre. A few of them, who seem sincere, even advise us to return to Montmartre. This is easy to say, but it was hardly for our own convenience that we moved all the way out here.

NOVEMBER 26, 1887—Our enlarged programs are going to make it necessary for us to find a rather large number of actors. Henry Céard—who has adapted *Captain Burle,* a novel by Zola, for the stage—introduced me to Henry Mayer, a young actor from the Vaudeville, whose experience will be a valuable contribution. Jean Jullien immediately requested Mayer for his play, *The Serenade,* which we are going to give. This Mayer is a pleasant and intelligent fellow who was growing stale appearing in curtain-raisers at the Vaudeville, and who is impatient to prove himself.

DECEMBER 5, 1887—Céard has managed to obtain authorization from Claretie for Mlle. Emilie Lerou of the Comédie-Française to come to our theatre to play a leading part in *All for Honor,* if she wishes to do so. This of course rather wrung the heart of my old friend Barny, who has a good deal of talent, but I explained to her that our Théâtre-Libre is growing rapidly, and we must strengthen our forces if we are to cope with so many different plays.

DECEMBER 9, 1887—Good news! I have been asked to go to the Théâtre du Parc in Brussels next January to give several performances. Moreover, another Belgian director, at the Théâtre Molière, has just engaged Sylviac to give *Sister Philomène* there.

DECEMBER 10, 1887—Emile Paz having submitted his resignation to me, Montégut, a nephew of Alphonse Daudet and a reporter for the *Intransigeant,* has volunteered to replace him as secretary. His many friends among the critics should help calm the situation.

DECEMBER 12, 1887—We are now rehearsing Jean Jullien's curious first play, *The Serenade,* every evening in the Rue Blanche. It was clear to me that we needed to present an exceptional program to smooth over the incidents of last month, so I have advanced the date of Banville's play, *The Kiss.* His name and Zola's will insure interest in our program.

DECEMBER 19, 1887—I gave a small part in *The Serenade* to a young actor named Gémier, who came to me from the Bouffés-du-Nord. But Jean Jullien, who was unwilling to accept the newcomer, and distrustful of his thin frame, waited until I was absent (detained by a distant rehearsal of *The Kiss*), and told Gémier he was dismissed. I was extremely annoyed, since it seemed to me that Gémier had something, and I have no idea where I can find him again.

DECEMBER 20, 1887—Honors already! I have been informed that I will be decorated by the Ministry of Public Instruction on January 1. Alas! I would much prefer a little money, for I feel myself embarked on a frightening adventure which will take me heaven knows where. Yet, ironically, this is the one thing of which I cannot speak, without destroying the indispensable confidence and security of all my colleagues.

DECEMBER 22, 1887—Although the weather was beastly this morning, Banville was kind enough to come all the way up to Montparnasse to see a rehearsal of his *The Kiss*. The theatre was very drafty, and I was deathly afraid that the old poet would catch cold, but he was so engrossed in watching the play that he seemed quite unaware of the weather. I had him sheltered by folding screens, and he listened to us with a most affecting politeness. It pleased me to feel that he departed satisfied with us.

DECEMBER 23, 1887—I thought as much. The attraction of the two great names of Zola and Banville on our program quite overcame the small grudges left from last month. Moreover, Montégut worked hard, and carefully organized the ushers and the box-office. The theatre was filled to bursting last night. Jean Jullien's *The Serenade,* written with the novelty and daring of an unusual comic form, stimulated both astonishment and genuine interest. Yet Banville's play was the real triumph, approved and applauded almost line by line. When the curtain descended, the house gave a long ovation to the author, who was in one of the boxes. This great success was a marvelous preparation for the tragic effect of *All for Honor,* which was considerable. We could not have hoped for a better evening.

DECEMBER 25, 1887—All the papers call Banville's play a masterpiece, and insist that it be accepted by the Comédie-Française. Jean Jullien's play clearly caused a sensation; his comedy of middle-class life is said to herald a new and original talent.

The other evening, I was standing on the little stage in Montparnasse after the acclamations for *The Kiss,* and overheard Banville say to Zola: "They act like angels; where the devil did they learn to speak verse?" to which Zola replied: "Here, I believe, are the actors we have needed for a long time."

DECEMBER 29, 1887—Everyone is agreed. *The Kiss* must go to the Comédie-Française, and Henry Fouquier began today's column in the *Gil Blas* with these words: "The Théâtre-Libre is all the rage; what a long way it has come since the first months of this year!"

DECEMBER 31, 1887—Henry Bauer devoted a fine article to us this morning, but seemed somewhat desirous of interfering in our affairs. He is disturbed over my choice of Méténier as adapter of *The Power of Darkness.*[15] I am determined, however, not to tolerate any interference in the theatre; so many varied talents and temperaments are now involved with it that we must remain an independent field of battle, or we will quickly degenerate into a coterie or clique.

---

[15]Although Antoine singles out Bauer, many critics of the time feared that Méténier, a specialist in Parisian *argot,* would make the opposite mistake from Halpérine, the previous translator, whose work was condemned for being too literal.

JANUARY-JUNE, 1888

JANUARY 8, 1888—I lunched at Séverine's home in the Boulevard Montmartre, across from the Variétés, in a dining room decorated in a rather theatrically rustic manner. Alexis and Labruyère were there, and an artist from the *Cri du Peuple,* Eugène Rapp. The latter seemed quite unwell, but Séverine watched over him with a maternal solicitude.

Séverine has been Vallès' secretary, and she spoke of him often, with a faithfulness and enthusiasm which endeared her even more to me. I was greatly encouraged by my visit, and felt in her home a warm and intelligent sympathy which I needed very much.

JANUARY 12, 1888—Here I am in Brussels. To tell the truth, it was only at the insistence of Mendès—who arranged the matter with Candeilh, the director of the Parc—that I decided to come for a week and present *The Kiss, Tabarin's Wife,* and *Jacques Damour.* Marie Defresne has come for *Tabarin* and the troupe of the Parc is furnishing the other actors. We enjoyed great success last night; the director, an old trouper who is a little suspicious of all these new ideas, was none the less impressed by the receipts. I was worried about my debut before the general public, particularly because of my rather weak voice and my complete lack of professional training. Yet everything went very well; indeed, the three short plays—with Tabarin, Pierrot, and the tattered commoner—were so sharply drawn that they easily and inevitably gained their effect.

JANUARY 14, 1888—Mendès, as well-known in Brussels as in Paris, introduced me into artistic circles, where I found a passionate interest in the Théâtre-Libre. Kistemaeckers, whose home is a center for the upcoming young Belgians, greeted me with the same enthusiasm he showed in welcoming the naturalists and in launching the first works of Huysmans, Descaves, Paul Adam, and so many others. Equally interesting was a visit with Edmond Picard, a noted lawyer with considerable influence, who received Mendès and myself most cordially in his sumptuous home on the Avenue de la Toison-d'or. Although these two groups were formerly hostile, they seem to have agreed to support the efforts of the Théâtre-Libre in Belgium, and both gave us important help. Candeilh, who found us very profitable, has already asked for additional productions. I am dazzled by this success. In a single evening I gained the earnings of a month's work at the Gas Company.

JANUARY 15, 1888—"Sir, you probably do not know me," a visitor said to me yesterday in the Rue Blanche, "for, after having made my debut with great success at a very early age, I was childish enough not to follow it up, and so I have been completely forgotten. I have just spent ten years in complete idleness, and the desire has re-awakened in me to go back to work."

It was M. de Porto-Riche, the author of *The Drama under Philip II* which, as a matter of fact, I had applauded at the Odéon somewhere around 1876 in the enthusiasm of my first romantic ardor. My companion went on to say that he had matured, and that while his first play was steeped in Parnassian influence, he sees things differently today—that the insights brought by the Théâtre-Libre have been decisive for many of his generation. He then offered me a short prose play which he would be happy to see us accept.

This Porto-Riche has most attractive features, an engaging voice, and the profile of an Italian of the Renaissance.

I read *Françoise's Luck* that same day, and while I found it engaging, I must admit that I was not swept off my feet. It seems to me that the other works I am presently considering have more that is genuinely new in them, and that this is more suggestive of the Dumas of *The Wedding Visit* than of Becque. Yet there is a sensitivity, a vibration, a warmth in the little play by this newcomer which the writers of the romantic theatre of the previous generation never had.

JANUARY 16, 1888—Our rehearsal room in the Rue Blanche has created a lot of curiosity, and we would be quickly over-run if I had not decided, from the very beginning, that only the authors and actors of the house should have access to it. Thanks to this precaution the spot remains intimate; only our own circle is ever found there. The large room in the rear is devoted to the work of rehearsals, which friends of the upcoming authors can watch provided they maintain a strict silence. Near the entrance we have a room for chatting, gossiping, and smoking. Many come now almost every evening, and it is truly moving to see the atmosphere of cordiality and co-operation in which all these young people pool their ambitions and hopes.

The foreign papers are becoming interested in us. I have received clippings from a few English papers.

*　　*　　*

JANUARY 30, 1888—We get no respite; the competitor of the Parc at Brussels, Alhaiza, director of the Molière, is organizing some literary matinées, and has asked me to go over there to give *All for Honor*. It is a great strain, but we need the money badly. Despite all the stir, subscriptions are slow in coming; moreover, we are well into the season and cannot hope for many new subscriptions before next year.

FEBRUARY 1, 1888—A declaration signed by Rosny, Lavedan, Descaves, Paul Margueritte, and Guiches has appeared on the first page of the *Figaro*.[16] It is a resounding abjuration of naturalism and is causing a devil of a row. Although these signers are my friends, I feel rather disheartened by this apostasy which pits them publicly against their master. I fear that this is only one incident in the silent battle two of the marshals have waged for several months

---

[16]Lavedan was not one of the signers of this famous manifesto, although he joined the rebels later (*vide* February 15 and March 27, 1888). The fifth signer was Bonnetain. The manifesto accused Zola of being "incredibly lazy" in his experimentation, and blamed the obscenity of *Earth* on Zola's physical and mental state. Antoine puts this manifesto far too late; it appeared in the *Figaro* on August 18, 1887.

over their great friend. Alas! Even the best minds are afflicted by these weaknesses of vanity—but should they not, for the sake of their disciples, keep them hidden? Especially here, when nothing in temperament or talent could logically gather together the signers of this paper.

Descaves began as a fanatic realist, and remained one despite the influence of his friend Huysmans. He has nothing in common with the stylish Lavedan, whose reactionary and clerical spirit is in turn completely opposed to the restrained and powerful vision of Rosny. As for Paul Margueritte, his quiet and sensitive nature has understandably suffered from the rather brutal surroundings he has been in for several years, but I can't understand at all why Gustave Guiches should be included—probably just to swell the ranks, for I don't think Zola ever even admitted him to his circle.

FEBRUARY 4, 1888—*The Power of Darkness* is really a large undertaking. Still, I have been able to put together a fairly satisfactory cast: Mévisto will be reliable as Nikita, and Méténier finally talked me into casting his brother, who has never acted, as Mitricht. I can rely on Barny, Luce Colas, and Lucienne Dorsy, all of whom have already proven themselves in our earlier productions. Thanks to Pavlovski, who put us in touch with political refugees living on the left bank, we have at our disposal a marvelous lot of authentic costumes. The warehouse of old Hartmann has furnished us with some very fine items for our settings, and we will have real Russian objects for properties.

FEBRUARY 5, 1888—Outsiders are often both fascinated and incredulous upon hearing that our troupe is almost entirely composed of simple amateurs, who carry on regular jobs during the day. Cernay, who plays Piotr, sells canes; Pinsard is an architect, and, as a matter of fact, a rather popular one; Tinbot works at Firmin Didot's establishment; Mlle. Barny is a seamstress; the young actress who plays Marina works at the telegraph office. Among the others, there is a wine merchant and the head book-keeper at a bank. In fact, the only real professionals in our troupe are Henry Mayer and

Mévisto, who sings the *Paulus* at the *café-concert,* and whom I have brought back to play in Méténier's *In the Family.*

FEBRUARY 6, 1888—The appearance of *The Power of Darkness* at our theatre is stimulating intense curiosity, and an interesting survey about it has come out in the recent papers.[17] The great dramatists have been asked for their opinion of the play, and here are some of their answers:

> . . . . From the point of view of our French stage, I do not believe that M. Tolstoi's play is possible. It is too melancholy, not one of its characters is sympathetic, and the language spoken, by Akim for example, would be quite incomprehensible to a French audience. Nikita, so straight-forward, yet so strange, would seem merely irritating at first, and eventually quite odious . . . .
>
> (Letter from M. Alexandre Dumas *fils.*)

> . . . . It has a cruel truthfulness and a real beauty; but it is written to be read and not to be seen and, to my mind, is unpresentable. Whatever one might do to make it suitable for the stage would only spoil it without gaining any benefit . . . .
>
> (Letter from M. Victorien Sardou.)

> . . . . It is less a play than a novel in dialogue form; its length alone makes it impossible for a French stage . . . .
>
> (Letter from M. Emile Augier.)

SUNDAY, FEBRUARY 12, 1888—The presentation of *The Power of Darkness* was a triumph; Tolstoi's play was universally hailed as a

---

17Antoine's arrangement of material is somewhat confusing here. The implication is that the authors quoted are predicting the failure of his own production. Actually, the quotes are concerned with the authors' reactions to the earlier translation by Halpérine, which Zola and Antoine himself also considered unstageworthy. Thus the quotes, which seem to be directed against Antoine, are actually in agreement with him.

masterpiece. We had the best and most influential critics imaginable; M. de Vogüé, bursting with enthusiasm, came to find me to say that he was going to have an article on us in the *Revue des Deux Mondes.* The reverberations have been so great that I have been asked to give a public presentation. These receipts will certainly be most welcome, for I no longer have a cent, and I scarcely know how we will be able to give the next production.

FEBRUARY 13, 1888—Requests are coming from all sides for a performance of *The Power of Darkness,* and the management of the Vaudeville has offered me the Chaussée d'Antin room for it. The translators were half inclined to accept, but I pointed out how ungrateful it would be to desert the theatre which Hartmann so generously put at our disposal. We will therefore remain in Montparnasse.

FEBRUARY 15, 1888—Our next evening will be composed entirely of works from the pens of the authors of the famous Manifesto of the Five concerning *Earth.* Bonnetain and Descaves will present a three-act play, *The Wad.* Paul Margueritte will appear in person in a pantomime, the music of which was composed by Paul Vidal, the author of the delightful score which accompanied *The Kiss.* The fourth of the rebels, Henri Lavedan, has co-authored with Gustave Guiches a play in two scenes, *Quarter Hours,* which will end the evening. It was Zola himself who first encouraged me to devote a whole program to his five adversaries, and the whole literary world is waiting with great curiosity to judge the work of the dissidents.

THURSDAY, FEBRUARY 16, 1888—The public sale for *The Power of Darkness* at Montparnasse is going marvelously, but alas, an incredible amount of snow fell during the morning. Our suburban theatre is so remote that I am much afraid that this will mean the failure of our venture.

SATURDAY, FEBRUARY 18, 1888—Astounding! Despite sixty centimeters of snow, the theatre at Montparnasse was filled to overflowing yesterday, and we made more than 4,000 francs. The next production is therefore assured.

FEBRUARY 20, 1888—As I arrived at Pousset's this evening, Marie Aubry, one of our number, introduced me to a friend of hers whom, she said, wanted very much to have me read a play. He was a stylish but timid young man for whom I immediately felt a great sympathy, as did Ancey, who was also there. I learned that he is the nephew of our confirmed enemy Albert Wolff. I saw at once the irony of this young man coming to enroll himself among those whom his uncle is treating so roughly in his column in the *Figaro,* and it would make me very happy to return good for the old journalist's evil by launching his nephew's career in this same despised Théâtre-Libre.

MARCH 8, 1888—*The Power of Darkness* has created such a stir that Francis Magnard has asked me to come and present the highly controversial bench scene in an entertainment at the *Figaro.* I agreed, happy to be able to show my gratitude to an organization which has supported our efforts so strongly from the very beginning.

MARCH 10, 1888—Darzens, who has become the archivist of the Théâtre-Libre, is also our fencing-master; he has asked my permission to hang foils on the walls of our large room in the Rue Blanche, and on certain days there are furious bouts between him and the frequenters of the house.

MARCH 15, 1888—Good old Hartmann, who gave me such an unselfish welcome to Montparnasse, has an enthusiastic interest in the productions of the Théâtre-Libre. It is touching to see this old producer of melodramas regain the enthusiasm of his youth over our attempts at a new theatre. He has even tried to present *Sister Philomène* with his own troupe to the common folk of the suburb.

Yesterday evening he informed me that the sudden illness of his young lead was going to force him to shut down at Grenelle until Thursday, the date of his next production. Only too glad to take this occasion to show my gratitude for his good offices, I immediately offered to go and play Barnier, a part I still know.

I told Mendès about it at dinner, and he went down there with me. I was very impressed by a young man who shared the stage with me; his convincing warmth and the beauty of his voice seemed strangely out of place in these surroundings. After the curtain fell, I spoke to him at length. He was from a good family, he said, and when he failed the examination at the Conservatory, his love of acting had kept him for many months in Hartmann's theatres.

I told this young man, whose name was Grand, that he had very good qualities, that he did not have to remain there, and that I would be happy to see him at the Théâtre-Libre, where he would be given the opportunity to show himself to the critics.

Then, as soon as the play was over, I ran to the *Figaro,* where we were giving a scene from *The Power of Darkness* that same evening.

In the *Revue des Deux Mondes,* M. Melchior de Vogüé, speaking of the presentation of *The Power of Darkness,* says:

> It was Austerlitz. When the curtain came down in a tempest of applause on the final scene, the audience was enraptured. I never noticed an instant of relaxation or inattention during the whole four hours.
>
> Every time I question the intelligence of our French youth, or their speed in comprehending works alien to our taste, I am completely fooled.
>
> For the first time a setting and costumes truly borrowed from the daily customs of Russian life appeared on the French stage without comic opera embellishments and without that predilection for tinsel and falsity which seems inherent in our theatrical atmosphere.

MARCH 27, 1888—Taken as a whole, the reviews of the works of the Five were cool, possibly because public opinion has never really forgiven them for their aggressive manifesto, but more particularly because there was a new tone about this production, and this made the audience uneasy. Yet, the Five do not seem to have given up the battle, for in the course of the discussion re-animated by our production, they got together again to address the following letter to the papers. I don't like it, since nothing could diminish my admiration for Zola, and I have never cared much for useless and painful gestures.

To the Editor:

M. Emile Zola has spoken of our four names on the announcements of the Théâtre-Libre with flippant and bitter comments as unworthy of his great talent as they are of his high position in the literary world. He classifies us all as a new movement against naturalism, of which he is and will remain the high priest.

Yet our statements in the papers were quite specific. We said before, and we say again, that our three works are all different, the results of individual experiments, and that their simultaneous appearance implies neither a previous understanding nor a common theory. The absence of the fifth protesting artist, our friend Rosny, and the addition of a new name, that of M. Henri Lavedan, should suffice to prove this.

M. Emile Zola is also mistaken in speaking of a new art which we, laughably, are claiming to bring to the theatre. The theatre is not even mentioned in our "Manifesto," and even if it were we would not attack M. Zola the novelist. We know too well what tacit sympathy is owed to the author of *Bouton de Rose* and *Renée*.

> Paul Bonnetain, Lucien Descaves,
> Paul Margueritte, and Gustave Guiches.

MARCH 28, 1888—The program by the Five did not go badly at all; the authors showed talent, even though the literary public obviously did not approve of their demonstration against the master of Médan. *The Wad,* a domestic tragedy by Paul Bonnetain and Lucien Descaves, had a gripping roughness which was very effective.

Paul Margueritte's pantomime was quite original. He has made a specialty of Pierrot, and consented to a public appearance on the condition that I support him as the mute. *Quarter Hours,* two short acts by Henri Lavedan and Gustave Guiches, were quite effective in their cruel and incisive irony. Several critics challenged the dramatic character of these two scenes, calling them "slices of life."

We left the theatre for a merry supper in Paul Bonnetain's garret in the Rue Ballu, a place quite littered with beautiful things he brought back from Tongking.

Sarcey is very harsh in his column. He says that the two plays by Henri Lavedan and Gustave Guiches are simple, if gloomy, hoaxes.

MARCH 30, 1888—Zola was interviewed about the production of the works of the Five. Full of good sense and reason as always, he said he attended the production and found the experiment interesting. He personally felt, however, that it had not revealed the new theatre form which he had expected from the Five after their recent outburst.

APRIL 7, 1888—This evening the Porte-Saint-Martin gave a fine new play by Georges Ohnet.[18] What theatre!

APRIL 12, 1888—Willette has just founded a small illustrated journal, the *Pierrot,* and invited us to a party which he gave in a sort of lounge on the Rue Rochechouart. The room could have served as a skating rink or a swimming pool, and was certainly too large for the few dozen persons who were there. Everyone present came from Montmartre; and sympathetic groups huddled together to eat and drink, and, I must say, they drank a good deal.

I would not have even made a note of this rather Bohemian night of gaiety except for the extraordinary sight produced by the dawn coming through the windowed roof—pale and exhausted people, all in Pierrot costumes, the most glorious symphony in white imaginable.

---

[18]The play was Ohnet's *The Great Marl-pit,* and had a very successful run of 100 performances.

APRIL 22, 1888—Daudet gave a party to treat his guests to Paul Margueritte's original and personal talent in pantomime; and in order to please Bonnetain, another faithful friend, Daudet asked me and several others to give a short play of his, *After the Divorce.* Bonnetain's piece was rather insignificant, and in the crowded drawing-room on a shallow stage, we were not very successful. Margueritte, on the other hand, with his face floured, mimed the anguishes of *Pierrot, Assassin of His Wife* with a power which was truly the envy of professionals.

APRIL 24, 1888—Albert Wolff attacked Zola in the *Figaro* again this morning, challenging him to produce a play for the Théâtre-Libre by next winter. The journalist added that if he can not, nothing will remain but the drawing up of a report of failure for the prodigious novelist who, after boasting that he would divide all dramatists into opposing camps, remained at home playing bezique with William Busnach when the time came to act.

APRIL 20,[19] 1888—Our next to last production of the season didn't amount to much. *The Bread of Sin,* a three-act play in verse by Paul Arène based on a Provençal poem by Aubanel opened the evening,[20] and although this was greeted with enthusiasm by the Southerners, the evening ended badly with a poorly executed play by Emile Moreau. This was a three-act verse drama which Bauer had commended highly. I am troubled by this failure, not only because it comes at the end of the season, but also because it leaves me without a cent for the final production.

MAY 1, 1888—*Germinal,* adapted by Busnach from Zola's great novel, was an irritating fiasco at the Châtelet, and its failure will hurt all of us.[21] Why on earth was a vaudevillist allowed to tamper with this masterpiece? I was especially put out to find that Zola was

[19]A typographical error in the original. *The Bread of Sin* was presented April 27, so this date should presumably be April 28.
[20]Arène's play was actually based not on a poem but on another play, *Lou Pan dou Pecat,* given in Provençal at Montpellier May 28, 1878, and published in 1882.
[21]*Germinal* opened April 21, closed after 17 performances.

really much more interested in the play than he would admit, and one evening, when I heard him speaking about it rather passionately, I reproached him for delivering his work into such hands. He answered that even this was better than nothing, and that stage adaptations of realistic works were slowly but surely educating the general public. He may be right after all.

MAY 7, 1888—Le Corbeiller, a very genial fellow who is a writer on the *Débats* and a good friend of Ancey, has come on behalf of Mme. Aubernon de Nerville to ask me to appear in Becque's *The Woman of Paris* at one of her spring receptions. These are major events in Paris, and the proposal rather frightens me. I would be uneasy in such surroundings, and can hardly see myself appearing with a famous actress like Réjane. But it is clear that Le Corbeiller thinks he can help me out by pushing the Thèâtre-Libre in high society, and he insisted so strongly that I accepted. Becque has been advised of these plans and is apparently perfectly satisfied and even quite pleased that I have been chosen.

MAY 10, 1888—Yesterday evening at five we had our first meeting at Mme. Aubernon de Nerville's home in the Rue d'Astorg. She is a fine woman, quite plump, and very proud of her salon in which Becque is the great man at the moment. She welcomed me warmly and introduced me to Réjane, who immediately and with great charm accepted me as a comrade. The two other parts will be played by young society people, both well known in private theatres. We agreed to begin work immediately and I departed, somewhat reassured by Réjane's amiability.

MAY 14, 1888—We are rehearsing *The Woman of Paris* in the Rue Blanche before Becque, who is entertained by these performances and enchanted by Réjane's verve and spirit.

He arrives promptly for every rehearsal, and sometimes finds himself at cross-purposes with his actress. Réjane, like all truly individualistic artists, is apt to say "I would not do this myself," or "Personally, I would not say that." In the embarrassed silence which follows, Becque has a charming way of taking her about the waist and waltzing around the room with her—a gesture which settles the difficulty in laughter and youthful good humor.

Despite my shyness, I could not resist going to the Comédie-Française this evening for the premiere of *The Kiss*. This little masterpiece by the author of *Gringoire* was so brilliantly successful at the Théâtre-Libre that one could scarcely hope for it to do better at the Comédie, even with two interpretors of the first rank. In any case, it is a great achievement for us to have successfully stormed the doors of France's first theatre—doors closed until now even to Banville.

I am paying for it dearly, however. After the enormous success of the play at our theatre, I received many offers for presentations this winter in Parisian salons. My companions and I could surely have sold ten thousand francs worth of tickets, and this decision by Claretie forced Banville to ask me to give all this up. Naturally, I did so with the greatest of pleasure, but all the same, the money would have been a great help to me, for even at this late date I am still looking for some way to finance our final production.

Jean Richepin's *The Privateer* was an unqualified triumph. His verses caught the spirit of the land of Brittany and the great winds of the sea, and Got delivered them magnificently.

The evening ended a bit less brilliantly — not for Banville himself, for his play retained all its freshness and grotesque charm — but for the actors, who were neither as spontaneous nor as spirited as those at the Théâtre-Libre. The casting of a comic actor like Coquelin junior as Pierrot seemed a mistake to me. Banville's character is first of all a naive and ingenious being, with never a thought of being amusing, but Coquelin, with his consummate skill, sought his effects with the simperings of a pastry-cook. The antics were delightful, of course, but it seems to me that they should have been played down.

MAY 15, 1888—Banville has published *The Kiss* with this lovely dedication, which he sent me:

> I wrote this comedy when I was alone with my dear wife on the banks of the little river Abron. It is a country of fairies, and every day I was in it I read, as I had done before, Victor Hugo's *la Forêt mouillée*. The Kiss was performed once on December 23, 1887, by the artists of the Théâtre-Libre. Mlle. Deneuilly made a graceful and poetic fairy, and the excellent actor Antoine played the young Pierrot with a sure touch and an inspired and romantic imagination. Then at the instigation of my good friend Jules Claretie, the Comédie-Française took its good where it found it, with a disinterested munificence. It gave *The Kiss* for the first time May 14, 1888. Molière's great family gave me as interpreters Mlle. Reichenberg, whose name has become almost proverbially associated with perfection and who deserves an even more sublime word, and Coquelin junior, who possesses a tremendous comic and lyric spirit. In all, I had the pleasure of satisfying my critics after having faithfully obeyed my muse.
>
> Théodore de Banville.

MAY 16, 1888—Besides rehearsing *The Woman of Paris* in the afternoons in the Rue Blanche, I have been going over to Réjane's home in the Rue Brémontier two or three mornings a week to work over the big scenes with her. She is extremely sensitive, and immediately felt my sense of inexperience and my discomfort at rehearsing in the Rue Blanche under Becque's penetrating eye (a situation which truly paralyzes me). She therefore utilizes these sessions to increase my confidence in a thousand clever, tactful ways. She is just now at the peak of her reputation, and is currently appearing in *Decorated* at the Variétés.[22] She really has an admirable actress' disposition, as I see in working with her. We chat a good deal and our friend-

---

[22]Meilhac's *Decorated* had opened January 27 and was an enormous success. It was given 135 times in 1888.

ship increases daily. My self-confidence is increasing as a result, a development which is very good for me.

MAY 17, 1888—This afternoon Porto-Riche came to a rehearsal of *The Woman of Paris* in the Rue Blanche. I expressed surprise when he did not even nod to Becque, so he drew me aside while Becque was chatting with Réjane at the other end of the room and said: "Then introduce me to him." Rather astonished, I naively led him to the other, whose face stiffened a bit as he sharply responded: "At last, my dear friend. Yet I cannot spend my life making up with you."

MAY 18, 1888—This morning when I arrived at Réjane's home in the Rue Brémontier, she told me that Porel had just come to ask her to go to the Odéon to play Goncourt's *Germinie Lacerteux*. She is undecided and a little wary, fearing that her stylish, Parisian public would not really understand her in the role of an old nurse. I too was a little astonished by Porel's strange idea, for Réjane is not really old enough for the part, and Germinie seems to me a large, bony, mature woman, who is quite unlike this scintillating Parisienne. Yet I did everything I could to convince her to accept; she has so much talent that she would surely succeed, and the appearance of such an interpreter in a naturalistic play would be a trump for my friend Goncourt which would delight me. I even became a bit sharp with Réjane, reproaching her with loving only the artificial in the theatre and trying to make her see all this as an escape into the living and human art of the future.

May 26, 1888—Mendès, who is familiar with my financial embarrassment, being the only one to whom I confide such things, has had an idea. Our great success last winter in Brussels during our two trips with *The Kiss* and *The Power of Darkness* suggested to him a third excursion, the profits of which would finance our last production. It is clear to me that this absence will make us very late in finishing the season, but since there seems to be no alternative, I telegraphed Alhaiza at the Molière to ask him if we could give *The Bread of Sin* and *All for Honor* at his theatre.

MAY 31, 1888—Here we are stranded in Brussels. Everyone tells me that I was insane to come at Pentecost, when the town is deserted. Alhaiza himself is gone, and upon arriving, we found that our production was not even posted. As a result—what receipts! We got as little the second day as the third, and since I housed my actors in the Hôtel du Grand-Monarque, we are all left penniless, lacking even the money to return to Paris. And the last production of the season, now long overdue, still must be given!

JUNE 1, 1888—Still in Brussels. Mendès, who came with us, has been a delight throughout this whole business, and his good humor and confidence helps cheer me up. Every night at midnight I go to the Exchange to talk with my business manager Chastenet, who stayed in Paris to search for funds; whenever he gets two or three hundred francs together, he sends them by telegraph, and I am sending the troupe back, a few at a time. But since we still owe our bill at the hotel, I remain as security, and await developments.

JUNE 2, 1888—At last I have returned. Now I will get the wheels turning and find what we need for the last production. I will no longer be led to count on receipts from outside of Paris to finance the Théâtre-Libre.

It has become quite clear to me that our very success is going to force me to make a grave decision after this first season in Montparnasse. Henry Fouquier was both right and wrong when he predicted that the public would not come to this side of the river—wrong because, despite the worst weather imaginable, our performances were filled to overflowing by the artistic elite of Paris; but right because I am sure that a second winter here could not stimulate the same enthusiasm. We must therefore establish ourselves in Paris proper, and this doesn't really seem possible. No director will rent me his theatre for evening performances, and to give only matinees, as some have suggested, would be foolish. Finally, although we started out with few subscriptions, requests have been numerous since *The Power of Darkness,* and if we could announce our presentations for the coming year in the heart of Paris, there would be a real rush. This would give me the solid resources I need, for I really had to go out on a limb to finish this season, and I frankly don't have the courage to start all over again.

JUNE 3, 1888—Just when I was most deeply concerned about our next season, Frantz Jourdain—whom I know from Daudet's and the Goncourt-Zola circle—came to me with the most unexpected proposal. He is the scene designer of the Menus-Plaisirs in the Boulevard de Strasbourg, and he suggested to Derenbourg, the manager, that he rent me the stage two or three days for dress rehearsals for a low rental and a percentage of the season tickets.

JUNE 4, 1888—I have now met Derenbourg, who struck me as a dangerous, enthusiastic, yet practical man — a strange mixture for a businessman. He loves the theatre so much that he has gradually spent a large fortune in it — a fortune gained, I think, in the lamp business. Frantz Jourdain gave me his whole-hearted support, and our agreement was soon made. Beginning next season, the Théâtre-Libre will regularly give its monthly performance in the Boulevard de Strasbourg. There will be two performances of each bill — a dress rehearsal for the press as well as for authors and friends, and a performance open to holders of season tickets, the requests for which are already numerous.

I no longer have the good Hartmann's settings, and Derenbourg's theatre has none, so we must build them for each production, and I foresee this as a potentially serious expense. Yet, we seem inescapably led to this course anyway. More and more, discussions over our presentations are turning from the value or the tendencies of the work given to questions about interpretation or setting. There has been more debate about such matters than I would ever have thought possible. Even at Montparnasse, where we utilized only Hartmann's stock settings with some small additions and much ingenuity, we stimulated the curiosity of the spectators about these peripheral matters. Clearly it is not possible to do justice to the character and atmosphere of these new works in the old settings. So, establishing a complete and suitable new setting for each play will bring us success in a new direction, if I can accomplish it. But what will this cost, and where will it lead us?

Our friend Charpentier, the sculptor, is in the habit of creating a small medallion of each author we present, and this has gradually developed into a very interesting collection. His reproductions of Mendès and Banville in particular were so good that the series was sent to the Salon, where it was very successful.

JUNE 5, 1888—I have had a lot of trouble in casting Alexis' one-act, *The End of Lucie Pellegrin,* which is to close our season. The strange and beautiful leading role was particularly difficult, for although neither Balzac nor Baudelaire shrank from treating this subject, it seems far more daring when transferred to the stage. If the play were not by Paul Alexis, and of an indisputable literary value, I would have refused it. At last Mme. Félicia Mallet, who has been gaining quite a reputation for herself in pantomime, accepted the part.

JUNE 6, 1888—This evening Paul Alexis and I dined at Zola's house in the Rue Ballu—a small place of astonishing simplicity. The master is not satisfied with his surroundings, however, and wants to redecorate the place. Zola's pleasant and cordial wife prepared an excellent dinner; I could tell I was among people who knew and appreciated fine food.

We ended the evening in the study. Zola opened a box of cigars with a key that he carried on his person and then sat discoursing by the fire, his legs crossed, while I followed the movements of his delicate, mobile, and astonishingly expressive hands. While discussing *Madeleine,* an unpublished play which he is going to give me, he spoke of the time when he was working at the Hachette book-dealers.

Zola showed us to the door, and while we were putting on our hats and coats in the hallway, he said to his wife: "Very good. Success has not spoiled him. You see, he has not changed his overcoat."

JUNE 7, 1888—We have announced our move to the Boulevard de Strasbourg. The effect was enormous, and all the detractors of the

Théâtre-Libre who were predicting its demise for next winter have taken the blow rather ungraciously. All our first critics from the Rue Blanche have long since been silenced.

JUNE 8, 1888—Yesterday Réjane and I gave *The Woman of Paris* at Mme. Aubernon de Nerville's home. The afternoon performance was a real occasion, but as I feared, I felt unknown and at a loss next to my famous companion.

JUNE 10, 1888—Salis has carried through his plans for presentations at the Chat Noir. The stage on the first floor was too small for the actors required by his original plan, so he has set up a sort of puppet theatre instead. Henri Rivière has created Chinese shadow plays—which are marvels—on a screen of white linen.

JUNE 16, 1888—Ancey's one-act play, *Monsieur Lamblin,* was the success of our last program of the season, which was presented yesterday in Montparnasse. The audience eagerly responded to this pleasant comedy with its ironic flavor, and Henry Mayer played it very well. I think that Ancey is on his way up; during the intermission, I received a number of inquiries about him. Gaston Salandri's comedy, *Prose,* a middle-class tale full of original turns which I personally found very amusing, was also a success, although it is hard for a beginning playwright to sustain three acts—toward the end, one lets up a little.

For all that, I could see by the astonished expressions on the audience's faces that the emphasis of the evening was new and unexpected. We ended with the naturalists on the offensive, and the poets were especially displeased. *The End of Lucie Pellegrin,* by Alexis, clearly part of this new offensive, stimulated great curiosity without arousing much protest. The sincerity of Paul Alexis' art commanded respect, but still, I think we would do well not to go too far in this direction. Besides, it would be difficult to find, in such a genre, works of so incontestable a literary value as this one.

JUNE 17, 1888—The reviews are not kind. The least extreme demand that the theatre be fumigated after *The End of Lucie Pellegrin.* Of course, this is too bad, but I rather think that violent plays of this sort, if we are reasonable enough not to abuse them, are the blows that will set the theatre free. After such a production, other daring subjects that could not have been touched before will now get by without hindrance.

Sarcey inquires if we are nothing more than hoaxsters taking pleasure in mystifying our contemporaries, in which case he says that he would very much like to be in on it, being rather fond of practical jokes provided he is not on the receiving end. Poor Félicia Mallet was terrified by all this uproar, and wrote to the *Figaro* apologizing for having played the role.

JUNE 21, 1888—*Lucie Pellegrin* has created an enormous scandal. All the papers have of course seized this opportunity to repeat their old charges that our theatre is immoral and steeped in naturalism. They are careful to avoid recalling that we have given Villiers' *The Evasion,* Mendès' *Tabarin's Wife,* and Banville's *The Kiss.* What displeases me even more is that Alexis was weak enough to let himself be talked into a public presentation at Déjazet, although the performance was called "special" to avoid censorship. I gave him what I considered were good reasons for not going through with this, but he insisted, and I was forced to renounce the performance publicly. A slight coolness has resulted. How sad that an excellent man like Alexis, however devoted he may be to a literary ideal, may still let himself be led astray by the possibilities of a purely financial venture.

JUNE 24, 1888—All of these people really do have a point. When the 1887-1888 season is considered as a whole, it is evident that the Théâtre-Libre has grown away from its first definite bias toward the Parnassians—a bias which began with the success of *The Berga-masque Night.* Although the poets have shared in the season, the naturalists have contributed the most important efforts, with Hennique's *Esther Brandès,* Jean Jullien's *The Serenade,* Ancey's

Sister Philomène and *Monsieur Lamblin,* Bonnetain and Descaves' *The Wad,* and Lavedan's *Quarter Hours.* Even *The Power of Darkness,* the high point of the season, has been classed among the revolutionary works, although I personally feel that this is not quite right, for Tolstoi's masterpiece is very similar to classic Greek tragedy.

JULY-DECEMBER, 1888

JULY 1, 1888—The total deficit of the 1887-1888 season is 9332 francs, 20 centimes.

JULY 5, 1888—The good Alexis, apropos of the failing Déjazet production, attacks me in his *Cri du peuple,* treating me as a pawn and accusing me of consorting with Sarcey.

JULY 17, 1888—Renan has sent me this letter in answer to a question I sent him:

July 15, 1888

Dear Sir:

The idea that you were kind enough to communicate to me, coming as it does from a man of taste such as yourself, does me so much honor that I cannot say no. I was highly flattered by it, and I assure you that I myself have often thought that there were surely parts at least of *The Abbess of Jouarre* which might be very exciting on stage. Still, there are certain serious problems. If the presentation were not quite expertly done, the play would be completely ineffectual. There is really only one role in the work—that of the Abbess; it is a long role, full of nuances, and it demands a most talented and beautiful actress. If such an actress could not be found, a simple reading of the work would be preferable.

The success of the play in Italy was due entirely to the efforts of a single actress, Mme. Duse, a woman of great intelligence who, having read my book, took a liking to the character of the Abbess and absolutely insisted upon creating her on the stage. Apparently her success was stunning. Do you have anyone who could perform such a difficult task?

I should note that my experience with a short occasional poem that I wrote for Victor Hugo's birthday showed me that the French which I write is difficult for actors to memorize.

All this boils down to one question: do you have someone for the role of the Abbess who would be willing to make this great an effort for one or two performances?

If you present *The Abbess*, I want it given just as it is written, with its entire five acts. I know that it is quite contrary to theatre custom to continue a play for two acts more if its high point is in the third act; but my thought is absolutely incomplete without these final acts. In Italy they left out most of them, and I cannot help thinking that the action as a whole must have been seriously crippled by this omission.

Think it over again, dear sir. Your enterprise is so honorable and the literary experiment you propose seems so interesting that I would be glad to participate in it. But I don't think there is much hope of success. Think it over; consider your resources.

I will not be back in Paris until about October 10.

I remain, your most devoted,

E. Renan.

JULY 21, 1888—Renan's letter makes it quite certain that he will not authorize a presentation of *The Abbess of Jouarre* at the Théâtre-Libre unless we can produce an outstanding actress. I therefore went to the Boulevard Malesherbes to see Sarah Bernhardt, who has recently returned from a tour of America.

Covered with furs and stretched out on a chaise longue, she listened with apparent interest as I eagerly described the Théâtre-Libre, of which she was unaware, and painted a picture of the new theatre movement which was developing there. I tried to make her feel what a contribution her assistance would be to a budding

· 79

literary school, since she has a faithful public which follows her wherever she wishes. Then I tried to excite her about this glorious part, since she has really never had a role which was a real challenge to her genius, as a recent article by Mendès complained. All this did not seem to move her much, although she smiled pleasantly on my enthusiasm.

I then spoke of *The Abbess of Jouarre,* and mentioned a famous Italian actress, Duse, who had played the role in Italy. Bernhardt turned to an old lady, one Mme. Guerard, who had just come through the portiere of the neighboring room, and asked if she remembered the actress of whom I spoke. The old lady said she did, and then added: "Ah yes! Ah yes! Duse—not really worth much."

JULY 23, 1888—While Jules Claretie was passing through Brussels, he stopped to attend several performances of the celebrated troupe of the Duke of Saxe-Meiningen which was appearing at the Monnaie. He published an essay on them which was very pleasant, to be sure, but which betrayed a certain uneasiness about their innovations and their magnificent effects, the latter clearly superior to those at the Comédie-Française. I attended some of these performances too, being in Brussels on business, and welcomed the lessons they could teach. While there, I wrote a long letter to Sarcey which he printed in his column in the *Temps:*

> Dear Master:
>
> Your latest column has found me and disturbed me in this quiet corner where I am getting a bit of rest. I must tell you that I will soon return from Brussels, where I spent a fortnight observing this German troupe. You know that I am going to present *The State in Danger* this winter, and in connection with it, I have been thinking of an interesting experiment with crowds. It was therefore obvious that I should go to see the Meininger.
>
> I have used the word "disturbed" because in speaking of the Meininger you cling to your favorite theories, which M. Claretie's observations seem to confirm. What

a pity that you could not come up here to obtain a true impression, instead of seeing and feeling only through another.

For as long as I have been going to the theatre I have been annoyed by the way we handle our crowd scenes. Indeed, with the possible exceptions of *Hatred,* and the circus scene in *Théodora,* I have never seen anything which gave me the impression of a multitude.

Well, with the Meininger I have seen it! During several evenings at the Monnaie I found myself looking about for you. How happy I would have been to talk it over with you there, on the spot. They showed us completely new and highly instructive approaches. M. Claretie might have been right about *Julius Caesar,* which I unfortunately did not see, but *William Tell* did not remind me of the Eden[23] in the least, and I would be quite satisfied if Hamlet's court was anything like that of Leontes in the *Winter's Tale.*

Do you know what the difference is?

Their crowds are not, like ours, made up of elements put together at random—or people hired during the dress rehearsals, badly dressed and quite untrained to wear bizarre or constricting costumes, especially when these demand precision. Our theatres almost always demand that the extras stand stock still, while those of the Meininger must act and portray their characters. Do not assume therefore that they attract attention and divert the emphasis from the principals. No, the scene is an organic whole, and wherever one looks, he is struck by a detail in situation or character. This lends an incomparable power to certain moments.

The Meininger troupe contains about seventy artists of both sexes. Everyone who does not have a part is kept as an extra and so appears every evening. If twenty actors are

---

[23] A theatre in Paris.

needed, the fifty others—without exception, the stars included—appear on the stage in crowd scenes. Each may be the chief or corporal of a group of extras (as we think of them), which he supervises and directs while they are before the public. The obligation to serve in this way is such that when the wife of Hans von Bülow, one of the Meininger stars, found the task beneath her talent and refused, she was dismissed, even though her husband had the title and the duties of choir master to the Duke. He too left the ducal court as a result of this conflict.

In this way they obtain configurations of startling realism. But try to do this in our theatres and ask an actor of even the fifth rank to help fill up the salon of the Princess of Bouillon! So we are forced to accept the services of well-meaning fellows who scarcely know what they are doing or why they are there. I know this to be true, for I was an extra myself in bygone days with Mévisto at the Français. We took the job so that we could watch our favorite actors more closely than we could in the audience.

But every member of the Meininger submits to playing extras. Their leading lady, Mlle. Lindner, playing the Time scene in *A Winter's Tale,* was an extra in the judgment tableau, and mimed a common wife with as much conscientiousness and care as she brought the following evening to her interpretation of Hermione in the same play.

This is the secret of their crowds, which are superior to ours in every respect. And I am quite convinced that if you had only seen the arrest of William Tell and the apple scene you would have been as delighted as I.

There was another superb scene in this *William Tell*— the murder of Gessler. Gessler was stopped on a narrow path (formed by a sunken road at least eight meters from the footlights) by a beggar and his two children. This family barred Gessler's way with their bodies, and during a long scene of supplication during which Tell aimed at Gessler, they remained with their backs to the audience.

I am sure this scene would have convinced you that a properly shown back is most effective in giving the audience the impression that the actors are not aware of their presence and that the action is really taking place.

Since these new ideas are so logical and so inexpensive, why don't they replace the insupportable conventions which everyone unquestioningly puts up with in our theatres?

M. Claretie's word "mechanical" does not seem just to me. Isn't the Comédie "mechanical," repeating certain works for months on end? The Meininger have polished the mechanics of their crowd scenes, that is all.

The only real objection that I can make to them is this: in this same *William Tell,* for example, Schiller having written in a part for the crowd, all the extras cry the same phrase, *at the same time.* This is false and heavy-handed. Yet couldn't the lines of the crowd be broken up into a carefully orchestrated clamor? For example, if we wanted them to cry "Viva Gambetta!" do you know what I would do? I would divide my two hundred extras into ten groups or so—women, children, tradesmen, etc. I would have the tradesmen start off with "Vi . . . ," the women, with a faster rhythm, would begin when the others reached "Gam . . . ," and I would have the youngsters lag five seconds after all the rest. In short, it would be like coaching a chorus. I am quite certain that the audience would understand the "Viva Gambetta!" amid the din, and if the crowd's gestures, positions, and groupings were planned and varied with the same care that the Meininger employ, a unified and realistic effect would doubtless be the result.

In the crowd scenes, the protagonist who is the center of the scene can bring about strict silence with a gesture, a cry, a movement. And if the crowd then watches the actor and listens to him, instead of watching the audience, or, as at the Comédie-Française, contemplating the leads with a mute but visible deference, their listening would seem natural and so would their silence. In any case, all two hundred must seem really interested in what the dominant actor is saying.

I don't know anything about music, but I have been told that in certain operas Wagner split his chorus into different parts, and that each set of chorus members represented a distinct element of the crowd, even while contributing to a perfect ensemble. Why can't we do that in the spoken theatre? M. Emile Zola wanted to for *Germinal,* but the directors prevented him for budgetary reasons. His plan was to rehearse the crowd extensively and have them supervised by leading actors. As you see, this is the Meininger approach.

Please note that I have not been completely swept off my feet by them, as the saying goes. Their garish and oddly designed settings are not nearly so well painted as ours. They abuse the idea of practical elements, cramming them in everywhere. As for the costumes, even when they are purely historical, they are foolishly rich; and when no documents exist and a work of imagination and fantasy must be made, they display shocking taste. The lighting effects, although often striking, are handled with epic naïveté. For example, when an old man has just died in his armchair, a beautiful ray from the setting sun suddenly shines through the window, without any gradations, to illuminate his beautiful head—this solely to achieve an effect. Again after an extraordinary torrential rain, achieved by electric projections, I was annoyed to see the water stop abruptly, without any transition.

There were many things of this sort. The same stage carpet served for the entire play; the rocks of Switzerland were mounted on coasters; there was a squeaking floorboard in the mountains. The actors were adequate and nothing more; many wore their costumes badly; all the mountaineers had the white hands and clean knees that we associate with the Opéra-Comique.

Actors seem to have been hired for their strong voices

and large shoulders, the latter so they could show off the marvelous fabrics which the Duke himself purchases and which show a real extravagance. It is said that he spent 75,000 thaler for Schiller's *Marie Stuart*. The training of the actors is generally of the most rudimentary sort. Two or three are mentioned as having been educated at Vienna. Mlle. Lindner, whom I just mentioned, was a dancer a short while ago, and could hardly have suspected that she would soon be called, as she now is, the "true Maid of Orleans." Almost all the troupe, or at least the better half of them, made their debuts without any other theatrical education than a year or two spent as an extra and in small roles.

I was naturally very anxious to see *The Imaginary Invalid,* which they advertised, but did not give. In *Twelfth Night* and *A Winter's Tale,* they showed us three comic actors, one of which, Carl Gorner, is of the first rank.

Their repertoire is extremely varied. At Meiningen they even gave Henrik Ibsen's *Ghosts,* which I have in translation. It was the Duke's idea to give the play in private before the author and invited critics from the German press—much in the manner of the Théâtre-Libre. The play could not be given publicly, for it is quite subversive, and I am sure that in October you too will be rather astonished by it.

Another characteristic detail is that the actors and extras are strictly forbidden to go outside the frame, properly speaking, of the stage. No one ventures onto the proscenium;* and in twelve evenings, I never saw anyone put his foot within two meters of the prompter. The actors are also forbidden to look into the house, which is kept in darkness. Almost all the important scenes are played upstage, the extras turning their backs and watching the actors engaged at the rear of the stage. Of course you are aware

---

*M. Antoine means by this the part of the theatre which is, in most theatres, bordered on the right and the left by the directors' boxes [Sarcey's note].

of the stimulating innovations in all this. Why don't we try to appropriate what is good among them?

Nothing like this is to be seen in Paris, and I would have been delighted if you could have made the trip. You could have given us your personal reflections on these technical matters, which would have been useful for theatre people and interesting for everyone. I was told at Brussels that M. Porel came. The great directors and their scenic artists should have come too. Each would have gotten something out of it.

Of course, dear master, this letter is completely between ourselves. I only wanted to show you, in my usual bad French, that I am not wasting my time, and that I test something seriously before attempting it. I am going to put a few of the practices I have seen up here into the Goncourt play and into *The Death of the Duke of Enghien* by Hennique. I hope that if I can achieve what I want this will prove of interest to you.

> Your most sincere and grateful,
> Antoine.

AUGUST, 1888—I have just spent several days vacationing at Avesnes, a pleasant spot where I was once stationed. I am hard at work preparing our next season.

AUGUST 5, 1888—Mme. Charpentier has brought me a query from Abel Hermant, who wonders if I would be disposed to welcome a play he has made from his recent successful novel *Nathalie Madoré*.

AUGUST 8, 1888—A M. Taylor came to offer me an adaptation of *Madame Bovary* which he had made from Flaubert's masterpiece. I reproached him for this sacrilege by asking him to read this passage in one of Flaubert's letters:

> Since you are interested in my affairs, I will tell you that if my novel has never appeared on the stage, it is because

I am absolutely opposed to it. I found the only such attempt was quite unworthy of me, even though it was very good. Many theatres wanted it and it was all the rage for a while, but now it is over and forgotten.

Taylor left my house to take his manuscript to another independent theatre, recently opened; and the perpetration of this foul deed had already been announced when Flaubert's heirs arrived with an injunction to stop it.

SEPTEMBER 1, 1888—We have all returned to Paris, and our evening gatherings in the Rue Blanche are becoming more lively every day. Subscriptions are coming in, and for the moment we have no financial problems. We are all joyful at having a real theatre. I found a sort of warehouse with an attic at la Villette, set up by the designer Ménessier, and several workmen are there now, beginning work on the settings for our next plays. But I want only new and different settings, nothing like the current things. All this unfortunately will be quite expensive; we shall have to use all our resources immediately, trusting to our successes to replenish them as we did last winter.

SEPTEMBER 10, 1888—M. Georges de Porto-Riche read his one-act comedy—which we will soon give—to the actors yesterday. It is called *Married*. The title suggests the Vaudeville to me, but M. de Porto-Riche has thought of another: *Françoise's Luck*.

SEPTEMBER 13, 1888—The Odéon has reopened its doors with an adaptation by Paul Ginisty of Dostoievsky's famous novel, *Crime and Punishment*. Paul Mounet is truly admirable in it.[24]

SEPTEMBER 27, 1888—Fernand Icres, who sent me a very original one-act verse play that we will give this winter, died several days ago in his country. He was a tall fellow, thin and feverish, who elicited a warm sympathy from me.

---

[24]*Crime and Punishment* actually opened on September 15. Paul Mounet played Rodion.

OCTOBER 3, 1888—Today I lunched at Sèvres with Léon Cladel, and we spoke of a play that he would like to give me. The poet, a fine rustic figure, both sly and swarthy, sat between his daughters, two pretty brown-haired children who played about the table while hens entering from the garden pecked crumbs beneath our feet. Cladel's *The Elder* held me with the charm of its glowing verses and its images. He also spoke of another fine play, *Ompdrailles, the Tomb of the Warriors,* which he has in manuscript. At present, I said nothing to him, but I promised myself I would produce it later if it did not prove too heavy.

OCTOBER 10, 1888—We have 26,000 francs from season subscriptions. The first productions are therefore assured, but they must in turn finance the others.

OCTOBER 13, 1888—Vidal, having had two plays produced in the early days of the Théâtre-Libre and having later found himself pushed into the background, has written a letter to the *Echo de Paris* speaking of my "puny literary and commercial operations." This is what comes of trying to be master in one's own house.

OCTOBER 17, 1888—Thinking that we should open the season with one of our trump cards, I included Porto-Riche's *Married* in the four one-acts selected. But the author has proved difficult and uncertain, and has tormented his interpreters so much that we are not ready and must postpone his play until another time.

OCTOBER 18, 1888—As a result of the fire at the Opéra-Comique, the official commissions are preoccupied with safety measures in theatres. I have been warned that I must fire-proof my settings. This order was reasonable enough, but at the Beaux-Arts, the officials attempted to link this question with another which the Rue de Valois finds of great interest.

Since the opening of the Théâtre-Libre, I have always escaped needing the Censor's permit, contending that our performances are private. This argument went unchallenged so long (either through the inattention or the negligence of the officials) that it was at last accepted and I was left alone. Yet from time to time the indictment is slyly brought up again, and this time I am officially warned that we must request a permit for all *public* performances. I was quick to accept this warning, since it implicitly recognizes the private character of our productions.

OCTOBER 19, 1888—It occurred to me to have a different painter or designer illustrate each of our programs. This time Willette sent me a marvelous design which I hope will be the first of a most interesting collection.

OCTOBER 20, 1888—We opened our season yesterday at the Menus-Plaisirs with a packed and excited house. *The Butchers,* by poor Fernand Icres, proved interesting. It was followed by a lovely piece translated from the Italian, Verga's *Rustic Chivalry. The Lover of Christ,* a sort of mystery-play by Darzens, completed the evening.

Rustic Chivalry was put together with much care. It cruelly centered on the inexperience of a poor girl with rare gifts and magnificent beauty. In *The Butchers* I wanted a realistic setting and hung up actual quarters of meat, which created a sensation. The audience was also delighted, although I can't imagine why, with a real fountain standing in the middle of the square of the little Sicilian village which is the setting of *Rustic Chivalry.*

The audiences attracted by the stir we caused during our first season are basically quite different from the faithful and devoted patrons of our first efforts. Still, I am not alarmed by their present boisterousness during the productions. I have never been one to avoid a struggle, and what we absolutely must do is impose a respect and a habit of attention on these new spectators.

OCTOBER 24, 1888—Paulin Ménier, who was in rehearsal for *The Messenger from Lyon* at the Porte-Saint-Martin, has just broken his arm and Duquesnel has asked Mévisto to replace him in this major role. I tremble a bit for him.

OCTOBER 26, 1888—After Jean Aicard's *Old Lebonnard* had long since been accepted at the Comédie-Française, and was actually in rehearsal, some trouble arose as a result of which the irritated author noisily withdrew the play. Immediately I asked him for it. Even if, as is likely, it is not really the sort of thing we generally present, the controversy about it will make its production quite a little event. Parisian curiosity is always short-lived, and I am convinced that I must let slip no opportunity to keep up interest in the Théâtre-Libre. That is why *Old Lebonnard* would be good for us. Unhappily, the author is still a bit touchy, and is slow in answering.

OCTOBER 27, 1888—I know that for a long time my good friend Mendès has had a work of real stature which is particularly dear to him locked in his desk. It is a great verse drama, *Queen Fiammette,* which he has not been able to get presented, since theatres are closed to such large and costly works of uncertain success. I do not dare ask the poet for it, however, since we do not really have the money or the facilities to present a play with settings and costumes of the Italian Renaissance.

OCTOBER 28, 1888—Death of Emile Augier. In our little corner the author of *The Poor Lionnesses* and *Giboyer's Son* was the most respected of all the older generation, for in his middle-class social comedies he was one of our precursors and many young people still show his influence. He was one of the high points of our dramatic literature before Becque.

OCTOBER 29, 1888—I am finding it harder and harder to escape the different influences exerted on our theatre. Recently Henry Becque, who is the real master and leader of this whole new movement, has given us much support. Several of our friends are irritated by this, especially Céard, who has some unexplained grudge against the master of *The Vultures* and who has indulged in this violent outburst against him in the *Vie populaire:*

> In the new theatre everyone, masters and students alike,
> are joined in a united effort, devoted to the same new cause.

Now, in this gathering of bold spirits, the absence of M. Henry Becque is irritating, since everyone knows that he has made boldness his specialty. For want of anything better, M. Becque has deigned to bestow upon the Théâtre-Libre his extraordinary and fruitless guardianship. He has found it easier to give M. Antoine advice than to give him a play.

Certainly M. Becque's advice—that we shake off our apathy and support important works—is good. But why doesn't he follow his precious advice himself? The Théâtre-Libre has been waiting for an important work from the author of that uninspired vaudeville, *The Abduction*. It has waited in vain. One can only conclude from this that M. Becque is condemning himself in the case he makes against others, and that when he speaks of famous but worn-out authors he is talking about himself, as he so often does.

In any case, the Théâtre-Libre was created without him; it obtained its results without him; and without this timid, if recognized, revolutionary it will continue the struggle for independence at the Menus-Plaisirs which it began at the Elysée-des-Beaux-Arts and at the Théâtre Montparnasse.

NOVEMBER 1, 1888—It was just as I suspected. This evening Marie Desfresne told me that Mendès is very disappointed that I have not asked him for his *Queen Fiammette*. I gave the author all the reasons that I did not dare ask him for a work from which he expected important results when I could only give it two performances. Mendès was rather touched, and replied "Yes, but your Théâtre-Libre has become so important in the world of letters that I consider it my duty, when Zola himself has given you a play, to keep aloft the banner of the poetic drama there. My dear Antoine, you have made your theatre a battlefield not only for the public, but also for the literary schools, and until your experiment is over, you should give all sides an equal hearing. You should therefore give my *Queen Fiammette* during the same season you give the Goncourts' *The*

Nation in Danger and Zola's *Madeleine*." I answered that my theatre was his and that if he would be satisfied with our meager resources, we would do our best for him. I feel that our friend was quite pleased, and his devotion certainly entitles him to this.

NOVEMBER 3, 1888—Mendès has the bizarre idea of asking Capoul to play the leading man in *Queen Fiammette*. This makes me uneasy. No matter how curious people might be to see the famous tenor's debut in a regular play, I think his Toulousian accent would present a real danger.

NOVEMBER 6, 1888—Montégut has completely won back Louis de Gramont, one of the journalists who abused me most strongly the day after the unhappy box-office affair in Montparnasse. Indeed, we are presenting a play of his, which I think strikes a happy compromise between the old sentimental theatre and the boldness of naturalism.

NOVEMBER 7, 1888—Gramont's *Rolande* was a big success, just as I suspected. If the romantic drama of the daughter who is her father's judge is rather old-fashioned, it is relieved by the reflections of Hulot de Balzac, which give it vigor and form. Odette de Fehl was very successful in the principal role, and Luce Colas was truly extraordinary as the little maid.

NOVEMBER 10, 1888—Derenbourg and Gramont are very anxious to give a public performance of *Rolande*—a very coarse idea. I object to these public presentations, however lucrative they may be, for they betray our undertaking. The day when the general public is freely admitted to see productions now reserved for an elite will be the day when we become an ordinary theatre, and thus come into the grip of censorship.

NOVEMBER 13, 1888—Albert Wolff begins his column in the *Figaro* thus: "Goddam it all, to hell with peace and quiet and long live the Théâtre-Libre!" This is followed by a long diatribe in which he assassinates our character by bringing up *Lucie Pellegrin* again, and he requests that I replace the ushers of the theatre with elderly female attendants to whom one would give a small tip upon leaving. The truth of the matter is that the noted polemist has never forgiven me for the mistake he made when he wrote to me that the Théâtre-Libre would not be of interest to anyone.

NOVEMBER 14, 1888—I had to give in to the public performances. Derenbourg must be humored if we are to remain permanently established in the heart of Paris—a real feather in our cap. But he is a practical man who would never have lent me his theatre on such easy terms if he did not think he could make more money out of it. The public performances are going quite successfully, with good receipts, but I have made it clear that they cannot continue indefinitely,[25] for next month's production must be rehearsed and since most of my companions work during the day, evenings are the only time they have free.

NOVEMBER 17, 1888—Eugène Rapp has a most amusing cartoon in the *Vie moderne*—a series of silhouettes of Sarcey watching Gramont's play. First the noted critic stands motionless, leaning peacefully on his cane. Then little by little he is overcome by uneasiness, indignation, and wrath. In the sixth panel he flees, his arms raised toward heaven.

NOVEMBER 22, 1888—Mendès has just taken Louise France away from me. He asked to have her engaged at the Renaissance for his operetta *Isoline*,[26] for which Messager has written the music.

NOVEMBER 23, 1888—*Rolande* has been a financial success, but most of the money has gone to our landlord, and I badly need these precious resources to continue the season. We were quite surprised to see the grandduke Vladimir of Russia arrive last evening, attracted by the controversy over the Théâtre-Libre.

25*Rolande* was given 16 public performances at the Menus-Plaisirs.
26Presented December 26.

DECEMBER, 1888—Extract from a recent preface by Henry Becque:

It was not without reason that I mentioned M. Antoine's Théâtre-Libre. It has a director who is still quite young, yet who is highly perceptive in theatrical matters; it has dedicated authors whose lack of bias cannot be questioned; it has an enthusiastic troupe possessing two valuable qualities—simplicity and naturalness. Ever since the day this home of art opened, the educated public has flocked to it, and last winter it was the only source of dramatic life in Paris.

DECEMBER 1, 1888—Porto-Riche is finally satisfied, and has finished the re-writing of his one-act play. The title will be changed from *Married* to *Françoise's Luck,* and it will accompany Hennique's *The Death of the Duke of Enghien* on our next program.

DECEMBER 12, 1888—Our presentation last night of *The Death of the Duke of Enghien* was a real event. The work was heralded as marking a renaissance—a renewing of the historical play through the methods of the realistic school. Not only was there a definite attempt to reconstruct the feeling of an age, but the setting contributed greatly to the success of this attempt.

The council of war in the third act, illuminated only by the lanterns placed on the table, created an effect so new and unexpected that everyone is talking about it. Moreover, I had the good fortune to discover a costumer with an admirable collection of authentic costumes which he loans to no one but painters. The best of the lot was the very same one which Jean-Paul Laurens used for his famous painting. Of course, this was all very expensive, but what results! The habitual scoffers were completely overwhelmed. In the third act, two or three wags attempted to banter in the darkness, and Bauer slapped one of them.

DECEMBER 16, 1888—The large illustrated page of this week's issue of the *Vie Parisienne* is entirely devoted to "the ladies who go to the Théâtre-Libre." It is a sure sign of success.

In view of the enormous interest aroused by *The Duke of Enghien,* Derenbourg has naturally insisted upon several public performances in compliance with his contract. I resisted again, but I spent too much money for settings (that for *The Duke of Enghien* being particularly costly) and the future worries me. So out of regard for my administrator Chastanet, I agreed. Still, these squabbles over money are a ball and chain that it is very tiring to drag along!

DECEMBER 20, 1888—Even before the curtain went up, it was clear that the premiere of *Germinie Lacerteux* would be an eventful one. The fact that the alleged "audacities" and "license" of the Théâtre-Libre were going to take place in an official theatre stirred up a lot of indignation beforehand. As for ourselves, all our faithful followers were present, united and resolute. Bauer's tall figure dominated the orchestra and he was casting furious glances about him even before the play began. Seated further back, I found myself between Albert Wolff and Koning, notoriously hostile to Goncourt, and I had the feeling that anything could happen. Every group's representatives were ready—there were frequenters of the Garret and of the Daudet house as well as the most fanatic members of the Théâtre-Libre.

Porel's settings showed his usual great artistic taste. The many scenes were admirably planned, and looked like actual lithographs of the period, with their characters costumed after the fashion of Gavarni.

The public was immediately won over by Réjane in an unexpected role; the stylish Parisienne, wrapped in shabby clothes, was Germinie Lacerteux herself. But things went rapidly downhill—first murmurs, then grumbles and muttering, at last hisses and jeers broke out. Not once in all this more or less heart-felt hullabaloo did Réjane become confused or cease to dominate the house. She was especially admirable in the second act, during the luncheon scene where the children are served by the unhappy creature, who moves about the table suffering the agony of her pregnancy. The audience erupted in stunning wrath; jeers rained down on author and actors alike; the house demanded that the curtain be lowered; and Goncourt's friends themselves were silent, overwhelmed.

DECEMBER 21, 1888—As one could have predicted, the reviews of *Germinie Lacerteux* are quite vile. Goncourt is the quarry and is bayed after by everyone. Only Henry Bauer in his column dug in his heels and defended the play. All this has made me so furious that I cannot work, and I have decided to answer the attack, in so far as possible, by immediately producing as our next program *The Nation in Danger,* already announced as part of this season.

I told Bauer about it in this telegram:

Dear master,

I decided this morning that it would be advisable to advance the date of *The Nation in Danger.* Your fine article has eased my heart; a thousand thanks for it. I want to give the other play within six weeks and we will see then if the poor imbeciles from last evening will be at it again.

Sincerely, Antoine.

At half past midnight I met Bauer's secretary, Auguste Germain, at Pousset's. He told me that in Bauer's absence he had opened my note and included it in tomorrow's column. I was taken aback, for I did not at all intend it to be made public. But Germain told me that the paper had already gone to press, and it being one thirty in the morning, I decided to let it go.

After the premiere of *Germinie,* we had supper at Daudet's. About twenty friends were there—Scholl, Zola and his wife, Mme. Ménard-Dorain, etc. Porel and Réjane, who were expected, begged to be excused. The stormy evening had exhausted Réjane. Everyone was deeply concerned, but each did his utmost to reassure the rather worried Goncourt. During a brief silence, Zola said: "Goncourt, I drink to you and your brother," and there was an emotion in his thin voice which impressed me strongly, for I thought of that other battle, with *Renée* at the Vaudeville, after which he sat alone over his supper at Paillard's.

DECEMBER 22, 1888—A storm of abuse has broken out in the evening papers. It is very annoying, but I am determined not to retreat a step. Even my friends at the *Figaro* disapprove of my action, as is evidenced by the comments with which Prével accompanies the insertion of my letter to Bauer:

> "The poor imbeciles" are three words of unusual impudence. They refer to a very large number of Parisians who found M. Edmond de Goncourt's latest play detestable and who do not wish, things being as they are, to dogmatically exalt goncourism.
>
> It is not pleasant to be classed as "poor imbeciles" by M. Antoine, but it is even more regrettable that the man who employs such expressions is an actor-director, who owes a certain respect to the public which pays him and listens to him.

All the rest of the papers have spoken in the same vein—each adds his word. My only course now is to keep my head, and I coolly and simply confirmed my attitude in this letter to Prével:

Paris, December 22, 1888

Dear M. Prével,

I did not wait for the occasion which you offer me to affirm aloud and in public what so many artists said after last Wednesday's performance. The telegram which you reproduced was not meant for the public, but I do not disavow a word of it.

You know very well that I have never been heard to speak ill of the press, which never creates a disturbance at premieres, having the inalienable right of commentary the following day, nor of the literary people who should form the exclusive audience of such productions.

The "poor imbeciles" are those who created not merely a disturbance, but a near-riot at the premiere of *Jealousy,* who begin to make jokes in the corners as soon as the gas is lowered at the Théâtre-Libre, and who jeered at M.

Dumény when he came forward to announce M. Edmond de Goncourt's name.

They are neither literary nor Parisian. They slip inexplicably into premieres and allow themselves the easy luxury of being both cowardly and vulgar. It is this group that should be put out. They do not pay; they do not understand; and they do not belong in a gathering of artists.

It is therefore against these that I protested, and I sincerely thank you for giving me the privilege of expressing my indignation at this gross insult to literature and dramatic art in the person of the great writer who penned *Germinie Lacerteux.*

Sincerely, Antoine.

DECEMBER 23, 1888—Things are happening too fast; I still have this *Germinie* business on my back, and although there is great interest in *The Death of the Duke of Enghien,* my poor Théâtre-Libre is in grave danger. We have stirred up feelings in the literary world that should be aroused only with great care. Our enemies are devoting themselves to organizing a scandal that will destroy the theatre at our next performance. They talk of demanding a public apology from me the moment I appear on stage for the presumed insults against the public and the press contained in my letter. We shall see. Whatever happens, I will not give in, and if necessary, I will close the theatre.

DECEMBER 27, 1888—This is serious indeed. Yesterday I was attacked three times in a single issue of the *Figaro*—first by Albert Wolff, as might be expected, then in the "News at Hand," finally in an article by Albert Millaud psychoanalyzing the "poor imbeciles." I was so disturbed that I went to see Francis Magnard, who has always been a good friend of mine, even in opposition to some in his house. The good man was highly amused, and his laughter gave me courage. "What," he said, "you get on the front page of the *Figaro* three times the same day, and you complain?" Then he explained to me that I have stirred up a hornet's nest by supporting

Goncourt so violently. Apparently there are issues involved that I never suspected. I learned that a large literary clique is pitted against the friends and followers of Saint-Gratien and of the Princess Mathilde.

Even so, Goncourt's friends, who did not make themselves heard at the premiere of *Germinie,* are still maintaining a silence which seems unnecessarily prudent to me.

DECEMBER 28, 1888—Bauer has been showing signs of a growing coolness for some time. Two or three times he has tried to interfere in our affairs, but I have paid no attention. At the same time, one of his comrades, Louis Besson of the *Evénement,* has supported us equally warmly. Therefore, when I could not think of asking Bauer for a helping hand in this "poor imbeciles" business—it all being rather his fault, even though I would not reproach him for it for anything in the world—I appealed to Besson instead. I wrote a note for him to publish, which only added fuel to the flames. The *Echo de Paris* then attacked me, with Bauer siding against his friend. The on-lookers were delighted to see me lose a supporter, but they reckoned without the complexities of the literary world. Sarcey, like Henry Fouquier, had been rather irritated by the influence which he thought Bauer had over us, and, delighted by this rupture, he defended me with a racy and bantering good nature.

Prado was just executed. Méténier is a friend of the police commissioner of the Roquette quarter, and he got me in to see this sinister ceremony. I was forever cured of my unhealthy curiosity.

DECEMBER 30, 1888—M. de Goncourt, who has remained silent during all the days following the *Germinie Lacerteux* disputes, sent me a short note on his card asking me to visit him at Auteuil. His old Pélagie told me that the master was not feeling well and was upstairs in bed, but that she had been instructed earlier to bring me up. M. de Goncourt lay half dozing in a rather dim chamber on the second floor, the shutters closed. He told me that all the uproar had given him a fever and that he gladly spent whole days in bed. My arrival brought a bit of the air of Paris and the stories I told him of the events of the last few days produced a bit of animation in him. Our conversation about *Germinie* led him to speak of his brother, and he said that the literary world today is much different from what it was at the time of *Henriette Maréchal*. He told how excitement ran high among the youth in the schools after the tumult of that play's presentation at the Comédie-Française, and that there was even a duel in the Ecole Polytechnique fought by students who sided with him and his brother. I sensed that the old man felt a sort of unhappy wonder in that his friends of the Garret had been more silent than one might have wished. M. de Goncourt noted this with a rather haughty bitterness, and I found myself silently in agreement.

JANUARY-DECEMBER, 1889

JANUARY 8, 1889—Mendès is indeed a devoted and courageous friend. His *Queen Fiammette* will appear in our next program, and although he could be nervous and irritated to see his play presented at a time when it risks suffering the abuse which is being carefully nurtured against me, he is not. On the contrary, when I told him how sorry I was about all this, it was he who comforted and encouraged me.

JANUARY 17, 1889—The presentation of *Queen Fiammette* did not go as badly as I had feared. The reviewers, out of respect for Mendès, were easy on us. I had been warned for some time that I would be made to pay this evening for the "poor imbeciles" business, and that when I came on stage I would be forced to make a public apology. I felt myself in a tight spot when the curtain went up on the first scene, for the house was rather unruly. But instead of the hisses I expected, applause and a "Bravo, Antoine!" from Alphonse Daudet's box stopped any inclination toward rowdiness. The audience took out its spite on poor Capoul, whose Toulousian accent set off a truly disgraceful outburst. Although from time to time the lovely poetry of Mendès and the courage of Marie Defresne would win back the audience, the unduly long play—six acts in length—admittedly dragged. In the midst of all this, I got by almost unnoticed, and when I arrived without trouble at my last scene, I began to hope that I might escape the storm.

But as I edged cautiously toward the door behind me while giving my last verses, several spectators realized that I would not reappear, and I heard hisses at my back just as I slipped quickly out. Poor Capoul, who had been both courageous and charming, was quite grieved, and I too was very depressed, for I had invested up to my last cent in costumes and settings that were still insufficient. It was foolish. I had certainly warned Mendès that this would happen, but he is such a good sport that instead of complaining he thanked me with a long and warm letter which much heartened me.

JANUARY 19, 1889—I have come in for a good deal of personal abuse in the reviews of *Fiammette,* but I fully expected it, and don't mind in the least. My costume, which I must admit didn't fit very well, drew particular attack. Its accuracy disconcerted the public, who are accustomed to seeing in the theatre the cast-off clothing of the opera. They were especially astonished to see me enter with a large sword in hand wielded like a cane, an absolutely authentic detail copied from a number of engravings and portraits of the period.

JANUARY 22, 1889—*The Blue Officer* has just been banned at the Gymnase and Koning is furious.[27] I am laughing up my sleeve; these gentlemen rather approve of censorship, and it is indeed amusing when from time to time the blow from the stick lands on their own shoulders. Still, Koning, while filling the papers with his complaints, has not failed to assert that the Théâtre-Libre is to blame for all this.

*   *   *

FEBRUARY 1, 1889—We have given Henry Céard's *The Meek.* The play had certain sound qualities, although it lacked color. Vitu declares that having listened to M. Henry Céard's three acts with the most careful attention, he can only wonder what the author was trying to do in them, and must assume that he himself did not really know. Pessard writes in the same tone in the *Gaulois,* but the clumsiness of the review does justice to its author. I fear that Céard, who was relying on a work which had occupied him for years, will gain from all this only a redoubling of his customary misanthropy.

27*The Blue Officer* by Ary Ecilaw, pseudonym of the Countess Czapska, was banned on January 20, apparently at the demand of the Russian ambassador. The hero of the piece was the chief of the Russian secret police.

FEBRUARY 5, 1889—The repercussions of *The Death of the Duke of Enghien* have been such that the English impresario Mayer, who used to direct the Comédie-Française in London, asked me to go there to give a series of performances. He is paying handsomely, requiring that the smallest roles be taken along, with the settings and costumes exactly as they appeared in Paris. He is an affable, proper, and very open-handed gentleman, with whom it is very pleasant to do business. We have therefore crossed the Channel. We opened yesterday evening at the Royalty, and are playing before very elegant houses. I spend my days touring London, a city I do not know.

FEBRUARY 9, 1889—Our comrade Mayer, who enjoyed a personal success in *The Meek,* is leaving to rejoin Coquelin for a tour in America.

FEBRUARY 10, 1889—I let everyone else go on ahead and I have remained here to see at leisure Irving's famous Lyceum Theatre, where I spent last evening. They gave *Macbeth,* with Miss Ellen Terry and Irving himself. I was not at all dazzled by this great actor, who seemed to me a Taillade with less fire, but what impressed me as incomparable was his setting, of which we have scarcely a notion in France. The scene where the manor is awakened, and even more that of the banquet with the appearance of the ghost, are masterpieces, with lighting effects we have never dreamed of at home.

FEBRUARY 18, 1889—Porto-Riche's *Françoise's Luck* is now being given publicly at the Gymnase, along with a revival of *M. Alphonse.* Koning apparently really thinks that he is performing the functions of a Théâtre-Libre, but the conversations in the lobby indicate that Dumas' play already seems a little dated, and I really think that we are somewhat responsible for this.

FEBRUARY 19, 1889—This evening we read *The Nation in Danger* in the Rue Blanche.[29] It is a magnificent example of historical drama which has slept too long in the book. Edmond de Goncourt, delighted at this requital, attended the reading, done now by Hennique, now by myself. The actors were astonished that I would contract to do a play with so heavy a setting. I have decided to attempt a truly sensational crowd effect for the scene at the town-hall.

FEBRUARY 20, 1889—A quote from Zola, who was interviewed following a report that I would present one of his plays:

> In addition to its other advantages, the Théâtre-Libre has for director an artist who is talented, dedicated, and intelligent—M. Antoine. It is not right, however, to attribute the success of this enterprise to him alone. The truth is that he came at just the right time. Yesterday he would perhaps have succumbed; one may believe that tomorrow he would have not succeeded. He came today. M. Antoine is the bearer of an idea, and his star protects him. Like General Boulanger, he succeeds in everything, even in his mistakes.
>
> At this moment, in the wake of *Germinie Lacerteux,* he demonstrates both his courage and his knowledge of the theatre by presenting *The Nation in Danger,* a play which, though written in 1866, has not yet seen the light of day.
>
> To sum up, I think it is certain that, thanks to the Théâtre-Libre, a change in favor of our new school in drama is coming to fruition. The influence of this new school is making itself felt ever more strongly on the public, and the time is not far off when a legion of young authors will popularize it on all the other stages of Paris.

---

[29]According to the Goncourt *Journals,* this reading took place the evening of January 16. Goncourt describes the setting:
There in a large room, whose three high windows hung with red drapes give from the court the impression of a fire inside, was a crowd of faded ladies, greyish in tone, poor in dress, sad and wilted; a group of bohemian actors, unshaven, their faces never touched by clean linen; and in the center a few long-haired poets, like Darzens, their shirts open, with Messianic features and dressed like undertakers. Hennique and Antoine read the play, which was applauded after each act.

FEBRUARY 22, 1889—It is amusing that the revival of Sardou's *Marquise* met the same fate at the Vaudeville as *M. Alphonse.* Lemaître says that the evening left him with a most melancholy impression. It seems to me that Ancey, Jullien, Salandri, and others of our house are partially responsible for this.

MARCH 12, 1889—This morning I found a violent article by Félicien Champsaur in the *Figaro* under the title "The Dealings of M. Antoine" which complains that I did not welcome *The Smart Set,* a play which he sent me. Clearly, the same old grudges are behind this.

MARCH 16, 1889—Goncourt sat next to me, happy as a child, during a rehearsal of *The Nation in Danger,* and seemed ready to applaud in the darkness of the house.[30] As the act at Verdun ended, he said to me: "If this doesn't please them, what will?"

MARCH 18, 1889—We have finished a series of tiring rehearsals of *The Nation in Danger.* The huge thing has caused a lot of trouble and been very expensive, but this evening M. de Goncourt was satisfied, and his delight in seeing on the stage at last a work which he has always cherished amply repaid me. There will be a very striking effect in the staging of the third act, which takes place in the town-hall at Verdun. I repeated the lighting technique from *The Duke of Enghien,* with the overhead lamps illuminating the swarming crowd. It was a truly beautiful moment, and I was rather proud to see a thrill pass over the master's face. I had nearly five hundred [*sic*]

---

[30]Goncourt's own statement is rather different:
Rehearsal at the Menus-Plaisirs until all hours. Mévisto and Barny hoarse, almost voiceless, Mlle. Deneuilly playing as if in pain, Antoine, who insisted upon taking the role of Boussanel, having not yet gone over the part from one end to the other, and leaving me undecided whether he will be good or detestable!
Antoine was in a very bad humor and harangued everyone, even myself a little about a move Barny made leaning on a crutch — a move which forced her to measure the time of the accompanying line. And everyone nervous, ready for arguments and disputes: the electrician wanting to fight with an extra, and the Count de Valjuzon exasperated at finding himself badly costumed and threatening to quit the part. And those who were not ready to tear out their hair playing as if asleep, as if under the influence of some opiate. In the midst of all this confusion, little Varly put her pretty lips next to my ear to whisper: "Ah, how I pity you, Monsieur, to be interpreted like this."

extras flow into a rather small setting through a single door. They slowly filtered in, like a subtle tide, at last inundating everything from the furnishings to the characters, and in the semi-darkness with light falling here and there on the teeming mass, the effect was extraordinary.

MARCH 20, 1889—Céard is most unkind to *The Nation in Danger,* and when one knows all about his estrangement with Edmond de Goncourt, one cannot help being pained by the grief the old master of Auteuil must feel when reading this article in the *Siècle.* The former adapter of *Renée Mauperin* administers the most ingeniously cruel blows to the spots which he knows are the most sensitive in the old man:

> At this time, the two brothers had already published *The Mistresses of Louis XV, The Eighteenth-Century Woman, French Society During the Revolution and the Directory*—curious books certainly in their minute attention to the accumulation of detail, not really historical works in the ordinary philosophic and humane sense of the word, but rather literary catalogues of the brothers' private collections. They egoistically reduced history to the books they bought, to the lists they had in their own possession, readily considering negligible and valueless all documents of which they were not the jealous owners. Moreover, deluding themselves by a convincing affectation of coyness, they misconstrue the sense of a phrase of Michelet in the preface to his book on the Regency; they pretend that they have been given an unimpeachable certificate by historians by a declaration which subtly denounces their intransigent narrowness, even though it gives credit to the ingenuousness of their spirit. They apply all their literary skill to making a compliment out of a rather harsh appraisal which gives due respect to their small knowledge, but makes it clear that this knowledge is never without some confusion and even inaccuracy. But no matter, in 1866 MM. Edmond and Jules de Goncourt, always strong in their opinion of them-

selves, were still able to consider themselves the only true repositories of the complete knowledge of the men and events of the 18th century. Again, because they most artistically described the insignificant aspects of an era in an outburst of illusion rendered respectable and even touching by its very naïveté, they came to think that they had penetrated this era to its most intimate depths.

MARCH 25, 1889—The reviews of *The Nation in Danger* are not favorable. The Goncourts are spoken of with respect, of course, but their play is considered tiring. Sarcey chides me severely about my handling of the crowd scenes in the act at Verdun, but concludes with a couplet in which he gives homage to the Goncourts. What pains me the most is to see Céard join forces with the adversaries of the master after frequenting his Garret and serving as one of his executors. They quarreled as a result of a discussion over an adaptation Céard made from the novel *Renée Mauperin* for the Odéon. It makes me very unhappy to see men of such worth and talent act in such an unjust and impassioned way. M. de Goncourt is really no more reasonable than Céard. One day in speaking of the journalist, he said bitterly: "He has taken everything of mine, up to my waistcoats."

MARCH 26, 1889—Derenbourg, excited by the last production, keeps tormenting me to give several public performances of *The Nation in Danger*. It is a foolish idea, for the play will be expensive to present, will interrupt and encumber our regular work, and will not be profitable enough to make up for this. Unfortunately, M. de Goncourt heard the proposal and insisted so strongly that we must carry out the imprudent venture.

MARCH 28, 1889—*The Nation in Danger* was given a public performance. The receipts were small, Derenbourg suffered heavy losses, M. de Goncourt was disappointed, and I was subjected to an endless number of interruptions of my work. From now on, I will not go along so easily; people simply will not listen to reason.

APRIL 15, 1889—Zola arrived late this evening to the rehearsal of his *Madeleine*. Letting himself fall rather heavily into the great red divan in the house, he said that he had traveled from Paris to Mantes by train during the day for a book he is getting ready* and he complained that both his legs were nearly broken by the vibration.

APRIL 22, 1889—The Comédie-Française has just revived Augier's *Master Guérin,* and Got is admirable in it. I think once again that the Théâtre-Libre movement has something to do with the boldness they showed in restoring the original ending of the play.

APRIL 25, 1889—After reading his *The Elder,* Léon Cladel told me: "Now you see, at the Théâtre-Libre you always speak rather softly. This verse must be shouted at the top of your lungs."

MAY 1, 1889—This evening we gave Zola's *Madeleine,* taken from his novel *Madeleine Ferat.* Zola wrote the play at twenty-five, when he was employed at the Hachette book-dealers, and he then took it to every theatre in Paris without success.

MAY 3, 1889—Porto-Riche invited me to lunch, saying: "I am going to introduce you to a delegate recently elected by my friends, who is going to become somebody."

It was Léon Bourgeois, who had indeed just been sent to the Chamber by la Marne. He spoke long and well, with a free-flowing eloquence different from the "tone" of our artistic circles.

Porto-Riche carries his elegant name with melancholy. Although he lives in a beautiful apartment in the Saint-Honoré district, he always thinks himself on the verge of bankruptcy. When I admired the arms which ornamented his study, he said: "Regard them well, especially that sallet, a marvel which you will never see again, for I am going to be forced to sell it," forgetting that he said exactly the same thing about these lovely objects the year before. Like

---

The Human Animal [Antoine's note]. The novel, which appeared late in 1889, concerned the railways, and the principal event in it was a murder in a railway carriage. Zola was apparently gathering impressions.

many of the younger authors, Porto-Riche is afraid of being considered a wealthy dilettante, and speaks incessantly of his difficulties, a conversation which contrasts amusingly with the ease and elegance that surrounds him.

MAY 4, 1889—In our last production, it was clearly Ancey's *The Inseparables* which carried the day. Its success was great and it was applauded act by act, scene by scene, line by line, as Vitu says—although he adds that he never heard anything more repulsive or depressing. The opening volley was fired by Léon Cladel's *The Elder,* a youthful work which was received as such, with great respect.

MAY 5, 1889—Zola, in an interview, said that he was quite surprised at the relative benevolence of the reviews of his *Madeleine,* and that he is not used to such consideration.

MAY 6, 1889—In his column this morning, Henry Bauer, who was once so cordial, finished by saying: "If it wishes to continue to prosper, the Théâtre-Libre will be naturalistic or it will not be at all."

I disagree completely. I think that too narrow a formula means death, and that we should, on the contrary, remain quite ready to welcome everyone. I already feel very acutely that we in the Rue Blanche are becoming a clique; the old guard at the Théâtre-Libre are disturbed by my eclecticism. I must move carefully, and steer a middle path between Bauer, who is ready to show his bad humor when he feels that he is not being heeded enough, and Mendès, who is more clever and devious in his influence, but no less dangerous. Zola, who knows the enormous influence he could exercise on me, is always careful to avoid interfering, and just now, though I am surrounded by writers and important men, he is the only one I feel to be truly great and clear-sighted.

MAY 10, 1889—The other day Goncourt did me the great honor of officially inviting me to his Sundays at the Garret. I turned down the invitation, however, and when he pressed me to tell him why, I recalled to him that one evening last year at Daudet's, Porel was mentioned in my presence, quite aimiably, but with the sort of veiled irony I always sense in authors discussing their interpreters. Someone told about a certain evening when Porel, seated at the piano, had talked to them for some time about music, singing and playing to the discreet amusement of the assembly. I told Goncourt that this little lesson had not been lost on me, and that I had resolved that very evening to always remain in my own circle so that I would never be "seated at the piano." There really is a sort of freemasonry against directors and actors among the dramatists—I imagine it is in unconscious revenge for the rather heavy tyranny to which they must submit during the rehearsals of their plays.

MAY 15, 1889—Hector Pessard, the critic of the *Gaulois* and a sort of sub-Sarcey without much brilliance but with a solid bourgeois good sense, took me gently by the arm the other evening at a dress rehearsal. "My dear Antoine," he said, "Stoullig has asked me to do the preface for his next *Annales* and your Théâtre-Libre seems to me to be the obvious subject this year. Since I want to be as thorough as I can, we really ought to have a chat. Come to lunch tomorrow at my home."

The next day found me at his house on the Rue Blanche, a pleasant little dwelling where I was cordially welcomed to his table. Upon my arrival, I was forced to take an obsequious interest in a young she-monkey, as large as a small girl. The creature was quite bothersome, and circled about the table to the affectionate delight of the masters of the house.

I was prepared to bend every effort to rally Pessard to our cause, and came hoping to win over to the new theatre this intransigent bourgeois, who criticizes us unmercifully after each production.

As we talked, I did not notice the monkey approaching me. It stole from one of my pockets a flask of ammoniac which I use for a cold, and suddenly bolted down the contents of it and fell over backward with almost human cries. This fit of hysterics upset the whole house, and the lunch came to an abrupt end with Pessard in great distress over the health of his animal.

MAY 20, 1889—Yesterday, on my way to the Menus-Plaisirs to consult Derenbourg about plans for our next production, curiosity led me to slip into the theatre where they are rehearsing *The Watch-Dog,* a new play by Jean Richepin. Taillade was rehearsing before the poet, who was seated at a small table on the apron. I became so interested in watching the actor that I was late for my appointment. Scrupulously careful, indeed almost finicky, he was never satisfied, but went back over certain replies five or six times. The great tragedian was never more handsome than when surprised in this secret work, with the worklights modeling his magnificent features.[31]

MAY 25, 1889—The end of the season was difficult, and I am glad to see it finished. We are in debt, and were able to get to the end only by selling subscriptions ahead for next season, which is only a form of borrowing.

JUNE 1, 1889—For six months the papers have been talking about *Old Lebonnard,* a four-act play that Jean Aicard had accepted at the Comédie-Française. Everyone was very enthusiastic about it, but once rehearsals were under way, troubles began. Apparently, the actors at the Française eventually realized that the play was still a long way from falling into shape. It was a most pitiful situation; the actors in it gave up their roles one by one until at last Aicard kicked up a row and withdrew it. I immediately offered the Théâtre-Libre to the poet, and he has at last decided to accept our hospitality.

JUNE 3, 1889—On our last program we gave a delightful and moving play by a young Russian, Count Stanislas Rzewuski, who has a most curious character. He was among the first subscribers signed up for the Théâtre-Libre, and often visits the Rue Blanche. One of the most well-informed men on contemporary European literature, he has established himself at Paris, where he is consuming a considerable fortune in gambling. They say that even in the highest circles, when

---

31*The Watch-dog* opened at the Menus-Plaisirs the following evening, and was one of Taillade's greatest successes.

it is his turn to distribute the cards at baccarat, he deals while continuing to read one of the innumerable little books with which his pocket is always crammed. With his *Count Witwold,* which proved very pleasing, we gave Méténier's *The Stewpan,* but this sort of play is wearing thin. The evening began with an adaptation by Ernest Laumann of Edgar Allen Poe's *The Tell-Tale Heart,* which attracted some interest.

JUNE 5, 1889—Jean Jullien and some of his friends have founded a weekly review called *Art et Critique,* in which he plans to defend our ideas and those of the upcoming generation.

JUNE 10, 1889—In his modest lodging on the Rue Madame, Jean Aicard read me his famous *Old Lebonnard.* In the very first scenes, I recognized that the play was a little too much in the tradition of the *"Ecole du bon sens"* for the Théâtre-Libre, but since there has been such a stir about it and it has been publicly withdrawn from the Comédie, I feel that it must be welcomed to our theatre, although it is more than likely that the company will not be very pleased.

Moreover, it is a theatre piece, as Sarcey says, and if its verses are willfully flat, the theories that Aicard proposes to advance publicly before the premiere and in a satiric prologue, giving an idea of the rehearsals of the play at the Comédie, will give the evening a very "forward-looking" appearance.

The author read in a warm and lilting Southern accent. At one point, I found him on his knees on the carpet before me, his manuscript in his hand, acting his play with every device of a consummate actor. I felt the justness of Got's observation: "You took in the Committee by reading too well."

JUNE 13, 1889—Félicien Champsaur pokes fun at current literature in his column this morning, describing it in terms of an imaginary parade. He proposes to hoist me up on a garbage truck.

JUNE 15, 1889—The directors of the theatres of Paris are complaining that the Exposition, which opened this evening, is drawing off most of their audiences.

Mévisto, less wise perhaps than I, has just accepted an offer from Porel to enter the Odéon.

JUNE 20, 1889—In the course of casting *Old Lebonnard* with Jean Aicard, I suggested to him the lad I met at Grenelle for the role which Le Bargy was to have created. Thus this morning, with an address which old Hartmann gave me, I climbed up to Grand's small dwelling in a remote section of Montparnasse, and dropped in on my future leading man, in shirt sleeves, who jumped with joy at the news I brought him.

JULY, 1889—Viewed as a whole, this season does not seem to me to equal the preceding one. Surely Ancey's *The Inseparables* and *The Duke of Enghien* were important contributions, but the poets, to whom I opened wide the doors, have really brought nothing. Jean Jullien's *The Date of Payment* was only a visiting card compared to his new and original *Serenade. Rolande* was an average modern play seasoned with the sauce of the house, and Céard's *The Meek* was not theatrical enough. Zola's three acts and *The Nation in Danger* were literary curiosities, valuable mostly because of the great names of their authors. I am beginning to realize that the Théâtre-Libre must follow new currents; I only wonder if the results will be sufficient to assure a sustained and fruitful campaign.

* * *

JULY 10, 1889—In the papers I am spoken of for the Cross! Some of the press is already worked up, and I think rightly so. I don't know who started this story, but at least it will serve the purpose of informing me what sort of feelings are held about me. Rather unpleasant remarks from Saint-Germain and Tessandier have been reproduced. Saint-Germain has sent a most genial apology, but all the same, we are in the midst of vacation, and they could surely leave me alone until September.

JULY 20, 1889—Ancey and I are spending the summer in an isolated little inn at the far end of the Bay of Douarnenez. Ancey is working on his *School for Widows* and I on my next season. Ajalbert has come to join us. This is truly a delightful vacation, but it would be more delightful still if I were not so terribly short of money.

Just now, upon going into Douarnenez to pick up my mail at general delivery, I was surprised to find a letter from Alphonse Daudet, sent from Champrosay, which said: "My dear Antoine, I am here with Goncourt, and we remembered that we have not yet retained our box for next winter." In the envelope was a money order for three hundred francs. I was deeply touched by this example of delicate sensitivity in Daudet, who must have heard from someone how difficult life is for me in the summer.

AUGUST 26, 1889—As I expected, Hector Pessard's preface for the *Annales du théâtre et de la musique* is rather severe. He reproaches me for not having regenerated the theatre—in three years! And yet I never contracted nor promised to regenerate it. In short, he really lays on the stick for twenty pages—an attack which, as a matter of fact, has brought protests. Lemaître himself reproaches his colleague for not recognizing that many of the plays which we presented had something that was lacking in most of the well-made plays being given at the same time in the regular theatres.

SEPTEMBER 1, 1889—Villiers de l'Isle-Adam has died, after living for a long time far from the public eye, without anyone even being able to find out where he was. The whole literary world mourns the great writer.

SEPTEMBER 2, 1889—*Old Lebonnard,* which we are just now beginning to rehearse, will really cut a strange figure next to *The School for Widows, The Duke of Enghien,* and *The Serenade.* Aicard boasts of having done something new by creating bourgeois poetry:
"I want red beef and soft-boiled eggs,"
but the play is not in our line. Long faces surrounded me at its reception. I have explained what a good thing it is to open our ranks to include a favorite son of the official theatre, pleading that his fit of

revolt is a contribution which our campaign should use. Aicard has also composed a sort of prologue, which will give the public all the necessary background before the presentation. It shows a rehearsal at the Comédie-Française with the director and actors on stage, and he has enshrined some delightful comments in it which were blurted out by the actors.

September 10, 1889—Aicard has just read me his quite spirited prologue for *Old Lebonnard*. The announcement of it has stimulated great curiosity. I have distributed it to my actors, who will make up as the members of the Comédie. We will avoid the expenses for scenery which are gradually ruining us, for the scene represents a bare stage with the simple furniture and accoutrements of rehearsals.

September 15, 1889—I am particularly interested in everything in the current Exposition relating to the theatre. I have spent several evenings at the Esplanade des Invalides where a troupe of Annamese actors are giving presentations of extraordinary interest. Nothing in the place suggests the Western way of doing things; there is a simple platform, no footlights, only tables and chairs, and a wild orchestra which takes some getting used to. Once one has done this, however, the impression is gripping. The nasality and gutteral chants of the splendidly garbed and painted actors are soon forgotten and one ends by following the drama with as much interest and enthusiasm as a play in French. The plays are great national epics, lasting for several hours, and requiring no properties or furniture. The other day an actor gave a most admirable imitation of a man escaping from a cage where he had been shut up for years, loosening his stiffened members little by little during a desperate flight across the rice fields. Another's imitation of a god—half man, half monkey— was one of the most amazing things I have ever seen.

October 3, 1889—Claretie is very disturbed over the announced prologue at the Théâtre-Libre and sent word to Aicard that such a demonstration would cause a definitive break with the Comédie.

Aicard wrote a public answer to this letter, saying that it is a mistake to threaten him with reprisals.

OCTOBER 9, 1889—All this *Old Lebonnard* business has filled the papers for two weeks; there are poems, reports, fantasies—everyone is getting in on it. Sarcey has devoted himself to parrying the blows and saving the face of his beloved Comédie-Française.

OCTOBER 12, 1889—The return of Coquelin the elder as pensionary to the Comédie, after his recent desertion for profit-making tours, is causing some discord, but Coquelin has such popular prestige that he remains master of the situation. Still, there is a lot of uproar about the house, and it comes at a bad time, when we are going to call attention to the Committee in our prologue to *Old Lebonnard*.

OCTOBER 15, 1889—At the rehearsal, Aicard showed me a short note concerning *Old Lebonnard* which Got had left once at his house: "For three days we have conscientiously tried to put the third act on stage. It is impossible."

OCTOBER 22, 1889—Premiere of *Old Lebonnard*. The prestige of the Comédie is still so great that the now-famous prologue *In the Guignol* not only seemed bothersome and out of place, but led to so severe a chill that we feared for the play. It was a great success, however, especially in the third act, and Grand, who made his debut this evening, was really quite good. All this was accomplished with no help from Lugné-Poë, who fluffed his lines in the last act.

NOVEMBER 1, 1889—Sarcey apparently will not forgive me for a long time for my irreverant attitude toward the Comédie. Yet if we were not altogether in the right in this *Old Lebonnard* business, we were not altogether in the wrong either, and our success with the public was quite pronounced.

A very clever and skillful director, this Antoine, but I'm hanged if I understand why he has the reputation of

116 ·

being an actor! He delivers verse in a boring monotone—no sparkle, not a word that glitters or stirs. He doesn't get his bearings until the big scene, and there too his only movement is a rather pathetic re-entrance, the only kind his voice will allow. Still, I applauded because he is, after all, the soul of this little world and with all his faults he is superior in intellect and force of will to actors who possess only natural gifts and technique. But Antoine, actor—it's a joke!

NOVEMBER 3, 1889—Burguet, our companion in the first productions of the Théâtre-Libre, has just left the Conservatory and gained great success in a small part at the premiere of *The Struggle for Life*[32] at the Gymnase.

NOVEMBER 5, 1889—Aicard has written this letter to Sarcey:
Monsieur Sarcey,

In your latest column, you directed defamatory imputations against my person, against which I lodge the strongest disclaimer, reserving my explanations and proofs for the proper quarters.

I demand that you insert this disclaimer in your next column. I am sure you will agree that it is only right that it pass before the eyes of your regular readers.

Sincerely yours,   Jean Aicard.
The other answered thus:

I do not hesitate to insert this denial, since a denial has been made. In the profession which I follow, one should always bear in mind the famous saying of Doctor Blanche: "When they are in that state, you can't argue with them." I am satisfied in saying that M. Jean Aicard's play is worth nothing and that the Comédie was quite right in not presenting it.

NOVEMBER 10, 1889—The memory of the fire at the Opéra-Comique

---

[32]A play by Daudet, which opened October 31. Burguet played the part of Antonin.

still terrifies the public so much that Chastenet tells me that in choosing their places, the subscribers of the Théâtre-Libre always ask to be put at the ends of the rows, near the doors.

NOVEMBER 18, 1889—The dismal failure of *The Woodcutter's Wife* certainly comes at a bad time for the Comédie.[33] Sarcey himself is discomfited, and says: "It would accomplish nothing to hide the reception the public gave this play on opening night." This is causing much delight at the Rue Blanche, and several wags wondered if M. Charles Edmond might bring me his *Woodcutter's Wife* with an explanatory prologue.

NOVEMBER 20, 1889—Ancey told us this evening how in his youth he had written a sonnet in praise of Delaunay. The famous actor answered a note from him, and granted him an interview. Ancey was told by the eternal young lead: "Well now, sit there and begin." Ancey recited his poem after a fashion, and then Delauney arose: "Yes, that's not bad, but more intonations are necessary," and began in his turn to recite his own eulogy with great ease and consummate art. Then he asked: "When will you present yourself to the Conservatory?"

NOVEMBER 25, 1889—This evening we were visited in the Rue Blanche by two new-comers—Tristan Bernard and Pierre Véber, two witty young journalists who jot down a survey of contemporary happenings in the *Gil Blas* each week. This survey, called the *Chasseur de chevelures,* is illustrated with scintillating vigor by Jean Véber.

NOVEMBER 27, 1889—This evening we gave Ancey's *The School for Widows,* which in my opinion is an important work. The daring of the subject did not disturb the audience and its success was great; a dialogue of extraordinary movement, precision, and depth quite swept away the house with enthusiasm. This is certainly the newest, the boldest, and at the same time the most classic play since Becque.

---

[33]Edmond's play opened November 13, lasted only six performances.

I have worked very hard with Mayer and Mlle. Henriot to get across the interior workings of these scenes and their multiple movement; It is perhaps the first time I have realized the power of the unconsciously comic. A phrase which would be revolting if delivered by an actor who realized the enormity of what he was saying can become a stupendous jest if it simply slips out in the sincerity of the character. I find that the Théâtre-Libre, without any of us planning it, but simply through its unswerving devotion to the sense and spirit of its works, is in the process of creating something new in the actor's art. Thus in Mirelet's frightful situation in the fourth act we find a striking transposition of *The School for Wives* and of the famous: "I will justify myself no further about that," of Arnolphe to Agnès. Here Agnès is a prostitute and Arnolphe a pimp, but this is humanity and life. The first scene, the funeral, turned out to be astonishingly funny, and Janvier and Clerget played it marvelously.

DECEMBER 4, 1889—Mme. Allemand, who directs the Scala and the Eldorado in our neighborhood and who never misses a presentation at the Théâtre-Libre, is so enthusiastic that she earnestly asked Ancey to let her use *The School for Widows* for one of her musical entertainments.

JANUARY-JUNE, 1890

JANUARY 10, 1890—Brieux makes his living as editor-in-chief of the *Nouvelliste* in Rouen, and therefore cannot often make the trip to Paris. When I have to see him, it is I who travel. Thus I came this fine sunny morning to the top of the Bon-Secours district, where he has a small and simple cottage. We jogged down into town for a pleasant lunch; and since Brieux had to work on his paper, I went there with him. I was amused to see this smiling, energetic fellow taking on the crushing responsibilities of a provincial paper almost single-handedly, becoming in turn a Magnard, a Scholl, a Thomas Grimm—reporter, feature writer, or sociologist. At this moment he is even publishing technical studies of the docks of Le Havre and Rouen. Such varied labor will be most helpful in the young man's development by giving him a sense of reality and a knowledge of the public which will be invaluable in his career as a dramatist.

JANUARY 12, 1890—Turgenev's *The Bread of Yesteryear,* which we gave yesterday, did not get by unchallenged. Yet it is a beautiful play, with Russian scenes of admirable color and pathos. The reviews are not bad, but the audience was odious. It must be admitted that Lugné-Poé was very clumsy, and had to be "carried" the whole second act.

We also gave a violent one-act play by Henry Fèvre, *In Distress,* which went very well. The evening was to have been completed by *The Unfaithful One,* a one-act verse play by Porto-Riche, but when I was unable to get Coquelin senior to create the title role, the author withdrew the play to take it to the Vaudeville.[34]

---

[34] Porto-Riche actually took his work to the Théâtre d'Application, another small theatre presenting original scripts. It was produced there before going on to the Vaudeville, where it was presented March 25, 1891. Porto-Riche never got Coquelin; M. Laroche played the title role in both theatres.

JANUARY 12, 1890—This evening I met Zola, who drew my attention to an article by Jacques Saint-Cère[35] concerning a Scandinavian author who has just had a work presented with enormous effect in Germany.

JANUARY 14, 1890—I went to ask Jacques Saint-Cère for his article. He is well informed on German matters, having been for a long time secretary to Paul Lindau, a journalist and theatre director there. Saint-Cère tells me that the play in question is a three-act drama about heredity, the title of which in French would be *les Revenants*. The author, Henrik Ibsen, virtually exiled from his country (he lives in Munich), is already considered in our neighboring country as one of the greatest dramatists to appear in some time.

JANUARY 14, 1890—Just while we were giving Turgenev's *The Bread of Yesteryear,* Koning revived *The Danicheffs*. The enthusiasm which greeted this play's first performance at the Odéon has already disappeared, and it seemed like pallid dregs next to the great wine of Turgenev.

JANUARY 15, 1890—Zola recently spoke to me of his candidacy for the Academy, saying that he doesn't have much confidence, despite the devotion of his friend François Coppée, but that he will see the matter through and stay with it as long as is necessary.[36] He feels this to be a continuation of the battle which he has fought so long and the duty of the leader of a school.

JANUARY 20, 1890—We are back at the Parc in Brussels and are giving some rather profitable productions, the proceeds from which are badly needed in our coffers in Paris. We are giving *Old Lebon-*

---

[35] Two articles on Ibsen written by Saint-Cère appeared in the *Revue d'Art Dramatique* in March-April, 1887.

[36] Urged by Coppée, Zola applied for Augier's chair and was defeated in December of 1890 by Freycinet. He remained a perpetual candidate, beaten by Loti in 1891, Lavisse in 1892, Challemel-Lacour and Brunetière in 1893, Heredia and Bourget in 1894, and Theuriet in 1896, after which the Dreyfus affair removed him from consideration.

nard, and although it was lightly dismissed by the papers, it is nevertheless attracting the attention of the public.

JANUARY 22, 1890—Kistemaeckers, an editor with whom I was chatting just now, told me how at a dangerous time he published the young French realists. This led us to speak of the Théâtre-Libre and the furious attacks of certain individuals concerned over its immorality. He smilingly took a tin box full of letters from the corner of his desk, and showed me some letters from one of our most inveterate adversaries concerning the publication of an unusually licentious book of which this very writer is the author! I brought a copy away with me.

* * *

JANUARY 29, 1890—A note in the papers says that I am "assured of the assistance of several financiers to construct a theatre in Paris." I have no such ambition, and would indeed be much happier if I could gain the acquaintance of one of these Maecenases just to be sure of finishing the season.

FEBRUARY 2, 1890—Méténier tells me that at the first reading of *The Zemganno Brothers*—a completely private affair at Goncourt's home, with only Mme. Alphonse Daudet and her husband invited—he looked up from his manuscript to see tears running down the cheeks of Edmond de Goncourt, who in his close life with his departed elder was the true Gianni.[37]

FEBRUARY 5, 1890—I shared what I was able to learn about Ibsen and his *Ghosts* with Zola, who strongly urges me to give it at the Théâtre-Libre. He has promised to check among the foreigners who constantly call on him, and to find someone who can translate the play.

FEBRUARY 7, 1890—Porel, who has a flair for great spectacles, presented Goethe's *Egmont* at the Odéon. It was a very beautiful

---

[37]This reading actually took place on January 7, 1889. According to Méténier, it was Antoine who first suggested adapting this novel to the stage.

evening, but the French public remained indifferent, as it always is to such magnificent things.

FEBRUARY 15, 1890—Grand and I have been going every morning for a number of days to practice on the riding track at the Nouveau-Cirque in the Rue Saint-Honoré. The good Médrano, inexhaustibly patient and obliging, is training us in several tricks of the trade, so that we will not appear too clownishly awkward when we portray the Zemganno brothers.

FEBRUARY 15, 1890—I just now received a visit from one M. Hessem, whose name seems to me clearly a pseudonym. He is a small, rather sickly person, blond, and timid. He gave me the manuscript of a play entitled *Ghosts,* written in a scholarly hand—regular, but fearfully cramped—with this accompanying letter from Zola:

> Dear M. Antoine:
>
> Permit me to recommend to you M. Louis de Hessem, who is in the process of translating *Ghosts,* the play by Ibsen of which we spoke. I think that you will find this play to have an individuality which, if not as arresting as that of *The Power of Darkness,* is yet of at least equal literary interest.
>
> Cordially yours, Emile Zola.

FEBRUARY 17, 1890—I have read *Ghosts*. It is like nothing in our theatre; a study of heredity, the third act of which has the somber grandeur of a Greek tragedy. But it seems too long to me—which may be due to the translation into French from a German text, itself an adaptation from the Norwegian. Apparently this is what slows down and obscures the dialogue, but even so, we should not hesitate.

FEBRUARY 20, 1890—During the rehearsal just completed, I analyzed Edmond de Goncourt's profile with curiosity; it is truly one of the most distinguished I ever hope to see. Braquemond's etching faithfully catches the style of this head with beautiful silver hair, fine falling mustaches, and the peculiar unkempt elegance of that white silk neckerchief which the old man never gives up.

Despite the friendliness and relaxation he shows in our midst, where he is treated as a dean of letters, the great writer remains somewhat aloof from all the young men who flock about him. Once when Méténier, in Southern exuberance, placed a hand on his shoulder, a certain indescribable haughtiness passed through the eyes of the master, and he all but made the gesture of dusting himself off a bit.

FEBRUARY 23, 1890—This morning we had a dress rehearsal of *The Zemganno Brothers* in the theatre. During the second act— charmingly set in the courtyard of the two brothers' home—when Sylviac stepped over the threshold, I immediately realized that his horse was not to scale. To make things right again, we are going to have to look for a small pony.

FEBRUARY 25, 1890—*The Zemganno Brothers* was received coolly at its premiere this evening. Yet the play has a delicate emotion which should charm the Théâtre-Libre audience, which, to judge from its complaints, seems to be growing rather tired of violent works. There really seems to be an antipathy against Goncourt which neither time, nor the age nor high position of the master, can extinguish.

It was pleasant to put the play on stage, and I enjoyed directing it, yet I feel a great concern this evening. I spent a good deal of money, and now that the intoxication of the production is over, I feel the weight of my heavy responsibilities. These financial matters must, of course, remain secret, especially from the authors, and when Goncourt thanked me, I showed an impassiveness which he took for indifference and could not understand.

FEBRUARY 26, 1890—In Porel's defense, one must give him credit for tenacity and perseverance. He accepted Ancey's three-act play, *Grandmother,* and presented it this evening at the Odéon. The heavy-handed interpretation lacked imagination and humor, and a hostile house became indignant, almost disgusted by its coarseness.

I am quite sure that despite all of Hennique's apprehensive precautions and diplomatic advice, his play, which is to be presented next, will not escape a similar fate—a first-class funeral.

MARCH 2, 1890—I am still disturbed about *Ghosts.* Its length seems excessive for an audience so quickly bored as that of the Théâtre-Libre. Yesterday evening at the end of the rehearsal in the Rue Blanche, I asked Mendès, Céard, and Ancey to remain after the others had gone, to listen to a reading of it and to give me their advice.

I told them that, in my opinion, there is something great in it, which I would not want to compromise by a clumsy production. Perhaps cuts are necessary, and it seems to me that this should be done by a literary man, one of our own dramatists, who would take the responsibility and who could do justice to this great discovery. I wouldn't want to trifle with a work of this importance myself. They were all three struck by the new accent and force of the drama. A short silence followed the reading, and I asked for their sincere advice.

Mendès, whose impression was of the greatest importance to me, spoke first. He leaned back in his chair with his characteristic gesture of tossing back his hair, saying: "My dear friend, this play is impossible here." Céard, no less direct, said: "Yes, it is quite beautiful, but it is not clear enough for our Latin minds. I would like to see a prologue, which would show us Oswald's father and Regina's mother surprised by the young Mrs. Alving—in short, a dramatization of the narrative the Chamberlain's wife makes to the pastor. After this exposition, the French public could securely enter into the drama." As for Ancey, he said simply: "It is magnificent; it doesn't need to be touched. If you are afraid of slow places, and it certainly has them, perhaps because of the translation, make the cuts yourself out of the small talk which your actors don't care for anyway." In sum, all three were struck differently, according to their temperament or mentality, but I feel that none of them would care to assume the responsibility of putting it on stage.

MARCH 3, 1890—The good Adrien Bernheim, in his column in the *Nation,* deals severely with Ancey's play at the Odéon, an opinion shared by all the other papers. Sarcey says that the play was a dismal failure, even though up until now he has strongly supported the author of *The School for Widows* and *The Inseparables.* He is no easier on *The Zemganno Brothers,* even though it is a new play, devoid of coarseness, which combines in the theatre for the first time what Goncourt calls "the modern picturesque" and the world of acrobats and the circus.

MARCH 5, 1890—The Variétés has presented *Monsieur Betsy,* a play by Paul Alexis and Oscar Méténier. I refused it myself because these authors no longer have any claim on the Théâtre-Libre, which is reserved for the new. I really must confess that this fantasy seemed much closer to vaudeville than comedy to me—and at the Variétés, Réjane, Dupuis, and Baron played it in the proper style. In any case, within a single week, the Théâtre-Libre influence has entered the Odéon with *Grandmother* and the Variétés with *Monsieur Betsy.* Several critics noticed this and showed signs of being disturbed.

Albert Wolff, aware of this danger, once again pounced on us. His *Courrier de Paris* is dedicated to "a young man" to whom he says: "You know that we are waiting for you, and when you come we will give you such a success that the dramatic carnival from which we have been suffering for some time will soon come to an end." Then, after three columns of venting his spleen on us, he adds: "The young man who will free us from all this cannot be far off. We shall bear him in triumph." But I am looking for this young man, too, and how I would laugh if—and I think this most probable—he should come from our theatre.

MARCH 6, 1890—René Doumic is the only reviewer who seems to have discerned the good qualities of *Grandmother* through the gloom, and he says that Ancey will not emerge diminished from this affair.

This is really good! Hennique's *Love* failed this evening at the Odéon. Porel continues to heap blame on Hennique, who has done everything to pacify him.

MARCH 7, 1890—Since the Comédie-Française has announced that it has accepted *Catherine,* by Henri Lavedan, I am quite determined to emphasize that this author too made his debut at the Théâtre-Libre, and not long ago.

*   *   *

MARCH 9, 1890—A comment that has been current for some time, even among our adversaries: "Clearly, the Théâtre-Libre has not given us particularly beautiful plays, but one cannot deny that it has shown us how bad most of those were that we saw before its coming."

MARCH 11, 1890—The censor has just banned *Mahomet,* by M. Henri de Bornier, which was beginning rehearsals at the Comédie. So much the better. Censorship can never commit enough blunders and damage, and when its blows fall on official backs, it serves them right.

MARCH 12, 1890—Eugène Brieux—whose first play, *Artists' Households,* we are going to give—is a thin youth with delicate features, blue metallic eyes, pointed moustaches and beard. He lives in Rouen and has just rediscovered an old school chum at the Théâtre-Libre. This is Gaston Salandri, with whom he perpetrated his first comedy, *The Old Maid,* which was submitted to Sarcey. When the critic had read it, he looked searchingly into their eyes, asking severely: "Is this in earnest?" and both almost wept in distress.

Sent to Rouen for the elections of 1885, Brieux remained there as editor-in-chief of the *Nouvelliste.* He has made an important place for himself there, and has had a drama and a comic opera given at the town theatre.

MARCH 13, 1890—In an open letter, Alexis and Méténier have sharply challenged Albert Wolff for treating the Théâtre-Libre as an unsavory haunt, and Hennique wrote to Magnard in connection with *Love,* asking if Sarcey had the right to say that a play would make no money at all. We in the Rue Blanche have firmly decided to let nothing pass unchallenged, for it seemed to me that we have been mistaken to leave the field open until now to those who have the public ear and who work against us without fear of contradiction. Zola has supported us by writing to Bauer:

Paris, March 10, 1890

My dear Bauer:

My old friend Hennique came to me very disturbed by an article by Sarcey on his play, and he would like to enlist you in his behalf. The opinion which he puts forward in a response with which he will acquaint you is one that I too have often expressed; and I join him in thinking that certain critics are on very thin ice when they are so hard on talented young writers, depriving the latter of any success by abusing the influence these critics have on the public. This is an abominable act, even from a strictly commercial point of view, for imagine a young author who needs the receipts of the evening to eat. What a wretched thing you would be doing then if you said to the public: "Do not go." The question is a stimulating one, so see if it would not be worthwhile to consider it with your usual devoted interest.

Cordially yours, Emile Zola.

MARCH 15, 1890—I would like very much to find a way of comparing the original Norwegian text of *Ghosts* with the translation that I have at hand. I spoke of this to Darzens, who said: "I have a highly literate friend who was a lumber agent in the North for a firm in Le Havre and who lived in that country for some time. If you wish, I will ask him to make me a word-for-word translation of the original text. Let me be responsible for the work; I will answer for everything." It was therefore agreed that he would do whatever was necessary.

MARCH 15, 1890—Amiens has joined in; they are going to establish a Théâtre-Libre there.

MARCH 17, 1890—Word has come that the Théâtre-Libre of London has just given Ibsen's *Ghosts*.[38] The entire English press condemns the play as revoltingly immoral and obscene. The *Times* speaks of "the lugubrious and malodorous world of Ibsen."

MARCH 18, 1890—The rehearsals of Jean Jullien's *The Master* are going well. If these peasants do not disgust my audience, it will be a great success; it is the first study of real flesh and bone men of the earth in the theatre since George Sand.

MARCH 18, 1890—A painter whom Jean Jullien brought to the theatre did a painting, "A Reading at the Théâtre-Libre," which he has shown me and which I find most interesting. I would have liked to buy it, but alas, I don't have a cent.

MARCH 20, 1890—In his column in the *Soleil,* M. Claveau says that the naturalism of the Théâtre-Libre, for all its swagger, has been on the down-grade for many a long day.

MARCH 20, 1890—Ajalbert just informed me that he has obtained permission from Goncourt to make a play from *Elisa the Slattern.* When we announced this in the papers, there were protests and demands if this were really necessary.

MARCH 22, 1890—Last night Eugène Brieux made his debut at our house with *Artists' Households*. It contains much ranting and many commonplaces, but, as I expected, an extraordinary parting scene between Sylviac and myself in the third act was strikingly effective. The cause was a dialogue whose life, tone, and truth made it clear why I had given a play apparently much less taut and daring than those we usually give. Brieux, who came to Paris for several

---

38The March 13 production of this play was the first offering of J. T. Grein's Independent Theatre.

rehearsals and the premiere, returned to Rouen quite happy.

MARCH 22, 1890—Sarcey says that Brieux's play is a very puerile thing and a failure, and the reviews in general are severe. Jules Lemaître feels that the author should be given a second chance. Adrien Bernheim, in the *Nation,* calls the play "inconsequential and unproductive chit-chat."

MARCH 23, 1890—Jean Jullien's *The Master,* a strong and restrained study of peasant life given the same evening as *Artists' Households,* was considered a real success by almost all the reviewers. Janvier and Luce Colas were first-class. What makes me laugh is that the critics, so chary just now of realistic plays, did not recognize that we have never given a more truly revolutionary work than this one. Jean Jullien's play buries forever the insipid peasant stories of George Sand.

MARCH 23, 1890—*Germinie Lacerteux* has just been revived at the Odéon.[39] There was no trace of the storms which attended the premiere; a quiet audience listened to the play with interest. Sarcey in his column vainly repeated that his opinion—that it is a play of pretentious mediocrity—had not changed. Still, he was obliged to admit that the large audience did not appear to share his misgivings.

MARCH 24, 1890—Janvier, who just triumphed in *The Master,* is only twenty years old. He still works at an insurance company, and even with the success which has just welcomed him, he hesitates to commit himself entirely to the theatre. His friend Arquillière, who was also much applauded in *The Master,* is just twenty too. He is still a house painter, as he was three years ago when I welcomed him to Montparnasse.

MARCH 24, 1890—The Théâtre-Libre of Berlin has just given Henri Becque's *The Vultures.*[40]

---

[39] Antoine is mistaken by a year here. *Germinie* was revived March 2, 1891.
[40] Again, an error of a year. Otto Brahm gave Becque's play, called in German *Die Krähen,* in March, 1891.

MARCH 27, 1890—Auguste Germain, Bauer's secretary, has just released a letter to the press announcing that since I have not presented his play *The Peace of the House* within the agreed time, he is withdrawing it from our theatre. Good riddance! I really only took the play under pressure from his circle, to avoid the trouble that I have seen coming for a long time. Bauer has backed up his secretary in the *Echo de Paris,* and they are attempting to get up a campaign—for they have been lying in wait for me in that quarter for some time.

MARCH 30, 1890—The Germain affair, as I expected, is becoming more serious. Bauer has taken it over and started a column in the *Echo de Paris* with the heading "The Antoine Incident." Since I attempted to answer and the letter was not printed, I had to appeal to the courts for a trial to obtain the necessary rectification. Succeeding articles end each day with a "to be continued," promising a new broadside for the following day. All those I have offended, all the people whose plays I have refused, all the enemies of the Théâtre-Libre are rallying for what the *Echo de Paris* calls "the execution of the capitalist of the Théâtre-Libre."

APRIL 1, 1890—In a letter to the *Gil Blas,* Céard explains that upon reflection, he did not think it possible to make an adaptation of *Ghosts,* since the work must keep its essentially local psychology. Of course, we never considered laying a hand on Ibsen's play; there was never a question of doing anything more than lightening a text the abundance of which made us rather fearful for the slow scenes. Moreover, it is probable that this is the fault of the translation, for when Darzens brought me the original text, I was surprised to find it much shorter than the French manuscript. Perhaps in Norwegian, as in German, a word can only be translated by four or five of ours.

APRIL 1, 1890—In a major article in the *Revue des Deux Mondes,* Brunetière considers the current dramatic movement at length, reproaching Ancey, Brieux, and Jullien for thinking of their studies as works. He does not appear entirely hostile, however, and seems to agree to the usefulness of a possible reform. This is a very important straw in the wind.

APRIL 2, 1890—I went to one of the regular receptions at the Charpentiers' this evening, half-hoping to meet Bauer there in public at the moment when our controversy is at its height, but he did not come. Zola most touchingly insisted upon publicly demonstrating a particular friendliness toward me. He hailed me in a loud voice: "Well, my poor Antoine, a pretty kettle of fish! Ah well, come drink with me at the buffet." Daudet and Goncourt came too, anxious to register their feelings in this matter. I left the Rue de Grenelle with Mendès and we walked down the boulevard together. He spoke to me at length about Bauer, and I sensed that he was not particularly sorry to see me in open combat with his eminent collaborator on the *Echo de Paris.*

It has been announced that Albert Carré has accepted Germain's play for his Thursday matinées.

APRIL 3, 1890—The violent campaign in the *Echo de Paris* goes on and on. My friend Séverine has come to my rescue with a fine article in the *Gil Blas,* and a reaction is already forming. Fouquier and Magnard have briskly taken up my defense, although of course with all the circumspection imposed by the brotherhood.

APRIL 5, 1890—We were speaking of Daudet the other evening, and someone (I no longer remember who) said that no one shows a more sincere and considerate charity than he for the distressed folk who come to him. I am not speaking of his immediate following, for whom he unceasingly exerts himself with editors or newspaper publishers, but of the innumerable solicitors attracted to him by his reputation. He often helps out some poor devil in whose eyes he sees a request for aid which timidity keeps in the suppliant's throat; moreover, he always has a cup in his anteroom with a louis or two in it, which the pseudo-mendicant can pocket before leaving, without the embarrassment of asking alms or of giving thanks.

*   *   *

APRIL 10, 1890—Jules Lemaître's comedy in four acts, *The Rebel,* was a big success at the Odéon.[41] The critic of the *Débats,* for all his reservations about our productions, was apparently crafty enough to borrow what he needed from us for his entertaining, if opportunistic, success.

APRIL 20, 1890—Darzens brought me the translation of *Ghosts* today. We compared it with the one I have at hand, and found that there is indeed a world of difference between them. I have therefore decided to give Darzens' translation, and he has already established relations with Ibsen, who has kindly written me the following letter:

> Sir:
>
> I hasten to reply to your pleasant letter which I had the honor to receive today.
>
> Since the founding of the Théâtre-Libre, I have followed the activity of this interesting enterprise with the closest attention, and I was very pleased to learn, two years ago, that you were planning to present my play *Ghosts* in the theatre which you direct.
>
> The translation which M. Darzens made and sent to me seems most suitable and conforms closely to the original. Despite my obligations to M. de Prozor, therefore, I see no objection to giving my consent—which you have so graciously requested—to the presentation of M. Darzens' translation at the Théâtre-Libre.
>
> I await the fruits of your labors with great interest. In thanking you for the warm welcome you have given my work, I remain, etc.
>
> Signed: Henrik Ibsen

And here is his letter to Darzens:

> To Monsieur Rodolphe Darzens:
>
> I was honored to receive your letter, and later, a copy of your translation of my play, *Ghosts.* Please accept my most

---

41An error of a year. Lemaître's play was presented April 9, 1889.

sincere thanks for both and also my apologies for not responding to you until today.

I was pleasantly surprised by your grasp of Norwegian, and the friendly interest which you show in my literary work gives me great happiness.

The word *Haandsraekning* has no double meaning. It has the idea of friendly aid in danger. Oswald means by this word that if it is necessary, he wants someone to agree to give him poison if he is incapable of taking it himself.

Fraternal greetings to you. I remain your devoted

Henrik Ibsen.

MAY 2, 1890—We have given Louis Mullem's *A New School,* together with Boniface and Bodin's *Aunt Léontine* and *Jacques Bouchard,* a first play by Albert Wolff's nephew.

Aunt Léontine was enormously successful. The savage comedy captivated the audience in its very opening lines, and even while I was acting in an extremely funny scene in the third act, I was aware of Sarcey in the balcony, for he literally doubled up with a burst of laughter so loud that the whole audience looked at him. Then they all began to laugh for so long that we on stage were unable to regain our composure during the rest of the scene. The critic of the *Temps* gave Boniface and Bodin's play an enthusiastic eulogy, without recognizing that it is perhaps one of the most revolutionary plays we have given. The two authors were talented enough to coat their pill with vaudeville turns, which got it by. As for the unhappy Pierre Wolff, he certainly got a drubbing from everyone, and Doumic says he is sorry that this hoaxter was not accompanied home, as he deserved, with catcalls and hisses.

MAY 3, 1890—I am really too lucky. Pierre Wolff's play, *Jacques Bouchard,* is certainly the most violent work we have ever given. Although there was no part in it for me, I wanted to be on stage to watch Albert Wolff's expression during the performance. I there-fore played the almost mute wine merchant who spends the play rinsing glasses behind the bar. The furious uncle left the theatre as soon as the curtain descended. Pierre Wolff is now one of our circle, and we have become such good friends that we will spend our next vacation together in Brittany. Ancey, who is also very fond of him, agrees with me that deep down within this lad there sleeps a real gift for dialogue. He has the spirit of his uncle, whom, moreover, he astonishingly resembles.

MAY 4, 1890—Mullem, the author of *A New School,* which we gave at our last performance, is a member of the *Justice* group which includes Clemenceau, Pelletan, Geffroy, Millerand, Pichon, Charles Martel, and others. This group is producing some of the most interesting writing in Paris.

MAY 8, 1890—Someone asked our budding young author, Pierre Wolff, for an autograph, and he wrote: "When we are walking down the street and hear the words slut, jerk, for Chrissake, and so on, we don't even turn around. On the stage, however, these same words always astonish the audience. Why?"

MAY 13, 1890—Sarcey was certainly impressed with our *Aunt Léontine,* for he talked about it again in yesterday's column. He says that Adolphe Brisson gave a much-applauded reading of the play in the Salle des Capucines, and also that he had seen the authors, Maurice Boniface and Bodin, to tell them of his intention to have the play presented in a boulevard theatre. He doesn't know Boniface—who declined the offer, saying that he would prefer to leave this battle behind him now that it is won, and to begin another with a new play. Sarcey declares that he is quite encouraged to see that the sap is still flowing. He speaks of Henri Lavedan, also from our house, who is about to be represented by a major work at the Français, and mentions Ancey, too, saying: "There is no lack of authors."

Our horizons seem to be broadening, but those in the Rue Blanche who think that we have permanently forced open the doors are sadly deluded. Each striking success pushes them ajar, but at the least lapse, we shall find them shut in our faces. I seem more aware than anyone that this will go on for years and years. At the moment, the outlook is very bright; the year seems to be ending most propitiously. Still, I chuckle to myself because I know that the play I have just received from Descaves will stir up a fine fight.

MAY 20, 1890—In preparation for my next season, I have had a red brochure printed which will be sent to our subscribers and to the press. I have gotten into the habit of keeping our supporters abreast of the affairs of the Théâtre-Libre and of our future plans. I cannot help wondering if the hour has not come to approach the general public, in a theatre which is totally our own, where we could demonstrate the dramatic reforms that are certain to come. I have drawn up a scheme for a theatre and plans for a house which I have seriously gone over with my friend, the architect Grandpierre, who is an intelligent and forward-looking spirit. This brochure has caused a devil of a row, for it really answers genuine needs, and the Parisian public, with their charming lack of reflection, already consider me installed in a boulevard theatre, without even asking where I would find the necessary money.

MAY 26, 1890—*Ghosts* is ready. I distributed parts to Arquillière, Janvier, and Barny, keeping the character of Oswald, one of the loveliest roles an actor could play, for myself.[42] I have made cuts, but took care to touch nothing essential.

MAY 28, 1890—Ibsen is sixty-two years of age and must know the theatre very well, for it seems he was designer and director at the Norwegian Theatre in Christiania for five years. Voluntarily exiled from his country, he rarely stays in one place for more than four or five years. I hoped for a time to get him to come to Paris for the production of his play, but it didn't work out.

Albert Wolff is indignant because in my red brochure I printed the letter he sent me during our opening productions when I asked

---

[42]The casting was: Oswald, Antoine; Manders, Arquillière, Engstrand, Janvier; Mrs. Alving, Barny; and Regina, Luce Colas.

for his support. He has answered with a violent harangue on the front page of the *Figaro*. Mendès is urging me to answer, but I hesitate to enter into a direct controversy with one of the editors of a paper which has always been so favorable toward my efforts. I went to Magnard to ask him if he thought a reply from me would be out of place; on the contrary, he seemed to find the whole business quite amusing, and warmly advised me to take up the gauntlet.

MAY 29, 1890—I therefore went to Carnavalet to look for back issues of the Figaro from '67 and '68 and—sure of my position—I gave an interview to Jules Huret, a reporter from the *Echo de Paris* whom Mendès sent to me. Here is the heart of it:

Why do you want me to answer M. Wolff [M. Antoine said to me]. I have no desire at all to do so. It is quite simple—he gave me a licking I deserved, and I accept it. Yet I understand that he is not satisfied. As a matter of fact, I have observed that this man, who had spirit in 1860, has not only lost that spark in the last three years (which is not a crime in itself), but has lost with it that simple good will which should be an attribute of his high position. In order to open, the Théâtre-Libre needed between 6000 and 8000 francs. I published a small blue brochure wherein I set forth my views and my disinterested ambitions. I asked M. Wolff for ten lines of publicity in one of his columns to draw attention to this brochure. I asked only one thing—that it be read. I was very young—and very naive! I foolishly thought that I needed only these ten lines signed by Wolff for all Paris to embrace my project. M. Wolff disdained to write them. Obviously, he was right, since I have succeeded without him, and even, less than a month ago, presented a play by his nephew, M. Pierre Wolff. But surely I have a right to remember that he refused to help me, and that to avoid a conflict in prerogatives, he sent me to Vitu and Sarcey! One would certainly have thought him capable of maintaining this scrupulousness in the future, however, instead of devoting two hundred and fifty lines of insults, half to me and half to my work, on four different occasions, when I was no longer asking him for anything . . . .

Yet when all is done, one finds that M. Wolff brings luck to those whom he renounces and disparages. Massenet is not doing badly at all; Manet, they say, will enter the Louvre, and Zola, the Academy, with all due deference to their old adversary. In short, the Théâtre-Libre can only be flattered to be included in the "gallery of those condemned by M. Wolff." The company does not displease me . . . .

MAY 30, 1890—We gave *Ghosts* last evening. I think its effect was profound in some quarters, but the majority of the audience went from wonder to boredom, although a real agony gripped the room in the closing scenes. I can say no more of it except by hearsay, for I myself underwent an experience totally new to me—an almost complete loss of my own personality. After the second act I remember nothing, neither the audience nor the effect of the production, and, shaking and weakened, I was some time getting hold of myself again after the final curtain had fallen.

MAY 31, 1890—Before *Ghosts,* we gave *Fishing,* a rather crude but interesting one-act by Céard. It was a sort of scene à la Paul de Kock—of Henry Monnier pushed to the tragic—and did not especially succeed.

*   *   *

JUNE 2, 1890—Naturally, Albert Wolff could not refrain from answering and denying having written the things I quoted. I therefore wrote the following letter today:

Monsieur the Director of the *Echo de Paris:*

The letter which you printed this morning, in which M. Albert Wolff once again shows his willingness to talk about the Théâtre-Libre, clearly forces me, if only out of respect for the *Echo de Paris,* to support by direct quotation the allegations which I made in the presence of M. Jules Huret.

Here are M. Albert Wolff's own words: "Curiosity recently led me into a mire of blood and filth called *Thérèse Raquin.* Delighting in coarseness, he (Zola) has already published *The Confessions of Claude,* which was the romance of a student and a prostitute. He sees woman as M. Manet paints her, the color of filth with rosy makeup. I do not know if M. Zola has the power to write a subtle, sensitive, substantial, and decent book. It takes will, spirit, ideas, and style to renounce violence, but even so, I should like to suggest a change to the author of *Thérèse Raquin* . . . ." (*Figaro* of January 23, 1868.)

In the rest of the article, M. Albert Wolff proposed to M. Emile Zola that he follow the example of M. Jules Claretie, who had just then published a new book.

Concerning M. Massenet, what M. Albert Wolff calls a pleasantry in his answer to me took up an entire column in the *Figaro* of February 4, 1868. There was a rebuttal from M. Massenet, who had just started writing, and a whole series of comments in the press, ending with a letter from M. Théodore Dubois (*Figaro* of February 9, 1868), the conclusion of which I quote:

"Your reading public is rubbing its hands together and saying: 'Ah! Ah! This Wolff is really quite funny, but he has no idea of the value of this work,' and sir, you wantonly bring discouragement to a young composer who could have spirit and a future."

In the course of the archeological labor that circumstances forced upon me in order to find the quotations just given, I saw this one also:

"That man deserves ridicule, and if ridicule can still kill in France, the author of *The Trojans* should no longer be concerned with anything but a pleasant little monument." (*Nain-Jaune* of November 7, 1863.)

And again, at the time of Wagner's *Flying Dutchman:* "All this is tremendously reminiscent of one of Hervé's most delightful follies, *The Crazy Composer.*" (*Figaro* of February 4, 1868.)

Finally, on April 19, 1868, announcing the appearance of a volume of short stories: "*Médan Evenings* is not worth a line of criticism. Except for the short story by Zola which opens the volume, it is of the utmost mediocrity." De Maupassant's *Ball-of-Fat* appeared in this volume.

I therefore said nothing inaccurate to your reporter, M. Jules Huret, and that is all I seek to prove. No one will be surprised that I have forbidden myself to comment on these statements; writing is not at all my trade.

M. Albert Wolff cannot doubt my profound respect for his grey hairs, but should he be unaware of it, I publicly express it here to him again. I beg him to accept my full apologies for this regrettable incident, and my assurance that I will be his most respectful witness whenever he chooses to consider literature and dramatic art as they apply to me.

I am, Monsieur the Director, etc.

A. Antoine

JUNE 2, 1890—After the enormous repercussions of *Ghosts,* I immediately began preparing, despite the incomprehension of the public and Sarcey's hostile witticisms, to strike a second blow with another of Ibsen's works. I have at hand *The Wild Duck,* which Lindenlaub, a reporter on the *Temps,* and Armand Ephraïm brought me. It seems to reveal another side of the master's genius—to the pathetic grandeur of *Ghosts* is added a picturesque life, an uncommon quaintness. With Grand and little Meuris, we will have two incomparable interpreters for the characters of Gregers and Hedwig.

JUNE 4, 1890—Ajalbert and I invited M. de Goncourt to dinner at Lathuille's to read him the adaptation of *Elisa the Slattern,* with which he was quite pleased. We agreed to have a second reading at Daudet's after Ajalbert has made a few small changes which the master suggested to him.

JUNE 5, 1890—At Berlin's Théâtre-Libre, two of Germany's greatest actors, Kainz and Reicher, have agreed to play two of the parts in a play by Gerhart Hauptmann, a new author.[43] Can you see our own Mounet-Sully and Coquelin senior premiering the play of a young author in our Théâtre-Libre?

JUNE 8, 1890—The battle with Albert Wolff worked to my advantage, because it is now recognized that I am able to defend myself. Albert Wolff is taking a terrible beating in many papers. The old polemist, who is after all an excellent man, has surely not yet recovered from it. His nephew Pierre—one of the regulars at the Théâtre-Libre, and much embarrassed to be caught between his friends and an uncle of whom he is very fond—describes to us the consternation in the old gentleman who has been accustomed to terrorizing Paris for so long.

JUNE 14, 1890—Well! We had a fine brawl last evening, completely unforeseen. For our last production we gave *Myrane,* a brilliant fantasy by Bergerat which the audience found entertaining, and we were supposed to finish with *The Capons,* a one-act play by Lucien Descaves and Georges Darien. It showed two good bourgeois fellows who were ruminating over the events of the war. I don't know why, but the audience took the ironic words the wrong way and a disturbance broke out which quickly degenerated into an indescribable uproar. When the pointed helmets of the German soldiers who were marching before the house appeared through the panes of the window, these inoffensive properties put the audience into a rage. I was showered with hisses and shouts for thirty-five minutes before I could name the authors. It was truly a strange sight; some people standing on their chairs and shouting, while the friends of the house applauded furiously. I even saw two of them jump from the balcony and drop with all their weight on an adversary in the orchestra. When the house cleared, half an hour later, the battle continued on the Boulevard de Strasbourg. Our friend Henry Lapauze completely lost his voice from shouting.

---

[43] The play in question is presumably *Das Friedensfest,* given June 1.

JUNE 20, 1890—Paul de Cassagnac has published a frightful tirade against Descaves in the *Authorité,* under the title "The Infamous Play." The really strange thing, however, is that this article, under the same name, has been reproduced in more than thirty provincial papers. Other papers, moreover, are in agreement: "The Too-Free Theatre," "False Artists," "The Nation's Shame," *"Sursum Corda"*— every sort of ephithet is employed.

JUNE 30, 1890—The end of our third year. I thought it of great interest, and I feel strongly that a new school is gathering and co-ordinating its action in the group that has grown up around us. *Old Lebonnard* must be classed simply as a sensational trifle. Ancey's *School for Widows* was very successful, especially after Jean Jullien's *The Master,* which was so completely different— demonstrating the many aspects of the new movement. Brieux's comedy, *Artists' Households,* seemed very promising. Moreover, we had *Aunt Léontine,* a comedy of the first rank, showing a lively and keen observation and developed with the greatest skill. These plays surely represent the young dramatists. The high point of the season was of course the play by Ibsen, which introduced a new kind of drama, despite misunderstanding and hostility. Our enemies have exploited to the full the riot at *The Capons,* but after all, the play dealt with life and war, and a theatre like ours can only exist in a super-charged atmosphere.

JULY-DECEMBER, 1890

JULY 20, 1890—After an excursion to Brest, I have settled on the coast at Brignogan with Ancey, who wanted to come at least as much as I did. Our friend Pierre Wolff has come to join us, and we spend delightful hours walking and all working on the next season. Pierre Wolff read us his two-act play, *Their Daughters,* which seems interesting and lively to me.

JULY 25, 1890—A dispute has arisen between Count Prozor and Armand Ephraïm and Lindenlaub over *The Wild Duck.* Count Prozor claims to possess exclusive rights. Most happily, I took precautions against this by dealing with Ibsen himself, who could not refuse a second play to the theatre which presented him for the first time in France.

AUGUST, 1890—An article in the *Figaro* this morning brought me news of three of the amateur actors who participated in the first production of the Théâtre-Libre. They were members of the *Société de la Butte,* three revolutionists who have since become famous: S. H. Malato, Pauzader, and Guy Prolo.

SEPTEMBER 1, 1890—We have 17 francs 50 in the till to begin the season. The total deficit for the 1889-1890 season was 12,778 francs.

SEPTEMBER 15, 1890—We have returned to Paris, and begun rehearsals of *Honor,* a five-act play by Henry Fèvre which will be presented in October.

SEPTEMBER 17, 1890—The Théâtre-Française has revived Vacquerie's *Jean Baudry,* and Got is incomparable in it.[44] Despite its author's romantic tendencies, it is a play which is not far from what we are seeking. I could not resist the opportunity to go again to hear the great actor, master of us all in modern comedy.

OCTOBER 1, 1890—Received this letter from the Beaux-Arts—which pleases me very much, since it helps to refute the legend of pornography at the Théâtre-Libre:

M. the Director:

I have the honor to inform you that by a resolution dated this day, I have appropriated to you the sum of five hundred francs, representing four subscriptions, two for the ministry and two for the Beaux-Arts. I am happy to recognize, by this mark of interest, the services which you are rendering to dramatic art.

For the minister
the director of the Beaux-Arts:
Larroumet.

OCTOBER 15, 1890—I don't know why, but Arquillière is consumed by a desire to enter the Conservatory. He asked me to approach Dumas *fils,* who has great influence, on his behalf. I therefore went to see the master, who can hardly be expected to hold a favorable opinion of the Théâtre-Libre people. There is no denying that our regular diatribes against the three pillars of dramatic art and the recent story of their interviews concerning *The Power of Darkness* are not the sort of things to make them very sympathetic toward us.

I waited in a downstairs vestibule in the Avenue de Villiers while a valet took up my card. I heard a hearty voice, and Dumas himself leaned over the banister: "Come on up, come on up, my dear Antoine. I am only too glad to see an artist of your worth and a man of your intelligence." He continued my panegyric to a visitor,

---

[44]Surely Antoine is speaking of the revival of Laya's *Duc Job* (September 16, 1890). *Jean Baudry* was revived a year earlier (September 17, 1889) for the third debut of Paul Mounet, and Got did not appear in it. In *Duc Job,* on the other hand, Got played the part of the Marquis de Rieux, the same part Antoine played in a production of this play at the *Cercle Gaulois* in 1887.

unknown to me, who was there, and quite disconcerted me with so warm and unexpected a graciousness. I therefore set forth my request, interrupted every moment by the most cordial and adulatory affirmations. I left Dumas' home certain that the Arquillière matter was settled.

He was, of course, rejected at the examination three days later.

OCTOBER 16, 1890—I have been sent information from Berlin on the free theatre there, the Frei-Buhn [*sic*], which was founded by a correspondent on a German paper who saw the Théâtre-Libre in Paris. The curiosity and agitation there over this enterprise are intense. The troupe is not made up of ordinary amateurs like ours. The greatest names of the German stage consider it an honor to be allowed to support the young organization. There are already more than seven hundred subscribers, and the Lessing Theatre, which corresponds to our Odéon, has been placed at their disposal.

OCTOBER 20, 1890—I had difficulty in casting the ingenue part in Henry Fèvre's *Honor,* a middle-class study of an unrelenting ferocity, but full of talent and force. Fèvre was the collaborator of poor Louis Després in the condemned book, *Around the Steeple,* which sent Després to prison—where he was treated like a common criminal, despite his tuberculosis and the protests of men of letters. He died behind bars.

Fèvre's ingenue, seduced by a bourgeois, a friend of her father, is driven to abortion to prevent a scandal. The situation frightened all the actresses, but at last Mlle. Théven had the courage to accept the part.

OCTOBER 24, 1890—Last evening the Porte-Saint-Martin presented *Cléopâtre,* Emile Moreau's skillful adaptation of Shakespeare's masterpiece, for a very good house. [45] The success owed much to a most sumptuous setting by Duquesnel and to the acting of Sarah Bernhardt, who entered (wrapped in a rug which was gradually unrolled) with such a burst of youthfulness that the house gave her an ovation.

---

[45]Sardou collaborated with Moreau in this adaptation.

OCTOBER 31, 1890—*Honor* went off without a hitch, thanks to the stability and quiet power of the work. The reviewers did not take it at all badly, realizing that after all, there was no intention of scandal in the play. It is with bold plays like this that we will eventually awaken a genuine reaction in the public against the vacuity and lies of the Romantic theatre. Lemaître says in his column that the play has real merit and that it raises important moral questions.

NOVEMBER 1, 1890—Séverine has written a fine article on Louise France, one of the most interesting persons in the Théâtre-Libre. The actress has experienced everything of theatre and its miseries, following an eccentric path through low-class concert halls, prowling about abroad from Egypt to Brussels, and then, later, coming to us. Here she has been acclaimed for the parts she has created in *Lucie Pellegrin, Rolande, Aunt Léontine,* and as the old servant in *Honor.*

NOVEMBER 2, 1890—What a pity that Porel, with his great talent in historical production, insists upon giving adaptations of Shakespeare. His presentation of *Romeo and Juliet* is admirable, but what a production we would have had if he had given us the masterpiece intact!

NOVEMBER 6, 1890—I arrived at Pousset's last evening to find Georges Courteline at Mendès' table. He is still employed, I believe, in public instruction or at the Cultes, but is already well-known for his extraordinarily gay and animated stories and tales. I have been noticing the rather silent and timid fellow for some time around Mendès, who has a visible admiration for him. I induced him to do something for the Théâtre-Libre, if only a one-act piece, for I am sure that his powerful comedy will bring a pleasant note now in our dearth of truly cheerful authors.

NOVEMBER 8, 1890—This short note has appeared in all the papers that were willing to accept it:

It has been announced that the minister of Beaux-Arts has taken four subscriptions at the Théâtre-Libre. Antoine sanctified by the Beaux-Arts, abortion designated a fine art, pimps honored by the ministry—hi, Alphonse, what a lark!

NOVEMBER 8, 1890—There are now two free theatres in Berlin; a schism has occurred and the *free stage* is now competing with the *German stage.*

NOVEMBER 12, 1890—Revival of *The Woman of Paris* at the Théâtre-Français. The presentation was not very effective, and we at the Théâtre-Libre, who were the first to present this masterful play, are not alone in ascribing its failure chiefly to a deplorable interpretation. Henry Fouquier himself says the same in his column.

NOVEMBER 13, 1890—This evening Scholl read us his short play, *His Wife's Lover,* which we will give next. I don't much care for this old-fashioned play, but the name of the famous reporter—who is moreover a delightful man—will be most valuable in neutralizing for once all his comrades in the papers.

NOVEMBER 14, 1890—Pessard, in attesting to the disappointment which Becque just had at the Théâtre-Français with *The Woman of Paris,* also complains of the interpretation, for all his faithfulness to the old formulas, and adds:

> Something I particularly noticed, for example, was that the actors in *The Woman of Paris* addressed themselves to the audience when they were really speaking to each other. M. Antoine's back hinders the scenic illusion less for me than these faces recounting their little affairs to the gentlemen seated in the orchestra.

Decidedly, we are making progress.

NOVEMBER 15, 1890—Becque just spoke to me about *The Woman of Paris* and the criticisms that M. Prud'hon is receiving from all the papers. He says that when he submitted the play to the reading committee, he had Coquelin senior in mind for the character of Lafont. Later he thought of Dupuis, of the Variétés. It is extraordinary how a dramatist of his breadth can be so mistaken about interpretation. I did my utmost to convince him that Lafont is a character who must not be comic, but must only evoke smiles. I cited the example of Vois, who created the part at the Renaissance, and who is still playing it, but Becque remained unconvinced. He looks back to the glittering theatre of Dumas, and he dreams of the actors of the past for his humorous and yet so pathetic gentlemen (like the lover of his Clotilde)—actors trained to flatter the public taste for light and pleasant theatre.

NOVEMBER 17, 1890—Sarcey, who naturally defends the interpretation of *The Woman of Paris* at the Comédie-Française, says:

> The set-back of Becque, an indisputable set-back (and those who do not wish to admit it need only await the reviews and they will be forced to sing a different tune), still leaves intact the esteem which we have for his talent and for the position he holds in the literary world. But the new movement has received a heavy blow from which it will be at some pain to recover. Unless things change, the proponents of this new movement would be ungracious indeed to claim that it is we who prevent their success by placing ourselves between their works and the public. We have supported with all our might the presentation of Ancey's *Grandmother,* Jean Jullien's *The Master,* and Becque's *The Woman of Paris,* and look at the result.

And elsewhere:

> At last the presentation took place. Dissimulation would be useless. *The Woman of Paris* was, as we say in theatrical jargon, a real lemon.

NOVEMBER 20, 1890—Aurélien Scholl, whose one-act play, *His Wife's Lover,* we are just now rehearsing, is truly one of the wittiest men in Paris. He has retained a touch of the Bordeaux accent which gives a lyric quality and a great charm to his pleasant voice. This grand and elegant old man dotes on his continual and daily fencing exercises, which have kept him quite slim. His famous monocle has set a fashion; his prestige is so great on the boulevard that a whole generation has come forward with this bit of glass in its eye.

NOVEMBER 22, 1890—M. Jules Schaumberger, editor-in-chief of a review in Munich, has just founded a free theatre there.[46]

NOVEMBER 23, 1890—Ajalbert and I went to dinner this evening at Daudet's, to read *Elisa the Slattern;* only Goncourt, Mme. Daudet, and her husband were present.[47] Ajalbert read the play, which is rather sketchy, but still picturesque and truly dramatic. The question arose as to whether the public would endure the lawyer's plea, which takes up the entire second act, lasting three-quarters of an hour, and there was general uncertainty. Daudet was the only one who said flatly that the thing was impossible.

NOVEMBER 24, 1890—This evening I was given the honors of Sarcey's column. The failure of *The Woman of Paris* at the Comédie-Française has been preying on my mind, and—not to convince Sarcey, but only to give the public something to think over—I could not resist putting down what I believe are the causes behind these repeated failures. For not only has *The Woman of Paris* (a work quite beyond discussion) failed, but so has Ancey's play, *Grandmother,* at the Odéon, and likewise that preposterous revival of *The Master* at the Nouveautés. I have set down the main part of my statement, before it is dispersed to the four winds:

Aren't you struck by this coincidence at all? Here we have three plays—*The Woman of Paris, Grandmother,* and *The Master*—all from the same source, all conceived in the spirit of renewal which activates the new school, and all three miscarrying, in three different theatres. Moreover, by common opinion, all have met with an inadequate interpretation, even with actors belonging for the most part to the elite among Parisian artists.

---

[46]An unsuccessful free theatre was attempted in Munich in 1891, but this note apparently refers to the *Intimes Theater,* founded in 1895. Jules Schaumberger was associated with this latter venture, although Max Halbe was the founder.
[47]According to the Goncourt *Journals,* this reading took place on November 29 at Antoine's studio, with a crowd of actors present.

How are we to explain this triple coincidence? Wouldn't it be of interest to seek its cause? Please note that I am not concerned with literary criticism; that is not my business. I am speaking only of the profession. Well, I think there is a major technical question involved which I can clear up, and which should be of interest to all future authors, and perhaps also to all intelligent and far-sighted actors concerned about their art and about the present-day theatre movement. This technical matter is what caused *Grandmother* to fail, what caused *The Master* to fail, and what caused *The Woman of Paris,* as you yourself noted, to fail, too.

The reviewers are generally agreed that the interpretation was mediocre in all three plays. In dealing with *The Master* and *The Woman of Paris,* they had the original interpretation as a point of reference. Since *Grandmother* lacked this point of reference, Ancey himself was rather excessively blamed for its failure.

Well! The simple reason for this triple coincidence—of actors who are ordinarily excellent being judged mediocre for one evening, and for this evening alone—is that not one of these three works was set or acted in its true sense. What the new (or renewed) theatre demands is new (or renewed) interpreters. Once cannot play works based on observation (or pretended observation, if you prefer) as one would play the traditional repertoire, or comedies based on the imagination. One must get under the skin of these modern characters, and leave the old baggage behind. A work which is *true* must be played *truly,* just as a classic play should above all be *recited,* since the character more often than not is only an abstraction or a synthesis, without material life. The characters in *The Woman of Paris* or in *Grandmother* are people like us, who do not live in vast rooms with the dimensions of cathedrals, but in interiors like our own—beside the fire, under the lamp, around a table, but never (as in the old repertoire) before the prompter's box. They have voices like ours; their language is that of our own daily life, with its elisions and its familiar turns, and not the rhetoric and noble style of our classics.

When Mlle. Reichenberg begins the first scene of *The Woman of Paris* in her stage voice, and M. Prud'hon answers in the accents he uses to portray Dorante, they immediately misrepresent Becque's prose—and they did so the other evening for three hours, without ever relaxing. The characteristic of the new theatre is always that the characters are unconscious of themselves, is it not? Like any of us, they make foolish and ridiculous mistakes without being aware of them. When most of our actors come on stage, they bring their own personalities instead of those of the figures they are to bring to life; they do not enter their character, their character enters them. Thus, the other evening we had Mlle. Reichenberg instead of Clotilde; MM. Prud'hon, Le Bargy, and de Féraudy, and not all the men of Becque.

And the salon! . . . Have you ever seen a salon like that in a middle-class Parisian home? Was that the residence of a head clerk? It completely lacked that little corner found in any of our homes—the preferred spot where one chats, the armchair where one relaxes when the day's work is done. I know the objection; the setting is secondary. Perhaps in the repertoire it is, and yet even if I am wrong, why not work out the decor, provided that it doesn't get out of proportion, since this can be done with care and without any sort of harm to the work? In modern works, created amid a movement of truth and realism in which the theory of environment and the influence of exterior things plays so large a part, isn't the setting an indispensable complement of the action? Shouldn't the setting be as important in the theatre as description is in the novel? Isn't it one kind of exposition of the play? Of course it can never be made completely real, because it is in the theatre, and no one would dream of denying it a certain minimum of conventionalization, but why not strive to keep to this minimum?

The dimensions of stage or auditorium are of little importance. If the opening is too large, why not frame it down in front? And as for projection, is it not well known that the acoustics of the auditorium at the Français are marvelous? The majority of other theatres, smaller by half, are less satisfactory in this respect. In any case, it is yet another reason to avoid these immense settings where, in the case of intimate works, the voice is lost. At the Odéon, *Grandmother* was played in a monumental salon, indeed the very one which completely stifled one act of *Renée Mauperin!* What do you think will become of a work full of life and intimacy in such a false atmosphere?

In my opinion, the movement was as poorly understood as the setting. The actors' movements about the stage were not determined by the text or the sense of the scene, but according to the desire or the whim of the actors, each of whom played for himself, with no concern for the others. Then, too, they were hypnotized by the footlights; everyone tried to get as close to the audience as possible. I was reminded of a theatre where in the time of gas lighting, so I have been told, all the actors burned the bottoms of their trousers in the great open jets.

Mlle. Reichenberg the other day gave a monologue while standing and embroidering, the way housewives knit on their doorsteps. Clotilde and Lafont never once directly addressed each other, yet on the street, after two such sentences, you would, with justification, say to your companion: "Look at me, blast it! I'm speaking to you!" The fact is that the new theatre is going to have to have new interpreters. I keep reaffirming this elementary truth everywhere.

The Master furnishes yet another example. This experiment, at the Nouveautés, was as baroque as it could be, and I said as much to young Brasseur. It was performed under the most adverse conditions. No play from our theatre was less likely than *The Master* to acclimate itself to such elegant, boulevard surroundings. Jean Jullien was pushed into making a mistake there, the results of which are only now becoming clear to him. He undercut a great artistic success without even gaining any appreciable pecuniary reward, and had the further misfortune of furnishing our enemies with arguments against the theories which underlie his work and the comrades who are struggling beside him.

Yet once he had decided on the performance, he applied himself to teaching his new interpreters the movements he had seen at our house. A similar setting was painted; good will and conscientiousness were pushed to the point of providing him with the same furniture and properties. And yet, as everyone noted in astonishment, this didn't solve the problem. The problem is simply that the boulevard actors can't move their legs in the way I have been describing. A cross made by Janvier, for example, is no longer the same when it is made by Decori; for Decori, with all his experience, has all the current craftsmanship in his legs, and—I must emphasize this—this formerly excellent craftsmanship becomes detrimental in the new theatre, and is not easily shaken off. Decori, who knew his craft, became irritated, while Janvier, who did not know it, simply moved where he was told to, with everyday motions. Decori has a special walk, a "theatrical" walk, which he will have a hundred times more difficulty getting rid of than he could have ever had learning it.

As a final example, at the request of the authors, I recently supervised a rehearsal by the troupe at the Menus-Plaisirs of *Two Turtledoves* and another play which would be presented in several weeks.[48] For Ginisty and Guérin's

---

[48] *Two Turtledoves* was given April 17, 1890. The other play was Audran's *The Mascot.*

one-act play, I attempted to suggest to the actors reviving the roles the walk France had originally used at our theatre. Well! The two actors were most pleasant, but at last I had to give up this idea, for they were sweating blood and getting no results. For the other play it was even worse. I gave up completely after one rehearsal. I could not even get them to simply go to a table or to sit down in an arm-chair without looking into the house or affecting a peculiar walk. Nothing could be done, and yet these artists without a doubt know their trade. Like the interpreters of *The Woman of Paris,* they do much more difficult things in other plays every evening, but they have lost the simple touch, and the ability to act naturally, *as if no one were watching.*

It is impossible to find actors who can speak for a long time while seated. They cannot begin a speech of any length without asking the director: "Don't I get up here?" For these actors, enslaved by the ancient rules and the Desgenais phrasemongers, the stage is a rostrum, and not an enclosed space where an action occurs. I remember that at a meeting at Ballande's in 1873 you gave an anecdote of an actor at the Palais-Royal—Arnal or Ravel, I think it was—who, having to hang up his hat, walked with deter-mination to the footlights, and searched with conviction for a nail on the fourth wall. You seemed to approve of this very much and it made a strong impression on me. This is how you corrupt the youth without being aware of it!

I will say no more; but I beg you to turn your attention in this direction, and watch. You will be struck by the discord between the works incorporating the new tendencies and the interpreters they encounter. It is an important prob-lem, and a curious aspect of the current theatre movement. I am personally quite pleased, for the outlines of the evolution are becoming clearer. Indeed, I would scarcely think of speaking out if it had not become a kind of sport to "jump on" the Théâtre-Libre—with kindness, true, but to "jump on" it all the same—every time one of its works runs into adverse circumstances. We should not be deceived about this—there are going to be more failures, more beatings; but the basic impetus has been given. The foundations have been laid, and the public is already becoming aware of our work. The critics used to say that our modest establishment was a passing fad and that one fine evening it would disappear as suddenly as it had come. You now know that our public is larger every year, and that as a consequence the field grows broader and broader. People come to me with new ideas, and I have great hope for them, but, good heavens, there is no need to get carried away and naively expect to win everything in a single blow—literary success, large receipts, and the conversion of the masses. Many plays will be posted before that—plays not even conceived as yet. For the time being, we must be content with looking back and seeing the advances made in the last five or six years.

Your devoted,   A. Antoine.

What surprises me is the cordial assent with which Sarcey accepts these observations and theories; and one must say on behalf of this singular man that, no matter how violent the arguments grow, he keeps an open mind about technical matters wherein he might go astray. He says, and truly I can believe it, that no one seeks the truth with greater willingness than he; and indeed, he followed my letter with a further substantiation of my remarks by recounting two anecdotes about actors resisting their authors.

NOVEMBER 26, 1890—The people in Marseilles have just set up a Théâtre-Libre there too, modeled on the one in Paris. I am told that the author of a one-act play *(Conjugal Duty)* given the opening evening will bear watching. He is a local young man named Emile Fabre.

NOVEMBER 27, 1890—This evening I paused for a chat with Pierre

Véber before his door in the Rue Richelieu, and he told me his idea for a play which would be even more Norwegian than those which are causing so much talk. The scenario would be delightfully mischievous. He would put everything into it—the pastor, the young woman who is about to take the boat, the fogs and the pines, the strange and misunderstood woman, and so on. He suggests that I announce this play as coming from an as yet unknown Scandinavian author, wagering with me that everyone will take it seriously. It is an amusing idea, and I think he could probably win the wager, but it would be a little beneath the Théâtre-Libre to lend itself to a hoax which, alas, would be all too successful if one may judge by the mistaken and distorted views which are expressed of Ibsen and his work.

NOVEMBER 30, 1890—Scholl's one-act, *His Wife's Lover,* was the principal attraction of our last evening. Scholl's comrades hold him in awe, and the reviews were most cordial. Biollay's three-act *Monsieur Bute,* a rather sombre story of torment, didn't cause much of a stir.

DECEMBER 1, 1890—During our last evening, we also gave a one-act play by Julien Sermet. This, *The Beautiful Operation,* portrayed in the most amusing fashion a dozen surgeons, ranging from the humblest district practitioner up to the Professor of the Faculty, all bustling around a patient. After a top-level conference, presided over by the Professor, they decide to operate, and enter the patient's room. The men of skill soon reappear shaking their heads; the operation has failed, the patient is dead. Despite its macabre subject, nothing could be more fiercely ironic than this little scene. It amused some and infuriated others. Most amusing of all is the wrath of Zola, who became furiously indignant over this little play—he, who should be the first to appreciate such violent realism.

DECEMBER 1, 1890—There is an inspector of the Beaux-Arts at the *Nation,* Adrien Bernheim, an excellent fellow, who has the bad habit, however, of always falling into step behind Sarcey, quickly crying "dead" whenever the other says "dull." This seems fair enough, since I am well aware that Bernheim, following the example of his illustrious comrade on the *Temps,* considers himself one of the knights-errant of the classical tradition. But after my letter to Sarcey, Bernheim proved less tolerant than his leader and descended upon me, teaming up for the time being with Bauer in predicting the imminent demise of the Théâtre-Libre.

DECEMBER 4, 1890—Rumor has it that Porel is thinking of leaving the Odéon for the Opéra. I have been sounded out as a candidate for the left-bank position, but I have little desire for it just now. We still have too much to do.

DECEMBER 15, 1890—Descaves, who has just published *Non-Coms,* is being prosecuted for writing it.[49] I was going to give a one-act play of his, *In the Ranks,* which we have even rehearsed a bit, but that will doubtless have to be postponed.

DECEMBER 15, 1890—Christian, an actor at the Variétés, has just died. He was one of the most entertaining comedians I have ever seen, and one could hear him several times in the same role—for every evening he improvised, much in the manner of the old comedians on the Commedia dell'Arte stages.

DECEMBER 15, 1890—Saint-Cère, the drama editor of the *Vie Parisienne,* is hard on the interpreters of *The Woman of Paris* at the Français. He says: "M. Becque, who has appealed the decision rendered on his play at the Renaissance to the decision of the Français, will perhaps appeal it once more—to the Théâtre-Libre." Alas, I do not have a regular theatre, but if I ever do become a theatre director for good and all, I am sure that one day I can do right by Becque's masterpiece.

49This is the first of several entries on Descaves, all in the wrong year. *Non-Coms* appeared in December, 1889, and immediately aroused the wrath of chauvinistic army leaders. Despite the pleas of the outstanding writers of the time, and the withdrawal of *In the Ranks* from the Théâtre-Libre (which earned Descaves an angry letter from Antoine), the author was brought to trial. Defended by Maurice Tézénas, he was aquitted on March 15, 1890.

DECEMBER 16, 1890—Becque has flared up against Sarcey's article on the revival of *The Woman of Paris.* He is even talking of bringing suit against the critic of the *Temps,* and they say that he has already engaged M. Tézénas as a lawyer.

DECEMBER 16, 1890—Another free theatre has appeared in London, this one organized by Beerbohm Tree,[50] one of the most distinguished artists over there. They give weekly productions, on Monday evenings, which are stimulating controversy in the papers for and against the young English school. The environment, however, hardly strikes me as suitable for a literary movement. The English theatre subsists on ephemeral works, facile but simple, sufficient only for a public interested in superficial distractions. Thus English cant, the severe censorship which Protestant rigor has imposed on all dramatic production, has centuries since dried up the sap of the great Shakespearian tree.

DECEMBER 17, 1890—The Odéon has presented an adaptation of *The Merchant of Venice,* by Haraucourt, in a most beautiful setting.[51] My poor friend Mévisto, who was engaged to create Shylock, was replaced at the last minute by Albert Lambert. All who come from the Théâtre-Libre, authors or actors, are continuously obliged to fight for their lives.

DECEMBER 19, 1890—It is irritating that while we can fight relatively effectively in the Parisian papers, the great provincial papers, the regional sheets, are in the hands of our enemies and can strike blows of which we are ignorant. For example, this morning the *Gironde* spoke of "Becquists" running rampant at the Théâtre-Libre; and while this attack would be parried immediately here, outside Paris it is disseminated unchallenged to the enormous public of a whole region.

DECEMBER 20, 1890—As could have been predicted after Sarcey's

---

[50]Tree's "Haymarket Mondays," while not greatly influential, were a pioneer experiment in repertory theatre in England. Antoine spells the name Beer Boom Tree.
[51]Once again, the year is incorrect. This production opened December 17, 1889.

savage attack and the other critics' assassination of its dress rehearsal, *The Woman of Paris* is not making a cent at the Comédie-Française. We all feel what a cruel blow this is for Becque, whose financial affairs would have been more or less put in order with the profits of a revival. So, to distract him from this, we thought of offering him a dinner with only a dozen carefully chosen companions. At the Café Américain, he was surrounded by Geffroy, Ajalbert, Rosny, Ancey, Wolff, Lecomte, and others. Deeply moved by this gesture and by the affectionate admiration which surrounded him, Becque seemed once again the witty and yet profound master whom we consider the true renovator of the contemporary theatre.

DECEMBER 22, 1890—M. Halgan, senator from the Vendée, just ascended the rostrum of the Senate to express astonishment that M. Larroumet, the director of the Beaux-Arts, had thought it necessary to subsidize the Théâtre-Libre by taking an official subscription. He spoke of the filth presented at our house, and there was a general movement of indignation. Larroumet, director of the Beaux-Arts, came to the rostrum and bowed a bit to the storm, but still declared that in addition to *The Capons,* an awkward play, and several others, it should be noted that the dramatic institution in question had given many interesting works, the influence of which was already making itself felt.

This would have been fair enough if the director of the Beaux-Arts had not spoiled everything by a white lie, declaring that the subsidy given is a way for the administration to maintain a necessary surveillance of what is going on in the theatre.

The Minister Bourgeois closed the debate with a wise and temperate comment, recalling the interests of the "young authors" who were finding occasions to make their talent known through "this house."

DECEMBER 23, 1890—There was a warm discussion over the casting of *Elisa the Slattern.* M. de Goncourt wanted Janvier for the role of the little soldier Tanchon; and I must admit that he will be excellent in the part, although I was also considering Gémier. I was worried about Elisa for a time. General Turr, the Austrian Ambassador, strongly recommended to M. de Goncourt a Hungarian actress, apparently quite famous in her own country, who wanted to try her luck in Paris. She came to rehearse the play in sumptuous dresses, but her accent was impossible. She is probably talented in her native idiom, but at last I simply handed the part to Nau, who was rehearsing a small supporting role and who will suit the character perfectly.

DECEMBER 23, 1890—This morning I dropped by Coppée's house, having heard that he has just had a one-act verse play, *The Pater,* banned because the action takes place under the Commune during the days of May, '71.[52]

Coppée lives in the Rue Oudinot, in a summer-house behind a parish-priest's little garden, and I found him by the fireside with a bowl of herb tea which he was taking for a cold. While his sister Annette fluttered about us in the little study, somewhat afraid that I would tire the invalid, I asked him for his play. I have known Coppée for a long time, since he frequented Montparnasse from the very beginning, and he sometimes comes to the Rue Blanche to chat. Still, my request surprised and moved him. It is a delicate matter, and he wants to think it over, but it is my hope that he will decide yes, since this skirmish is reawakening his Parisian gamin humor.

DECEMBER 23, 1890—We are in conflict with Koning, who announced Daudet's *The Obstacle* for December 26, even though the Théâtre-Libre reserved that date long ago for the opening of *Elisa.* Despite my polite protests, Koning took a perverse pleasure in not giving in to us. Daudet himself, in a pleasant letter, begged Koning to give up the date, in deference to his old friend Goncourt.

DECEMBER 25, 1890—Just now, while several of us were talking over the Descaves affair in the Rue Blanche, it occurred to us to

---

[52]*The Pater* was published late in January, 1890, and aroused almost immediately a storm of protest.

organize a protest against an author being prosecuted for his writings.[53] Darzens, always active, and Hennique, generous and enthusiastic, drew up the text immediately, and we all took cabs, for we had only forty-eight hours to gather the signatures of all the noted writers, without any regard for school. To begin, Darzens dashed over to the Avenue Trudaine, and an hour later triumphantly reported a signature to us, that of Georges Ohnet. This is a moving and elegant gesture from a man of letters who has so little in common with us.

DECEMBER 26, 1890—This evening we gave the premiere of *Elisa the Slattern.* Clearly, Daudet was mistaken. Although only a few small cuts were made, the plea in the second act proved totally acceptable. Indeed, as I delivered it, I felt that it was rather too short, and I expressed to Ajalbert my regret in not having kept the complete text.

The evening began badly with *A Christmas Tale,* a picturesque play in two scenes in which its young author attempted to fuse realism and mysticism. M. de Goncourt, who arrived late from dinner, came into his box just as the curtain came down amid loud hissing. He became quite pale thinking of poor *Elisa the Slattern,* which was next, but his play went quite well, and the audience was especially impressed by the act in the Court of Assizes—a fine success of staging.

The reviews this morning were very good. The hardest was our friend Pessard, who delivered a savage attack even though he declares that he left the theatre after the first act of a play that he says he is incapable of describing.

DECEMBER 27, 1890—Auguste Liner,[54] author of *A Christmas Tale,* which was so violently received the other night, is still in the service —a corporal in an infantry regiment at Vincennes. In this time of prosecution and prohibitions, I am afraid that the commotion his play has stirred up will cause him some difficulties.

DECEMBER 27, 1890—Descaves, who is being prosecuted for *Non-*

---

[53]See note to December 15, 1890.
[54]Apparently a misprint in the original. The dramatist's name was Linert.

Coms, is a model campaigner.[55] He showed us his record of sentences —during five years of service, he spent four days in the guard room and twenty days in detention.

DECEMBER 28, 1890—The papers are occupied with the Senate debate. All the reactionary journals, headed by the *Authorité,* talk of the "strange ideas" of the Minister. The enemies of the subsidized theatres have seized this opportunity to enter the fray, begging the director of the Beaux-Arts (in the *Temps* of December 25) to use his authority over the subsidized theatres so that he will not be reduced to admitting that *only Monsieur Antoine has some spirit of initiative.* They go on from this to ask what has been gained by the great subsidies given to the State theatres, since the Théâtre-Libre is doing its work with 500 francs. The article will doubtless win more friends for me, and yet God knows I had nothing to do with it.

DECEMBER 29, 1890—Daudet's *The Obstacle,* at the Gymnase, got good reviews, but the stir over *Elisa* still pushed it into the background. This makes me very unhappy, since it is an annoyance for people to whom I am sincerely grateful. Yet I did not provoke this conflict between the two productions. I feel that some coolness is going to be the result, and Goncourt is unwittingly going to aggravate it by speaking to all his friends of the success of his play, without even suspecting the minor irritation he is creating around himself.

DECEMBER 30, 1890—Our protest concerning Descaves is covered with the most illustrious signatures—Emile Zola, Alphonse Daudet, Edmond de Goncourt, Jean Richepin, Henry Becque, Mendès, Léon Cladel, Clovis Hughes, and others.[56]

DECEMBER 30, 1890—The Censor's banning of *The Pater* has caused an enormous stir. Coppée had finally kindly given me the play when Magnard called me to the *Figaro.* There I learned of a

---

[55]See note to December 15, 1890.
[56]See note to December 15, 1890. Fifty-four authors signed this petition, which appeared in the *Figaro* December 24, 1889.

fine trick by our friend Koning, who has offered to give Coppée's play at his theatre, the Gymnase. Coppée, who feels strongly that he would disoblige the *Figaro* by refusing, is seeking a compromise that will satisfy everyone. I was furious, although I didn't show it, since the play would no longer interest me on these terms. The only advantage for us would be to present it before our regular spectators, and I therefore let the matter drop. I will present the play in Belgium on our next trip, with my comrades who have already rehearsed it. Magnard, who is always kind, understands that I do not want to work with Koning, who has fought us so much.

DECEMBER 30, 1890—Ajalbert could not stomach Hector Pessard's account of *Elisa the Slattern,* and in an open letter protests against a critic attacking a play which he admits not having seen (for he says he left after the first act). Pessard is vice-president of the Critic's Circle, and the incident will probably have repercussions, for it once again brings into discussion the famous right of the critic.

DECEMBER 30, 1890—In light of the affluence of subscriptions, I must seriously consider the necessity of creating a third series of plays.

DECEMBER 31, 1890—Pessard has answered Ajalbert in the *Gaulois,* affirming that he did indeed leave the Théâtre-Libre after the first act of *Elisa the Slattern,* because, says he, his contract with the directors of the *Gaulois* does not force him to endure nausea beyond a certain limit.

DECEMBER 31, 1890—All this *Pater* affair is rather bad for censorship. They are disturbed at the Beaux-Arts over this stir and the sensation produced by the proceedings against Descaves, and I am sure they are afraid of a major shift in public opinion.

DECEMBER 31, 1890—In the period from 1887 to 1890, the Comédie-Française, the Odéon, the Gymnase, and the Vaudeville presented 154 unpublished plays between the four of them. During the same period, the Théâtre-Libre by itself gave 125.

JANUARY-DECEMBER, 1891

1891—Bauer has seen to it that the position of drama critic for the *Paris* has gone to Jean Jullien, who has become quite cool toward the Rue Blanche.

1891—I still regret that I never succeeded in drawing the two novelists from Médan into the battles for naturalism in the theatre since, aside from the master, they were unquestionably the outstanding persons in the group.

Huysmans has never had any desire to attempt the stage. At the most he has from time to time attended the plays of some friend at our theatre. His new book, *Down There,* is very successful. One can see him attempting to avoid realistic formulas, but the art and originality of his work are still somewhat out of the ordinary even in an era when the modern novel burns with such power of life and observation. The best pages of *Down There* are still those where Zola's method and analysis have left their imprint.

As for Maupassant, he is at the peak of his glory, too much in demand, "worth" too much to come to my little theatre to present a sample of the writing for which publishers pay him so much by the line. Céard has tried to serve as a go-between with him a number of times, and tells me that we must give up the idea. It is a great pity, for the author of *Ball-of-Fat* could have made a magnificent theatrical contribution toward the renewal we are seeking.

JANUARY 3, 1891—A savage attack by the good Pessard has appeared in the *Petite Gironde,* in which this excellent man speaks of the Marivaux of the sewer and the Musset of the cesspool. Since he holds a high position in the great provincial newspapers, we must endure this unprovoked assault without any possibility of answering back.

JANUARY 5, 1891—Got's interpretation of the role of Tartuffe has aroused new debate. The actor is attacked everywhere for having sacrificed the conventions of the character to bring him to life. Naturally, I went to see him. It was the most beautiful demonstration of acting conceivable, but in our fine country, it is not easy to depart from tradition, even when one is the dean of the Comédie-Française.

JANUARY 5, 1891—This morning in his series "Unhappy Monologues" in the *Echo de Paris,* Mirbeau attacks Pessard in the most ferocious and yet amusing manner. What a master writer of abuse, and what magnificent language, despite its injustices and its almost morbid exaggerations!

JANUARY 6, 1891—One afternoon recently, M. de Goncourt arrived in the Rue Blanche with a rather voluminous roll of paper under his arm. When he spread it out, I saw that it was a magnificent print of Bracquemond's etching of him, with a beautiful dedication beneath which made me blush with pleasure. In leaving, he formally invited me to go dine with him at Auteuil.

*   *   *

JANUARY 9, 1891—M. de Goncourt is giving his Diary to the directors of the *Echo de Paris,* after Mendès convinced them to ask the master if they could publish it. This has caused an enormous stir, even though I am sure M. de Goncourt was careful to exclude everything in his memoires which might lead to recriminations.

*   *   *

JANUARY 15, 1891—Yesterday the Théâtre d'Application gave a comedy in four acts by Léon Gandillot, Sarcey's Benjamin, which the author had submitted to me, but which I did not present since it seemed to me that despite his incomparable gifts, Gandillot is only a vaudevillist, and his play is really only a pale reworking of Ancey's *School for Widows.*

JANUARY 17, 1891—A committee of poets has been formed to establish a Théâtre d'Art which will soon give plays by Pierre Quillard, Rochilde, and Stephen Mallarmé in the Montparnasse theatre.[57] This is very good. The Théâtre-Libre is no longer sufficient; other groups are becoming necessary to give certain works that we cannot present at our theatre. I do not feel that this new theatre will compete with ours, but rather will complement it in the accelerating revolution.

JANUARY 18, 1891—When Sarah abruptly left the Porte-Saint-Martin in the very middle of performances of *Cléopâtre* to go to America, Duquesnel the director found himself caught short, and offered to present certain plays from the Théâtre-Libre to fill up the fifteen or twenty days he will need to get *The Lyon Post* back on stage. Since this director has shown himself the most pleasant and unbiased of men, we immediately organized these productions, the scenery for which we had in storage. The recent success of *Elisa the Slattern* suggested it immediately for several public presentations.

JANUARY 19, 1891—This afternoon about four, while we were rehearsing on stage, Duquesnel sent a request for me to go to his house. There he told me that he had just been informed that *Elisa the Slattern* has been banned, purely and simply. We are going to have to return some ten thousand francs worth of bookings which have already come in, and which we all need very much. In the meantime, we are now obliged to go on with the announced presentations of less revolutionary plays which will no longer permit us to hope for the great financial success we were anticipating.

JANUARY 20, 1891—M. de Goncourt sought for the most elegant way to thank me for our great effort with *Elisa,* and had the lovely idea of showing me personally through his private collection—the

[57]The Théâtre d'Art was actually formed a year earlier.

most beautiful museum of Far Eastern and Eighteenth Century objects to be seen at the present time. He therefore asked me to lunch in tête-à-tête with him in his beautiful dining room resplendent with tapestries by Boucher. The meal was served on the table with the plate and crystal of that period. Truly the elegance suited a great lord and great artist, and what touched me most deeply was that the master understood that I would appreciate all the honor which he did me.[58] When alone, he never dines in this room, and scarcely ever opens it except for guests of note like the Princess Mathilde or very close friends like the Daudets.

JANUARY 21, 1891—This morning Bauer, trapped by the attitude which he has held against the authorities for two years, was forced to swallow his ill humor and side with the Théâtre-Libre against censorship. The incident, growing larger, could have ramifications which the Rue de Valois did not expect, for Millerand has announced that he will bring the question before the tribune of the Chamber. A full-scale movement on the question of freedom of the theatre seems to be developing.

Goncourt, resigned but always a bit frightened by violent controversies, is unwilling to enter the fray personally. Séverine, as always, is courageously charging ahead. A young man, Pierre Baudin, who I think has influence in the Ecoles quarter, has published a virulent article in the Cité, calling public attention to the legendary ineptitudes of censorship—how it tolerates the music hall and reserves its most severe blows for literary works.

JANUARY 24, 1891—We are putting together The Death of the Duke of Enghien in the Porte-Saint-Martin theatre. When I asked the props boy for the riding crop which he has been lending me, the one Paulin Ménier uses in The Lyon Post, the poor boy, quite embarrassed, told

---

[58]It seems unlikely that a luncheon precisely like the one here described ever took place. Goncourt notes in his *Journals* on January 21 his impatience at not having heard from Antoine concerning *Elisa*, and specifically notes that he expected to hear from him the previous day, and did not. The dinner given in appreciation of the efforts made on *Elisa* took place on January 10, and on that date not only Antoine, but Ajalbert, Janvier, and Mlle. Nau were invited to Goncourt's home.

me that the great actor had become most indignant upon hearing that an object of his had been touched by the founder of the Théâtre-Libre, and had formally forbidden him to let me use it.

JANUARY 24, 1891—The Théâtre-Libre just won the Chamber hearing over the *Elisa* question. Millerand, deputy from the Seine, defended Ajalbert's work intelligently and energetically, saying that he had attended the dress rehearsal at our theatre, and that it caused no disturbance at all. He added that for public performance, it would not be unreasonable to request a few changes in the dialogue between the two girls in the first act—but that the Censor did not even request such changes, the motive for prohibition being simply stated as: general content. The speaker read several excerpts, which aroused a fit of comic modesty among our virtuous parliamentarians.

After quoting Sarcey, Faguet, Jules Lemaître, La Pommeraye, Edmond Lepelletier, and Henry Fouquier, who in their generally laudatory reviews never thought of raising the question of decency, Millerand asserted that the work, far from being immoral, was a noble cry of pity—an act of accusation against society—an act that might be considered violent, yet one of unusual signficance.

When the house continued to show embarrassment at hearing the terrible subject of prostitution discussed before the tribunal, the speaker observed that one of the ministers, M. Yves Guyot, had written an entire book on this social evil.[59] He finished by demanding whether—when the Censor allowed and tolerated music hall obscenity—it is to be tolerated that a great master like Goncourt, one of the literary giants of our time, should undergo such an outrage.

The minister, M. Bourgeois, had to mount the rostrum himself. He said that he was obliged to defend censorship, even while acknowledging that at times he regretted its existence. Without entering the debate, he attempted to show that the theatre inspectors were responsible persons, although he recognized that they had not satisfac-

---

[59]Guyot's book, *Prostitution*, appeared in 1882. Although Antoine does not mention why this book entered the discussion, it was because in it Guyot had spoken favorably of *Elisa the Slattern* (Chapter I, page 16) as a true picture of the poor prostitute, in contrast to such glorified courtesans as the more famous Camille of Dumas.

torily succeeded in purifying the music halls and certain public spectacles. He read certain passages in the play again, so as to re-arouse the expressions of reproach that he had observed during Millerand's speech. The listeners proved easily aroused, and he even obtained an approving interruption from Paul Déroulède and the Count de Maillé. He called M. Millerand his friend, and concluded by saying that he would be happy to lift the ban if the authors would consent to revise their play.

The *Figaro,* in its report, says that the Chamber got an hour's amusement out of this free-wheeling debate; but persons interested in literary history who some day will read the record of this session in the *Officiel* will find in the interrupting comments certain outbursts which are singularly revealing of the mentality and culture of the French Chamber in the year of grace 1891.

JANUARY 27, 1891—Now here is this *Thermidor* affair, which would be of relatively minor interest to us if the debate announced in the Chamber were not really a sequel to the campaign which the *Elisa* affair initiated against censorship. It has been found, with considerable reason, that the prohibition of Sardou's play, whatever its tendencies, clearly shows the ineptness of the Censor, and it is pleasing to see the *Gaulois,* which was so delighted a few days ago over the prohibition of a play by the enemy of its associate Pessard, cry "Bravo, Sardou," and enter the struggle against the Rue de Valois. In the interests of consistency, when *Thermidor* was banned I was obliged to put the Théâtre-Libre publicly at Sardou's disposal, and to give his play if he thought it worthwhile. To be honest, this was not much more than a gesture, but despite the innumerable difficulties of the undertaking, I am quite ready to go through with it if the author takes me at my word.

JANUARY 27, 1891—The *Figaro* has printed a cartoon about *Elisa the Slattern* by Francis Magnard, attacking censorship. It is a highly significant symptom when this great moderate and literary paper finally aligns itself openly against the bureaucracy and the harmful practices of the Rue de Valois.

FEBRUARY 1, 1891—Toché has written an amusing "Paris Evening" in this morning's *Gaulois,* which pretends that as a consequence of the advance I made toward Sardou for *Thermidor,* Claretie has just written a similar letter to Ajalbert, putting the Comédie-Française at his disposal for his *Elisa the Slattern.*

FEBRUARY 1, 1891—There is a fine cartoon by Forain in the *Courrier français.* It shows censorship personified by a horrible old man, armed with academic scissors, who is saying to Elisa: "First go get dressed at Georges Ohnet's, then we shall see."

FEBRUARY 1, 1891—Our productions at the Porte-Saint-Martin have gone on peacefully in the midst of all this uproar, with creditable receipts which have easily surpassed 2000 francs. We have given *The Death of the Duke of Enghien, Aunt Léontine,* and *The School for Widows.*[60] The papers were benevolent toward this experiment, which had the double advantage of seasoning our company and of putting us in contact at last with the general public. The works which, at their first appearance, the principal critics declared were incapable of withstanding a real test, proved that they could interest a general audience, and we have now shown that our repertoire is not inaccessible to the masses.

FEBRUARY 9, 1891—Sarcey, who came to see our public performances at the Porte-Saint-Martin, complimented us and acknowledged the talent of the actors, although he rather contested the attitude of the public, which led Ancey to protest in the *Figaro,* saying:

> There will surely be an eternal misunderstanding between us—the young—and M. Sarcey. He is extravagantly entertained by the ineptitudes which reduce us to tears; he is overjoyed; he dies with laughter. We do no more than request his advice. He gives it, and we take pains not to follow it. M. Sarcey's advanced age commands our respect,

---

[60] A fourth play from the Théâtre-Libre was presented with *The School for Widows —Two Turtledoves.*

but we deny him any literary competence so far as our own works are concerned.

FEBRUARY 16, 1891—We are now rehearsing, for our next production, a first play by a new comrade, Georges Lecomte. He is a tall young man, pleasant and eloquent, and I willingly spend hours on end chatting with him, for he has an expressive warmth which stands out amid the cynical surroundings of the Théâtre-Libre.

FEBRUARY 20, 1891—Some time ago, Mirbeau wrote a resounding article for the *Figaro* which called on me to stage Maeterlinck's *Princess Maleine*. I was reluctant, first because the author himself said that he had written the play for a puppet theatre, and second because I really don't have the materials, costumes, settings, or actors at hand to do it. Now this is being used against me in Brussels, and it is said that the naturalist clique at the Théâtre-Libre dissuaded me from the experiment. The truth is that I don't think that this would suit the nature of the theatre, and I would be undertaking a venture which would only betray the author.

FEBRUARY 20, 1891—After some dark hints appeared in the papers about the material results of our evenings at the Porte-Saint-Martin, I was curious enough to compare our receipts with those of other theatres. Now, while we were making an average of 1648 francs per evening in a theatre crippled by the departure of Sarah Bernhardt, the Odéon was making 943 francs; Mme. Mongodin at the Vaudeville, 1900 francs; the Gymnase, 1682 francs; the Palais-Royal, 1900 francs; the Variétés, 3000 francs, with *My Cousin;* the Châtelet, 1461 francs; the Nouveautés, 982 francs; and the Menus-Plaisirs, 238 francs. Well, then?

FEBRUARY 26, 1891—This evening the list was published of the people who will be summoned before the committee on censorship which the Chamber has chosen, appointing M. Dujardin-Beaumetz as the general secretary. They will hear Alexandre Dumas, Meilhac, Vacquerie, Sardou, Goncourt, Zola, Banville, Bergerat, Ancey, Bis-

· 171

son, Camille Doucet, Claretie, and Carré, and to my surprise, my own name ended the list.

MARCH 1, 1891—As might be expected, the papers are collecting comments about censorship and the actions of the committee chosen by the Chamber to examine the advisability of modifying the law. Zola says that he is for absolute and complete freedom, but he thinks that whatever legal opinion the parliamentarians decide upon will be a simple formality, and that nothing will really be changed. Sardou, singed in the recent *Thermidor* affair, merely fumes and rages. Carré says that as an author, he demands that censorship continue. In general, there is much doubt as to how all this will come out.

MARCH 2, 1891—Our production of Georges Lecomte's *The Millstone* did not turn out badly at all, and the debut was quite pleasant. The first two acts got off to a good start, and although the play slowed up by the end, the author got good reviews. Sarcey and Lemaître say he has a future. A one-act play by Ginisty, *The Leading Man,* provided a pleasant curtain-raiser. It was based on an anecdote concerning the actor Delaunay, and it amused me to make myself up like him.

MARCH 3, 1891—Here we are again in Brussels, where we have come to give *Elisa the Slattern.* These frequent trips are tiring and they hinder our work in Paris, but every month the same problem arises—to find a little outside money to finance the next production.

MARCH 3, 1891—It seems that the influence of the Théâtre-Libre has reached even to the Imperial Theatre in Petersburg, where *Aunt Léontine* has been given with great success. I was greatly surprised to find that the actors there—Andrieu, Hittemans, and Mlle. Thomassin—were able to capture the particular movement of a dialogue so different from that of the works they are accustomed to giving.

MARCH 6, 1891—We have been very successful in Brussels. We

found an audience here which simply accepted the works we brought them, without becoming involved in the sort of literary agitation that these works raised at home. I was quite concerned about Fréderikx, the critic of the *Independance belge*, whose position, in talent and authority, is analogous to that of Sarcey. He is not ordinarily easy-going, and I have been warned that we would have to endure his wrath. He was certainly not without his reservations, but he encouraged us and his attitude has had a lot to do with the financial success that we are having here—a truly welcome one, for our monetary situation is becoming more and more difficult in Paris. Most importantly, the subscriptions cannot increase, but the expenses grow incessantly greater, and our deficit is rising. Although I have said nothing to anyone, I strongly feel that we are headed for a pit into which the whole Théâtre-Libre will fall one of these days. It is terrible, because I cannot allow this distress to be seen, since it will immediately be used to thwart what we are doing. This is why these productions, for which I am being reproached in Paris, are a matter of life or death for the Théâtre-Libre.

MARCH 6, 1891—The Gymnase has just given an adaptation by M. Jacques Normand of Maupassant's famous short story, *Musotte*. The papers call it a first-rate Théâtre-Libre piece, skillfully adapted to the customs of society people, and it is enjoying great success. I went to see the production, and found that nothing of the masterpiece remains in it but a rather flat sentimentality. Even so, the fact that the most bourgeois audience can accept this midwife and this audacious situation is a victory. The populace is unwittingly moving toward a renaissance for which we have prepared and which will some day overturn all the old values.

MARCH 14, 1891—The death of Théodore de Banville has put us into mourning. The Théâtre-Libre owes him much, since his *The Kiss*, which he agreed to write for us, was one of the great successes which established the theatre. Once he said: "Writing verse is as natural to me as visiting my tailor." Now he is gone. He had been a Knight of the Legion of Honor since 1858; Marianne treats the poets well, as Bergerat says.

APRIL 25, 1891—Premiere of *A Loving Wife,* at the Odéon. Here at last is an important play—so important that its equal has surely not been seen since *The Vultures.* I was proud that this work was signed by one of the names from the Théâtre-Libre, for it was our theatre which in the past reopened Porto-Riche's way to the stage by presenting *Francoise's Luck.* The interpretation at the second Théâtre-Français is marvelous, starring Réjane, the most thorough-going artist of our time. With her masterful intensity and virtuosity, she seems to live this vibrant character. The third act remains weak— one feels that the author has not completely succeeded in expressing his thought—but the big scene in the second act was developed with the boldness, unerringness, and scope of the masters.

APRIL 28, 1891—M. George de Porto-Riche's *A Loving Wife,* which Porel received sight unseen at the Odéon, was first called *The Foe.* Pessard, even though he gave the play warm compliments, says that as a whole he had the impression of a closet drama rather than of a theatre piece. Vitu proclaims that he will not dwell on the shocking side of this singular experience, but he is prudent enough not to condemn it strongly. For those in my circle, *A Loving Wife,* with its new and vigorous tone, is an important play, a kind of play we have not yet seen. The boldness and frankness of the second act ring magnificently true next to the puppets in a play by Dumas *fils.*

APRIL 28, 1891—Very happily for us, Porel had no sooner scored a triumph in our literary competition with *A Loving Wife* than I was ready to parry with *The Wild Duck,* which we just presented. It was a strange performance. The audience started out hostile and bantering, but they were completely won over by the wonderful fifth act. There were some imitation duck cries and a certain amount of uproar, but the attitude of the reviews speaks volumes for the play.

APRIL 28, 1891—Pierre Véron in his review says that in writing *A Loving Wife,* M. de Porto-Riche has permanently abandoned romanticism to do homage to antoinism. I am more than a little proud of this sally, but I rather think that *A Loving Wife* is actually descended from the great work of Becque.

MAY 5, 1891—Sarcey's review of *The Wild Duck* is lamentable. This morning I got a clipping of it, which I want to preserve. It is clear to me that our "uncle" could not resist the fun of joining those who were joking in the darkness of the house; this has not hindered him, however, from speaking of the play as someone who has really understood it all, but who does not want to admit it. There is something so unpleasant in his pleasantries about such a work that they should be recorded:

> Ah! This Wild Duck! No one ever, no one—neither those who have seen the play, nor Lindenlaub and Ephraïm who so scrupulously translated it, nor the author who wrote it, nor Shakespeare who inspired it, nor God nor the devil —nobody has any idea what this wild duck is, nor what it is doing in the play, nor what it stands for, nor what sense it makes. Yet, aside from the duck, one begins to understand the play by the end of the third act, and by the end of the fifth act, with a retrospective effort, one can almost grasp it—always aside from the wild duck, of course. Oh, I do not delude myself by thinking I understand the duck, so don't expect me to explain it to you. I have already seen a number of exegeses on this duck, and I am not satisfied. Some have seasoned it with olives, others with rouennaise, others with orange slices—but I have no sauce at all to propose to you. I would not dare admit that I have no idea what Ibsen is trying to say, except that it is already generally acknowledged that I am a being deprived of all understanding. This confession, therefore, cannot worsen the opinion that the amateurs who presented *The Wild Duck* already have of me.

MAY 11, 1891—Jules Lemaître, in his column in the *Débats,* speaks of the work of the great Norwegian with admirable insight, and allows himself the mischievious pleasure of explaining the symbol of the wild duck to Sarcey, ending by saying: "That's all. What is so obscure or strange about that?"

MAY 19, 1891—A rabid devotee of Sarcey, Adrien Bernheim, advised me to go see *Grisélidis* at the Comédie-Française, and to take a lesson in staging from it. I must admire such a desperate affirmation of enthusiasm for medieval bric-a-brac in protest against our experiments.

MAY 22, 1891—Porel has just accepted Jean Jullien's new play, *The Sea.* He felt it necessary to inform the public of this through a disagreeable notice which remarked that the author of *The Serenade, The Master,* and *The Day of Reckoning* had been obliged, like so many others, to break off his early relations with the Théâtre-Libre.

MAY 24, 1891—I have just been notified that I must appear next Wednesday before the Committee on Dramatic Censorship which is working at the Palais-Bourbon. Got, Carré, Albin Valabrègue, and Georges Ancey are summoned for the same day.

MAY 28, 1891—We just gave *Nell Horn,* a five-act play which Rosny drew from his fine book.[61] It was a strange production, eventful but unsuccessful, and the reviews reflect this impression. The results were scarcely commensurate with the great effort I made. In the third act, which showed a Salvation Army rally in a London square, I used almost five hundred [*sic*] extras carrying banners, and three bands. For some inexplicable reason, this enormous display on the stage put the audience into an uproar. Since the noise on stage was so great that the spectators realized their jokes and gibes could not even reach us through the hullabaloo, they—for want of anything better to do—struck up in chorus the refrain of the Salvation Army song.

---

[61]*Nell Horn of the Salvation Army: A Novel of London Manners,* published in 1886.

Lost amid the extras, I became so enraged that I gave a signal on a whistle I had with me, and three hundred extras sent up a shout so violent and prolonged that the stunned and exhausted spectators were reduced to silence.

I remain firmly convinced that *Nell Horn* was a production of rare originality, but poor Rosny is not disposed to return to the stage soon after this mortification—another of our great writers driven away from the theatre, perhaps permanently.

MAY 28, 1891—The charming tone of this scandal sheet ought to be noted, because it is typical of the attitude adopted towards us in certain quarters:

> At the moment of going to press, when it is too late to recast my article, I am informed that the Théâtre-Libre has ceased to exist, and that its director, no longer able to make ends meet and yet unwilling to abandon his free art, has moved his activities to a poorhouse on the Boulevard de la Chapelle, 22 or 106 (the number could not be determined, but it would surely be the more gross).

MAY 29, 1891—The extras in *Nell Horn* cost me 1500 francs.

MAY 31, 1891—I spoke about censorship at great length before the parliamentary committee, and I felt that I detected in the majority of them a desire for its suppression. M. Dujardin-Beaumetz seemed to me one of the most ardent and determined, and his eyes sparkled with pleasure and approbation each time I thrust home. In sum, I demanded for the theatre the liberty enjoyed in all other aspects of French art, and Ancey, who was heard at the same time, upheld the same arguments in a more moderate fashion. He added an amusing stroke by telling how a Censor had asked him to suppress this sentence from *The School for Widows:* "I have just seen the curé of Notre-Dame-de-Lorette," because that was the Censor's home parish.

JUNE 1, 1891—Here is the statement which M. de Goncourt made before the Committee of Inquiry on Censorship:

> It is a fact that public interest has passed successively from Agamemnon and the kings of antiquity to the marquis of the seventeenth and eighteenth centuries, then from the marquis to the bourgeois of the nineteenth century, and the censors intend to draw the line at the contemporary "noble personage."
>
> These gentlemen have no idea that a hundred and fifty years ago when Marivaux published his novel *Marianne* he was attacked on the grounds that the public was only interested in the doings of nobility. Marivaux was obliged to write a preface in which he declared that he found interest in what were generally considered ignoble bourgeois activities, and he argued that those who were the least bit philosophical, and not the dupes of social distinctions, would not be annoyed to hear about the wife of a successful cloth-merchant.
>
> Well, a hundred and fifty years after Marivaux—and here I am speaking for myself—a philosophical spirit like Marivaux' should perhaps be allowed to descend to a housemaid, or to a base prostitute.

JUNE 1, 1891—A free theatre has just been founded in Copenhagen. It inaugurated its productions with Zola's *Thérèse Raquin,* under the presidency of the Minister of Public Instruction. We have come a long way from Paris.

JUNE 2, 1891—The opinions expressed by those examined on censorship have been made public. Vacquerie gave an eloquent plea in favor of complete freedom of the theatre, as did Goncourt and Zola. Alexandre Dumas *fils,* on the other hand, said that censorship was good—very good—and that the real writers never complained about it. Henry Meilhac and Camille Doucet were naturally of the same mind.

JUNE 9, 1891—We just gave *The Caudine Pitchforks,* by Maurice Le Corbeiller, a very pleasant fellow who is the drama columnist of the *Débats.* He has already given the Comédie-Française a most tasteful occasional piece in verse.

JUNE 10, 1891—Last evening we gave Pierre Wolff's *Their Girls.* Albert Wolff of the *Figaro* has never yet been able to stomach his nephew's debut with *Jacques Bouchard;* he has shunned us since, and at one time even fell out with his nephew. Matters were not improved by the controversy in which it was my fortune to give him a strong comeuppance. After all, we belong to a clique against which he has always nourished a deep grudge, and his squabbles with Zola are famous.

Wolff's curiosity about his nephew's new play was very strong, however, and besides, as a dramatic critic he was obliged to give an account of it. Thus, during the presentation, in which I had only a small role, I watched his reactions with malicious pleasure. The more successful the play appeared, the more stupefaction and confusion he showed, mixed with a rather touching emotion. When the curtain had fallen and I announced Pierre Wolff's name into the enthusiastic uproar of the house, Albert Wolff came up on the stage and told his nephew to take him to my office. Since we are only transient tenants, I am installed in a small unfurnished room, and when the author introduced his uncle, I was able to offer him only an old trunk to sit on. The old gentleman regarded me, deeply moved, his head nodding according to his familiar mannerism. I was taking off my makeup before a mirror when he asked his nephew to leave us alone. There was a long silence which I could not bring myself to interrupt, for I too was rather moved. After watching me for a long time, however, at last he spoke: "You are a chap with spirit and I am only an old fool. You have revenged yourself well. I thank you for my nephew and myself." I must confess that I was touched and pleased by this reconciliation. The morning papers say that *Their Girls* is a masterpiece, and that Henriot is Mme. Dorval in the flesh. Koning, a friend of Albert Wolff, is already speaking of asking the author for a play for the Gymnase.

JUNE 11, 1891—The suit that I brought against Bauer came up for a hearing today, but it has been postponed until July 29. Many friends have urged me to withdraw my complaint, but have I the right to do so? I have a great number of malcontents baying at my heels just now, and I must prove that I have nothing to hide, and that I do not fear to expose my life and my work to full daylight. Bauer too has his inveterate enemies, for certain contributors to his paper and noted rivals of his have surreptitiously advised me to stand fast.

JUNE 21, 1891—Courteline has written an amusing and fanciful article in which he pokes fun at those who reproached us after the production of his *Lidoire* for having given this play in a realistic setting. He concludes ironically:

> The play unfolds in a hussar regiment, doesn't it? A certain setting is therefore demanded—at the left, in the foreground, a tree behind a sideboard; then a stone statue of the Emperor of Brazil; at the right, in heaps, the works of M. Paul Perret; and in back, the burning of the Palais de Justice at Rouen, the red glare from which illuminates the despairing movements of the shipwrecked persons from the Médusa. You annoy me, my dear sir, with your realistic settings.

It is a most humorous answer to the attacks against the realistic setting, which have been growing in number for some time.

JUNE 25, 1891—My situation is difficult at the end of this season. Last month I wrote a note to Derenbourg asking him to advance me 6000 to 7000 francs in order to cover the last production and reach the summer. Yesterday I found my letter reproduced in the *Gil Blas,* which I find most unpleasant, for it publicizes a financial situation which should delight our enemies. Moreover, this was apparently done solely to irritate me at the very moment which I am setting up subscriptions for the coming season.

JULY 1, 1891—Marcel Prévost, whose *Confession of a Lover* has put him in the first rank among the new novelists, has graciously accepted my request for a play for next season. There is not the slightest doubt that it will be a real advantage for the Thèâtre-Libre to draw in one of the writers who promises to be a master in the future. We agreed that he will give me a one-act play adapted from an episode in *The Scorpion.*

JULY 4, 1891—All of these incidents of censorship, combined with the investigations of the parliamentary committee under the direction of the Beaux-Arts, should result in a sanction. Larroumet is leaving as director at the Rue de Valois, and even without knowing his successor, I feel that this is a great loss. In the numerous conflicts of recent years, Larroumet has always treated me with infinite kindness, and in the course of the visits I have made to him, I could discern under the discretion of the high functionary a real kindness for the upcoming dramatic generation.

JULY 6, 1891—This evening we gave the last production of the season—three one-acts: a story of peasant life by Sutter-Laumann; a rather amusing fantasy called *The Hanged One* by Eugène Bourgeois; and *In A Dream,* a very charming thing by Louis Mullem. The reviews are not bad, but I am looking forward to my vacation at Camaret to collect myself and rally my strength.

JULY 8, 1891—In the course of liquidating my accounts at the end of the season, I have been glancing over the disarray of a very grave financial situation. I have totaled up the figures for the subscriptions of the last three years: 26,000 francs for 1889, 42,700 for 1890, and 53,600 for 1891. This would be rather heartening if, at the same time, I did not see the costs and the expenses of the Thèâtre-Libre immeasurably increasing too.

JULY 12, 1891—Carvalho has announced an opera by Mascagni which has toured the world for next winter. It is *Cavalleria Rusticana*

—no other than Verga's *Rustic Chivalry,* which drew such sharp criticisms at our theatre.

JULY 15, 1891—Auguste Vitu devoted his most recent column to the Thèâtre-Libre, closing with these charming words:
> I almost forgot to mention that the management of the Théâtre-Libre put out a fine collection of obscene designs in the guise of a program. This made the party complete.

Now, these drawings were by Willette and Forain, and were given to us by the *Courrier français.* It's the same old technique of systematically spreading the legend of pornography through the provinces and in foreign countries.

JULY 20, 1891—Last year during one of the trips Ancey and I made to Douarnenez, near Brest, we passed the Point de Pois, which separates the Brest channel from the open sea, and were struck by the magnificent panorama of rocky cliffs and deserted beaches. When we left Paris this year, we went on around the bay without stopping at Douarnenez and came to this famous point, at the very end of which a little fishing village named Camaret aroused our enthusiasm. Here we will spend the summer—Ancey inland where he has found a little house, and I in an old ruined fort at the end of a pier at the entrance to the port, where I have settled myself, after a fashion, in a location which the commune is willing to rent to me for 25 francs a year.

JULY 30, 1891—I have received such a flood of manuscripts that there are almost 500 stacked up in my little fortress room at Camaret. I settled down to work on them, and last evening, as I read rather late into the night, I came upon a three-act play by a M. Charles Watterneau, *The Other Side of a Saint,* which put me into a fever and kept me awake the rest of the night. I have written to this gentleman to give him my impression, and to tell him that his play will certainly be kept for next year.

AUGUST 2, 1891—I am certainly in luck this year. Here is another manuscript, *Embellished Love*, by a M. de Weindel, who gives an address in Vienna. It is a remarkable work, a kind of *Game of Love and Chance*, mordant and tragic, which heralds a real dramatist.

CAMARET, AUGUST 5, 1891—Just as I completed a letter to the author of *Embellished Love*, asking him if he had anything else for me to read, I received one from M. François de Curel, 83 Rue de Grenelle, in Paris, ironic and yet joyful, which informed me that since I want to read something else, I have three of his manuscripts in my possession at this moment, signed with different names. Two are the plays I have already chosen, and a third is called *The Ballet-Dancer*. Naturally, I read that play last evening, and it too seems most remarkable to me. I did not take offense at Curel's strategem, but answered that I would certainly give one of his plays next winter, to begin with, and that I would present which ever of the three he chooses, although in my opinion, *The Other Side of a Saint* is the most important and the most likely to survive the great demands placed on new authors at the Thèâtre-Libre.

AUGUST 12, 1891—This morning I saw in the *Dépêche de Brest* that the burial of Auguste Vitu took place today. He was a talented man, although his ties with his own time often set him against us. I telegraphed to Paris for them to put a wreath from the Thèâtre-Libre on his coffin.

SEPTEMBER 3, 1891—Upon arriving in Paris, I went directly to M. de Curel's home. We were not long in agreeing on the choice of *The Other Side of a Saint,* and I told him not to worry about the other two works, which would be given afterward, at my theatre or elsewhere. He told me that he employed his little artifice in submitting his manuscripts almost as an act of defiance, imagining us to be a closed circle, narrowly realistic in our bias. He had taken his plays to so many theatres without any result that he was able to undertake this last step with a clear conscience and with no illusions about the results.

SEPTEMBER 10, 1891—We have put *Old Goriot* into rehearsal.

SEPTEMBER 28, 1891—The good Maurice Lefévre, a friend of ours, has launched an important investigation in the *Figaro* of the current trends in drama, at this opening of a new season. I was mentioned throughout seven long articles, but the last dealt with me exclusively:

> I have been asked why my discussion always comes back to the subject of the Théâtre-Libre, and one of my correspondents has done me the honor of ending his letter with a plea that I give him the explanation of this mystery.
>
> It is quite simple. I have used the Théâtre-Libre as a touchstone. Since its foundation, this theatre has been the subject of extensive discussions; some have applauded its attempts, others have fought them to the bitter end. It has about as many devoted friends as resolute enemies—to the latter it seems a kind of perdition, and to the former a kind of Monsalvat, where the Holy Grail of drama is found, with M. Antoine appearing as none other than Parsifal.
>
> The moderates support it as a testing ground where interesting ideas can be tried out, or as a laboratory where chemical preparations are being handled which some time in the future will enliven the old formulas. In short, and this is the heart of the matter, it cannot be ignored by anyone interested in theatre matters. A better basis for discussion cannot therefore be found—it gives a point of reference, and lends to these conversations the unity which is necessary for clarity of discourse. The devotees of progress have gone to battle in the name of the Théâtre-Libre, and it is against the tendencies and the esthetic of this theatre that the proponents of the old tradition have taken up arms.
>
> It is therefore only right, now that I have reported the personal comments of the combattants in the regular army, that I report the words of this guerrilla leader. Even among the conversations I have reproduced here, charges against

him were more numerous than statements in his support. Now it is the defense's turn, and the accused takes the stand. I will reproduce the various excerpts from my interview which most clearly show his state of mind at the beginning of this season:

"You are staging *Old Goriot;* meddling with Balzac is serious business."

"It is indeed rather hazardous, and perhaps we will produce a colossal failure. But the literary reputation of the Théâtre-Libre was established by such failures. What convinced me is that the thing is basically new, that it has never been done, and that, in the current confusion, bringing the great characters from the *Comédie humaine* to the stage will help remove some of the unknown element in the theatre's new direction. If we fail, so much the worse for us, but it is our duty to *search.* We are moving in the vanguard, like scouts, and if we risk falling in the underbrush from time to time, still we keep those who will follow us from breaking their necks. I am convinced that the task of the Théâtre-Libre is *not so much to produce successful works as to establish new directions.*"

"This definition certainly answers the objections. . . . Let us go on. How much of your program have you set aside for foreign plays?"

"I have set aside one evening for a foreign author, as I do every year. I cannot return to Ibsen or Tolstoi, nor do I wish to. The big theatres which are staging *A Doll's House* and *Hedda Gabler* are following the example our theatre set with *Ghosts* and *The Wild Duck*. I have therefore looked elsewhere for a new author, and I think I have found one in Spain."

"Although you want to remain as reserved as possible, aren't you ever tempted to reply to the different attacks which have been made on the Théâtre-Libre?"

"My dear friend, I have only been back from my vacation a few days, and you want to plunge me into battle immediately. I am infinitely grateful to you for devoting a small corner of your interesting investigation to the Théâtre-Libre; indeed, it seems to me that my theatre has been its principal subject. I have read the conversations you have quoted with keen interest, and at the beginning of the season, I really couldn't find a better spur than my comrades' slashing attacks. Six months ago I would not have resisted the desire to fight back, but now—bah! What would be the use? I have given up pointless controversies. Paris, logical and fair, is always reasonable about a new work. That is the whole secret of the Théâtre-Libre's vitality. What good do speeches on the side do?"

OCTOBER 2, 1891—Last night Porel gave Jean Jullien's *The Sea.* It was a success, and Albert Wolff, who has succeeded Vitu as critic on the *Figaro,* speaks highly of it. The production was creditable, but too theatrical, despite the research Porel put into the setting. He was so imprudent as to show the actual sea, instead of merely suggesting the area near it, and a rising wave painted on the backdrop did not recede during the whole three acts of the play.

OCTOBER 19, 1891—Mounet-Sully, after his recent fresh triumph at the Comédie-Française in *Oedipus,* is now speaking of leaving, complaining that he is being left to languish inactive. He would be foolish to leave, but unhappily, Sarah Bernhardt set a bad example for all the comrades she left behind in the Rue Richelieu.

OCTOBER 20, 1891—I am furious. A man named Chirac has just given a presentation in the Rue Rochechouart of three pieces of obscenity which have aroused the indignation of the public, and I know that they will tend to confuse our efforts with this filth.

OCTOBER 25, 1891—I have not yet gotten what I expected from *Old Goriot,* and yet I swear that no more conscientious or reverent work was ever done on Balzac. At the very outset, no one could understand why I appealed to Balzac to clarify the basic action, if he could.

Yet it seemed to me that this action had a tendency to become lost. The Théâtre-Libre has reached a plateau. I feel that some new impetus is on the way, but it has not come yet, and we must remain waiting.

The reviews were severe on poor Tabarant,[62] but generally indulgent toward the artists and setting. Céard was about the only one who gave us a bit of a dressing-down about the settings and furniture, knowing full well how unpleasant this is to me; but he gave credit to Grand, who played Rastignac marvelously. Unfortunately, all this has cost me a mint; and at the very beginning of the season, already so heavily burdened with old debts, I anticipate a year with yet heavier cares than the former ones.

NOVEMBER 2, 1891—After the disappointment of *Old Goriot,* I am a bit reassured at putting into rehearsal a work which, in my opinion, will mark a turning-point in our venture. François de Curel brings us something new which I think will take us away from what Jules Lemaître and others are beginning to call the Théâtre-Libre stereotype.

NOVEMBER 19, 1891—The mania for adaptations of Shakespeare still goes on. The Comèdie-Française in its turn gave a poetic version of *The Taming of the Shrew,* which succeeded largely through the efforts of Coquelin.

DECEMBER 7, 1891—Salandri's *The Ransom* aroused no opposition, but not much enthusiasm either. *A Fine Evening,* by Maurice Vaucaire, a charming and kindly poet whom I knew at the Chat Noir, was warmly applauded, and Henri Rivière, who founded the shadow theatre at Salis', created a marvelous setting for it, quite original in conception. But I was most excited by the production of *The Abbé Pierre,* Marcel Prévost's first play, based on an episode in his famous *The Scorpion.* It tells, with a terrible boldness and yet a marvelous tact, of a priest who hears his own mother's confession. This was presented with such great discretion that it aroused no

---

62The adapter of the work.

protest at all, but the critics are disturbed to see one of the master novelists of the future drifting toward the theatre, and they are exerting every effort to turn him aside.

DECEMBER 17, 1891—Yesterday the Ninth Chamber, presided over by M. de Boislisle, dismissed my suit against Bauer. The tribunal found that Bauer's article exceeded the bounds of criticism, but they felt that the declaration of M. Strauss, his defense attorney, did sufficent honor to my private life, and that my violent answer, which was read aloud, constituted sufficient reparation for the rest. The decision was just. This is all already ancient history, and no longer of much importance.

DECEMBER 19, 1891—Carré has just engaged Grand at the Vaudeville. This is a great loss for us, but at the same time proof of the services we are doing the Parisian theatres, by finding them new authors and new artists.

DECEMBER 20, 1891—My lawsuit with Bauer has caused quite a stir. Céard insists that the judgment given me was a mistake; he viciously attacks me, saying that the Théâtre-Libre is dead and that I should give way to someone new. As for Sarcey, he attempts to follow a middle path and does not hide from Bauer that, while he is delighted to see the courts uphold the rights of criticism, he does not excuse him at all for striking out in my direction with such fruitless outbursts.

DECEMBER 20, 1891—An examining magistrate has been named to press charges against this depraved person Chirac, who caused an abominable scandal recently with his realistic theatre. He is a fool and a lunatic, but his eccentricities were easy to exploit against us, and he has perhaps set back our contact with the general public several years.

DECEMBER 21, 1891—We just presented Ancey's *The Dupe,* with a pleasant one-act verse play by Marsolleau called *His Lack of Spirit.*

The former caused a sensation, for it shows the hand of a master, and Becque agrees with me that it is a kind of masterpiece. Fouquier finds it remarkable, and says that this evening furnishes good grounds for the discussion of evolution in the theatre. Bauer, naturally, thinks that the play is nothing more than a pot-boiler.

DECEMBER 22, 1891—I just had the unpleasant surprise of being summoned by the commission of authors. They intended to put me on an equal footing with other theatres, which would increase my burdens terribly. I hid nothing of my almost desperate financial situation from these gentlemen—Sardou, Halévy, and others—and, staggered upon hearing the truth, they were most understanding. This little conflict is already being exploited, however, and I feel hostility against me increasing daily. I have alienated many people by refusing plays, and the death of the Théâtre-Libre has been predicted so many times that our vitality alone has piled up hatreds, so that I wonder what I could have done to anger all these people. This causes me a weariness which I must keep hidden.

DECEMBER 26, 1891—Albert Wolff is dead. This causes me great sadness, even apart from the pain that I see in our poor Pierre Wolff, for since our reconciliation, the good man has evidenced a most touching interest in our little corner. His last days coincided with our recent production, and his nephew tells me that the critic was concerned over what other reviewer would be assigned to replace him at our theatre.

DECEMBER 26, 1891—The Théâtre d'Art founded by Paul Fort is prospering and growing in importance, and I am not the one to complain of it. They are going to give Marlowe's *Doctor Faustus* and a *Salomé* by Oscar Wilde. Our two amateur stages complement each other's activity for the greater profit of the young.

DECEMBER 27, 1891—M. Henry de Bornier has published an article in the *Patrie* the beginning of which is worth noting:

Shepherds, the wolves are at hand! They have descended long since and are prowling about your folds and your pens that are closed for the winter. Worse yet, they have entered the classic sheepfold called the Odéon, and before long they will enter the great sheepfold of the Comédie-Française —have no doubt about it. I tell you I have seen them on the square in front of the Théâtre-Français—the wolves, the thin wolves with long teeth. I don't blame them, these wolves; they are only doing their duty. But there will be a fine massacre all the same, and M. Jules Claretie will be dreadfully sorry, but he will only be able to stand by and watch the climactic scene of the last act. And I know well enough what they will say—these wolves emerging from the Théâtre-Libre and trained by M. Antoine. They will say: "It is our turn now, ewes, sheep, rams, and little lambs of Molière's fold. We are going to make you bleed merrily, for we are hungry and thirsty, and blood satisfies hunger and thirst alike." To M. Alexandre Dumas they will say: "You bore us with your *Demi-monde,* and you too, Pailleron, with your *World of Boredom;* we are of the world where throats are slit, and you are going to see it." To MM. Ludovic Halévy and Meilhac they will say: "My little Parisians, your hour is come; you had best make your confessions to the *Abbé Constantin."* And, of course, they will make only a mouthful of the author of *Roland's Daughter,* and I can almost hear them now: "Ah, there, little sniveling one. So you would refuse to marry your loved one because he has affected reluctance under the pretext that his father was a traitor? You are going to bleat for the last time."

This is how the wolves which I herald will speak and act; and they will bathe in our blood with the savage calm of wolves who are doing a duty. And those who should lead in the wolf-hunting will be disarmed, if they do not actually side with the wolves.

DECEMBER 29, 1891—M. de La Pommeraye's burial just took place.[63] He was an excellent man who surely passed on without the slightest indiscretion on his conscience. Singularly traditional in his ideas, he was none the less kindly toward those of the younger generation.

---

[63] Albert Wolff and La Pommeraye died the same day, December 23, 1891.

JANUARY-DECEMBER, 1892

JANUARY 4, 1892—The Committee on Censorship has published its report, a considerable document which will always be consulted on this question. It concluded by proposing that the Censor's influence be suppressed for a three-year trial period. What a victory if, as everything permits us to hope, Parliament ratifies it!

JANUARY 10, 1892—During a recent stroll with Brieux, I sensed that he was growing impatient because no progress is being made on his play *Bichette,* which he gave to Carré. He told me about it, and I immediately set about persuading him that a story of peasant life would be much more suited to the Théâtre-Libre, offering to stage it at once.

JANUARY 10, 1892—Every Friday, friends from the Garret and the Rue de Bellechasse dine together in the Place Gaillon at Drouant's. When I am able, I attend these gatherings, for it is a great pleasure to see Ajalbert, Geffroy, Hennique, Rosny, Descaves, and others again.

Last night about ten, as we were considering how to pass the remainder of the evening, someone mentioned the name of Bruant, who is making a fortune just now with his cabaret in the Rue Roche-chouart. Carrière expressed a desire to see him, and we climbed up to Montmartre together.

The singer's small establishment was filled with a rather elegant clientele, delightedly inhaling the guardhouse atmosphere under the picturesque vociferations of the proprietor. When I greeted him upon entering, he expressed concern over the people I brought, and asked me their names. Then, learning that Carrière and the others had come to hear him sing, Bruant immediately showed his other customers to the door, put up the shutters on his establishment, and became once again the quiet, timid, and charming fellow that I knew. He sang for us, with the most beautiful and profound feeling, the five or six things which had established his reputation. Clearly, for all the underworld flavor and daring and spirited use of slang which his pose requires, Bruant is a true, and perhaps a great, poet.

We lingered over our glasses very late, enjoying a vision too striking not to be recorded—the legendary Bruant in his felt hat and red shirt, which reputation has made so crude and common, once again becoming a fine and unassuming artist before these admiring companions.

JANUARY 15, 1892—This is infamous indeed. Some clever hand has distributed an article in the provinces and at Brussels under the capitalized title "The Théâtre-Libre Affair." The article suggests that the condemnation of that imbecile Chirac to fifteen months in prison —certainly punishment well deserved—applies to us.

JANUARY 25, 1892—In an article in the *Dépêche de Toulouse,* Camille Pelletan, who in my opinion is one of the deepest and clearest thinkers of the present time, says that the Théâtre-Libre has given plays full of spirit, but that none of them was obscene—that on the contrary, the most interesting literary experiments (in the best sense of the word) in recent years have been made there. I was moved by this eulogy, so much the more because this declaration in an important provincial paper is of a kind calculated to combat the vile and underhanded campaign carried on against us in every quarter in which I cannot answer it.

FEBRUARY 2, 1892—A double stroke this evening! Brieux's *Bichette,* changed to *Blanchette,* triumphed with every line. The third act slowed up a bit, but the success was still immense. As for *The Other Side of a Saint,* that was another matter. The audience received it stupidly, seeking every opportunity to condemn, but this morning, the reviews made M. François de Curel famous at one stroke. I did not appear in *The Other Side of a Saint,* and my nerves were so set on edge by the attitude of the audience that I went out into the corridors, where I grabbed a great brute, one of our subscribers, who was amusing himself by opening the doors of the boxes to boo. I forced him down to the box-office and his subscription was refunded to him then and there. He was stunned.

For all that, the play's value is indisputable and everyone agrees that it departs from our usual formulas. The results are even more wonderful in that the play was rather weakly presented. It is a kind of theatre that is so new, so completely internal, that it is extremely difficult to interpret. *Blanchette,* on the other hand, was presented very well. I dare to flatter myself, and Gémier was particularly admirable as the road-man. This evening has cut the ground from under our enemies' feet, and it will give me a chance to recover my breath.

FEBRUARY 5, 1892—News of the success of *Blanchette* has spread all the way to Rouen, and Brieux writes to me that we ought to give the play at the Théâtre des Arts there. This is a dangerous path to enter. Our trips to Brussels have already given us a lot of trouble, and, once embarked upon a program of public performances, we run the risk of destroying much of the individual character of our evenings.

FEBRUARY 8, 1892—This evening my delightful friend Rzewuski arrived in the Rue Blanche after the rehearsal, saying that he had just lost one hundred thousand francs at baccarat. "Well," he went on, "I have come here to seek a little balance and health. I will take you to supper." Fouquier was forced by his job as reviewer to attend Richepin's play at the Français, but he joined us later in a little room at Paillard's. The critic from the *Figaro* said, when he arrived, that he had been very hard on Jean Richepin and on his play *By the Sword,* which he rather brutally referred to as *By the Razor.* We dined until three a.m., enjoying Fouquier's dazzling conversation, which eventually turned to the subject of Greece. Then suddenly, the two incorrigible gamblers exchanged a glance and asked each other if they shouldn't stop back at the circle a bit before retiring, to see the end of the game. Both went off toward the gambling den with the vague hope of regaining in a few minutes the small fortune which Rzewuski had lost this very evening.

FEBRUARY 18, 1892—We had no choice but to accede to Brieux's request, and we gave *Blanchette* at Rouen last night. I must admit that our success was enormous, even though I feared that the physical surroundings would be overpowering. The Théâtre des Arts is an opera house, and I was afraid that the intimacy and life of the play would be lost in this Sahara. The receipts were superb—four thousand francs—and they give me confidence for Le Havre, where we are going tomorrow to give the play again. It is after all a little money, and we are feeling the lack once again.

FEBRUARY 25, 1892—The reviews of Curel's play make it quite an event:

> *The Other Side of a Saint*—though I would prefer another title (says Jules Lemaître)—strikes me as the most original and interesting play which the Théâtre-Libre has given us since Henry Céard's *The Meek*. The play has tedious moments, awkward spots, useless repetitions—the same things are echoed many times in it, and not at all where they should be for the clarity, interest, and movement of the drama. The play is a bit too close to a very good novel in dialogue form. Even so, it is truly beautiful, and has an exquisite quality. If it were signed Ibsen . . . .

René Doumic:

> M. Curel's play is composed of a series of conversations in which the characters tell about themselves and analyze themselves. The conversations are repetitious, and as a result, the whole lacks vivacity, but still, except for these reservations, *The Other Side of a Saint* recommends itself by rare qualities—a highly elevated conception, a delightful curiosity about the secrets of the internal life, the boldness to carry a study of a psychological case through to its end,

an analytic vigor pushed to its limit, and finally, the gift for breathing life into imaginary characters.

Sarcey:

> It is a study in teratology, brought to the theatre by a pupil of Ibsen. . . . With M. de Curel, as with Ibsen, everything happens by leaps and bounds in the most impenetrable darkness. The initiates cry: "Oh! How profound the psychology is!" but, my friends, I can make nothing at all of it. All of the characters give me the impression of puppets moving in the shadows. There is only one way to describe *The Other Side of a Saint,* and I must go to slang for that—it is a crashing bore. I cannot go so far as to say that it shows no talent, because there are certain indications of a solid and sober style in it—the style of a novelist, but of a dramatist, never!

MARCH 8, 1892—Last night we gave Henry Fèvre's *The Red Star* and *Alone,* a two-act play by Guinon. I have rarely spent so painful an evening as this one. In Fèvre's play I had the interminable part of a half-mad old scientist who devours his fortune and reduces his daughter to beggary through costly experiments to find out what is happening on Mars. I was loudly condemned for two acts, full of astronomical lectures, and had to stand fast before an uncontrolled audience that was determined to silence me. Fortunately, I knew my part very well, and I pitilessly poured out on their heads everything that Fèvre had been able to collect in the way of details about the Red Star. As I approached the third act, completely exhausted and in agony at the prospect of holding out for a good half-hour more, I was suddenly surprised by a complete about-face in the audience. At last a dramatic situation occurred, and impressed by this, they covered the end of the play and myself with applause.

Guinon's *Alone* is a middle-class tale, seasoned just to my audience's taste. Therefore, it was very successful. The reviews this morning were very hard on Henry Fèvre, but were full of praise for Guinon's clever concoction.

MARCH 10, 1892—M. Albert Guinon, the author of *Alone,* did not dare (I don't know why) to bring me his manuscript himself. Distrusting the theatre, which is readily represented in certain quarters as closed to new authors, he thought it best to employ an intermediary—the manager of the Rothschild house, with whom I am presently in contact since he is the one responsible for the renewing of subscriptions each year. This person, a most curious figure, let me understand with great tact that "certain gentlemen" were very interested in this author. Of course, this approach had nothing to do with my decision to accept the play. I took *Alone* because it is an interesting play and because its author seemed promising.

MARCH 12, 1892—I got a very intriguing telegram from Ginisty this evening at the Brussels Parc, where we are now performing. He says that Porel has resigned from the Odéon, that his succession is open, and that if I were to offer myself as a candidate, I would stand a very good chance. When all is said and done, I am very glad I am not there. I must say that I had no inkling of this dramatic turn of events; I do not feel myself ready, for it seems to me that I still have things to do at the Théâtre-Libre. Moreover, I know that Henry Bauer will be a candidate, and of course Marck, Porel's collaborator.

MARCH 18, 1892—I received a most unexpected surprise upon arriving in Brussels for our presentations. After *Blanchette's* great success, Brieux was strongly struck by Sarcey's advice, who thought that the third act should be rewritten to make it more optimistic. Brieux therefore brought me a new version, more subdued, and asked me to put it into rehearsal. We were overwhelmed by the duties of the production in preparation, and I could not find the time for such a major undertaking. So Brieux has written a letter to the Brussels papers acknowledging no more of his play than the first two acts. It was printed today, and it makes me look ridiculous.

MARCH 28, 1892—Marck, who was director of staging under Porel at the Odéon, has been named director, with Desbeaux as his general secretary—an excellent and very business-like choice. The boldness of these two directors is not likely to detract any from our efforts.

MARCH 30, 1892—We have toured Liège and Brussels, and have gone into Holland—Amsterdam, Rotterdam, and The Hague—with great success. I was surprised to find such curiosity and such comprehension in these Northern audiences for the works we brought them, however new. All in all, we were treated with infinitely more respect than in Paris.

*　　*　　*

APRIL 19, 1892—A revue by Mendès and Courteline, *The Merry Wives of Paris,* is playing at the Casino de Paris,[64] and I was supposed to appear in it. Mendès, always enthusiastic, planned on devoting a whole scene in his revue to me. But the poet was sensible enough to realize that these presentations would be harmful for the Théâtre-Libre, and he released me from my promise with the best humor in the world, and without a trace of bitterness.

APRIL 21, 1892—The rival matinees at the Vaudeville are becoming less and less a problem. The program which closed the season was composed entirely of one-acts and had to be reinforced with one of the pleasanter works from the Théâtre-Libre—Ginisty and Guérin's *The Two Turtledoves.*

MAY 2, 1892—Pierre Wolff's new play, *Their Daughters' Husbands,* was very successful, and Louis de Gramont's *Simone* was equally well received.

MAY 7, 1892—A frightful thing just happened to me here in Bordeaux, where we are stopping for four or five days. We were supposed to play in the evening at the Théâtre-Français, and the advance sales were very good. To pass the day, I was imprudent enough to suggest to Schurmann, our business manager, that we go

---

[64]This review was actually given at the Nouveau theatre, where it opened in October, 1891.

to lunch at Arcachon, and catch a train back in time for the performance. I don't know what evil spirit inspired me to take a boat tour, but I did, and just as we were thinking of returning to shore, a calm arose, the sail dropped, and we were left stranded. It meant that we would miss the evening performance. Realizing that of the two or three persons who were there, I alone was indispensable for the curtain to go up, I dove headfirst into the sea, fully dressed, swam three or four kilometers, crossed the point at a dead run, and, jumping over the railing, climbed into a compartment, streaming with water, just at the second when the train was pulling out. Schurmann, who had watched my departure with some skepticism, rejoined me two hours later, at the end of the first act of the *School for Widows,* played to a full house. What a lesson for me!

MAY 9, 1892—It is extraordinary. In certain large provincial towns one finds people better informed and much more up-to-date than many Parisians. There is a critic on the *Petite Gironde,* Paul Berthelot, who has extraordinary insight and spirit, and Gustave Babin, on the *Petit Phare* in Nantes, is among our most understanding and courageous defenders.

JUNE 9, 1892—There was nothing very stimulating about our seventh production. *The End of the Old Times,* another story of peasant life, had character, but paled beside *The Master.* The reviews were good, since Paul Bourde, the author, has an influential position at the *Temps.* No one seems to have noticed how admirable Gémier was as an old shepherd. People are accustomed to the characters of Janvier and Arquillière; Gémier's unfamiliar style is too subtle to have attracted any attention yet.

JUNE 13, 1892—Yesterday at M. de Goncourt's home at Auteuil, Ajalbert and I read a one-act play, *Down with Progress!* that the master is going to give us.[65] It is a pleasant fantasy, rather old-fashioned and repetitious, but with what language! And how glorious it

<hr>

[65]Goncourt unsuccessfully offered this play to the Odéon before bringing it to the Théâtre-Libre. He dates this reading on May 25.

is for the Théâtre-Libre to have this great name on its programs.

JUNE 30, 1892—At last we gave the final productions of the season: *Sin of Love,* a one-act play by Michel Carré and Georges Loiseau; *Mélie,* a scene in the manner of Méténier, which Georges Docquois adapted from a short story by Jean Reibrach; and, in the middle of the evening, three very curious scenes by Jules Perrin and Claude Couturier called *The Windows*—a short, original, and mysterious drama of remorse which proved quite sensational. Gémier, who appeared in it as a glazier and also in *Mélie,* is beginning to get the reviews he deserves.

JULY 1, 1892—Despite everything, the record from our fifth season is encouraging: Jean Jullien has been produced at the Odéon, Porto-Riche has carried off the season's greatest success with his *A Loving Wife,* Méténier has given *The Maid of All Work* at the Variétés, Hennique is at the Gymnase, and Lavedan has triumphed at the Vaudeville with his *Prince d'Aurec.*[66] One might predict that in ten years, three-quarters of the names that will appear on the Moris columns will have been written first on our programs. Naturally, all of these authors leave the house, and thus we avoid the mortal danger of overcrowding. Twelve authors out of the eighteen produced this year were new. This policy has been the secret behind several misunderstandings and painful quarrels, but it is my fond hope that it will later be seen that I was in the right.

As for the actors, Grand is now at the Vaudeville, Mayer permanently employed, Luce Colas with Carré, Damoye and Janvier at the Odéon. They have been replaced, and so much the better, since we cannot mark time with actors any more than with authors. Money is always the cloud on the horizon. Maintenance of my scenic warehouse at la Villette and the construction demanded by each new production are ruinous, but our experiments with setting have assumed great significance, and we absolutely must continue them.

66Jullien's *The Sea* was given on September 19, 1891; Porto-Riche's *A Loving Wife,* also at the Odéon, opened April 25, 1892; Méténier's play opened February 20; Hennique's *The Liar* (written in collaboration with Daudet) was given February 4; and Lavedan's play appeared June 1.

Our tours to Holland, Belgium, Bordeaux, Nantes, Rouen, and Le Havre will in part make up the deficit.

JULY 5, 1892—I dashed off to Camaret immediately, despite many inconveniences, for my vacation time is short. We have no money, and in order to get some, we are going to give productions in the South and in Switzerland during August.

JULY 6, 1892—I have moved out of my fort at Camaret, and rented an old isolated barn, quite on the large side and well inland, which I have leased for ten years at a rent of 120 francs per year—a figure well within my means. Moreover, the view over the dunes is splendid—the whole of the Iroise in the distance, leagues of sea, the cape of la Chèvre from le Raz all the way to Saint-Mathieu.

AUGUST 12, 1892—A young man who saw our touring production in Marseilles, Emile Fabre, has sent me the manuscript of a very interesting play which I have accepted for the Théâtre-Libre.

AUGUST 15, 1892—I absolutely must get back to Paris, for, even with the subscriptions for next season, I anticipate a very difficult year. The deficit is growing, and I must think of making money for my companions, whose dedication, while marvelous, is not inexhaustible.

Schurmann has proposed that we make a grand tour of France between August 20 and October 1. It will certainly be profitable for everyone, and I have agreed. We will take twenty plays, and I will be able to come back to Paris October 1 to begin the coming season without any cares for some time. Finally, both the authors and their interpreters probably need this first test of our repertoire before the general public.

AUGUST 26, 1892—Paulus, in an interview, just said: "Antoine, between ourselves, is a cowardly Chirac," adding: "Personally, when I sing, I always face the public." He is hard on the Comédie-Française, too, saying that its classicism is boring, although he admits he finds some talent in Mounet-Sully and Coquelin. This imprudent outburst has earned him a rather fine thrashing in the papers.

AUGUST 27, 1892—M. Paul Perret, the former critic of the *Liberté*, has been named reader at the Théâtre-Français. This is pleasant news for the young, for we have no more implacable and active enemy.

SEPTEMBER 1, 1892—Continuing our tour, we have reached Lyon, where we will stay from the 1st until the 7th. Our arrival caused quite a stir in the papers, although I received a severe reprimand during the day. The Secretary General of the Prefecture of the Rhone, to whom Schurmann applied for the visa we need, thought that I was that Chirac who made such a scandal in Paris with his disgusting performances.

SEPTEMBER 9, 1892—Before going on to our engagement in Geneva, we stopped here in Marseilles, where excitement is running high in the papers, as it did in Lyon. We have found a whole literary and artistic society here, formed by the intelligent impetus of a highly literate amateur, Auguste Rondel, who is madly in love with the theatre and devoted to everything connected with it. Many of the young people here have been enthusiastic partisans of the Théâtre-Libre for a long time, and one of them, Emile Fabre, has introduced us to the public through a fine article in his paper, the *Bavard*.

SEPTEMBER 21, 1892—The Comédie-Française just gave *The Jew of Poland*. Got was admirable in it, especially in the scene in the second act where he stirs the fire while listening to the sergeant of the militia. But for all that, the play did not succeed.

SEPTEMBER 30, 1892—Our presentations at the Théâtre Graslin in Nantes have been rather well-attended, especially by the upper classes. Several young society people who invited me to dinner expressed regret that I had not posted Curel's *The Other Side of a Saint*. I told them that the play was so out of the ordinary that I had feared I could not attract a provincial audience with it. Gustave Babin, the critic of the *Phare de la Loire,* and his friend Guisth'au, a young lawyer of Nantes, were so disappointed that I gave a presentation of Curel's play the next day for them alone, since all of the performers were along on the tour.

OCTOBER, 1892—The new directors of the Odéon have engaged Janvier, who will soon debut in the role of Basile in *The Barber of Seville.*

OCTOBER 1, 1892—Our summer tour enabled me to distribute 12,000 francs to my companions.

OCTOBER 5, 1892—We have at last returned from our tour. Schurmann, a very pleasant and agreeable traveling companion, never complained. Considered as a whole, this experiment demonstrates the power of our theatre for different audiences, since we traveled all over France. The public was hostile at first, but was bit by bit won over by the novelty and variety of a repertoire so completely unlike that they were accustomed to seeing. Ancey, so new and yet so uncompromising, imposed his work on them through its masterful craftsmanship and the flow of its dialogue. *Aunt Léontine,* with its hidden irony beneath what appeared to be the actions of an ordinary vaudeville, aroused wild delight in certain large towns, but disturbed the more simple audiences. The strange thing is that Ibsen, with his *Ghosts,* seems to have stirred the public most deeply. *The Power of Darkness* astonished and then revolted its audiences. Wolff was well received, and Courteline with his *Lidoire* contributed powerfully toward killing the wide-spread rumor that we are, for the most part, tedious people.

OCTOBER 27, 1892—Yesterday evening, a revue by Albert Millaud and M. Clairville was given at the Variétés. In an act about the theatre, I was portrayed, with all the usual jokes about the Théâtre-Libre. The actor who was supposed to represent me had two masks, so that when old Lassouche asked to see his face, the actor turned around, and the audience always saw his back. This was harmless enough, but Lassouche added a rather offensive bit of staging. He pushed the character representing me into the wings, clearly showing the scorn in which the old actor and his generation hold the artists of the Théâtre-Libre. That evening at dinner, I asked Mendès and Labruyere to go call one of the authors to account.[67] The matter was settled in the most courteous manner, and the author agreed to suppress the bit of staging which I found unacceptable.

OCTOBER 30, 1892—Henri de Bornier strikes a most encouraging note in his column in the *Patrie:*

> Often in this very column I have said that the authors of the Théâtre-Libre will be the masters of the theatre before long. M. Brieux entered the Odéon two months ago; yesterday M. Pierre Wolff planted the flag of naturalism on the elegant fortress of the Gymnase; perhaps tomorrow some bold soldier of M. Antoine's, with cannon and melinite shells, will destroy the great fortifications of the Théâtre-Français.

NOVEMBER, 1892—Since Ibsen cannot absorb the activity of the Théâtre-Libre indefinitely, despite the considerable interest of his work, I have looked extensively among the foreign dramatists for authors who could stimulate the interest and curiosity of the literary youth. I will soon give a curious play by Strindberg, *Miss Julie,* parts for which I have just distributed to Nau and Arquillière.

NOVEMBER 4, 1892—Yesterday we gave Gaston Salandri's three-act play, *The Hook,* which was not up to his first work, and a strange comedy by Maurice Biollay, *The Freed-woman,* in which Abel Deval and his wife, Mme. Marcelle Valdez, both just back from Russia, made their debut. Salandri is a bit disheartened. Our supporters from the early days have gone, and the theatre has been delivered over to our enemies. Yet his play was amusing, and Biollay's raised some

---

[67]Millaud, the other author of *Premier-Paris,* the review in question, died several days before its opening.

serious questions about hypnosis. All in all, the results of the evening were at least creditable.

NOVEMBER 5, 1892—Fouquier says a rather striking thing in his review of *The Hook* and *The Freed-woman*—that a uniform tendency is developing in the plays of the Théâtre-Libre and in those of others in the new school. This art is particularly directed against the family as it exists today, with its mystic concept of marriage and its utilitarian concept of heredity.

NOVEMBER 6, 1892—Jean Jullien savagely attacked all his old companions at the Théâtre-Libre yesterday in his column in the *Paris,* and added:

> Antoine was barely adequate in this play and in the one following. We could not recognize in him the actor of bygone days whose playing was so natural and sure that he could be interesting in a part which had nothing to it.

NOVEMBER 6, 1892—Henry Céard comes to the rescue:

> M. Antoine, desperately anxious to pass for a man of the world skilled in theatrical matters, fully justifies the scorn which Mme. Marthe Grandpré[68] heaps upon him for his awkward attitude and unseemly behavior in the role of a libidinous magistrate. Having said that out of respect for the authors of the two plays listed on last evening's program, we will be silent. Our silence is motivated by the tactics which M. Antoine has used against the editor of this paper in the past—actions which he is by no means the only one to inflict on the press. It is this that keeps us silent—not a high regard for a work which we would regret to see destroyed through the fault of an impresario— although we think, none the less, that the interests of art and of literature should be placed above the calculations of an entrepreneur and the presumptiousness of an actor.

Henry Bauer naturally supports this:

---

[68] A character in *The Freed-woman,* played by Mme. Valdey.

M. Antoine is supposed to represent an irresistible lawyer with a fascinating eye, an enchanting tongue, the elegance of a Brummel, and the hypnotic power of a Don Juan. Need I add that neither his appearance nor his thin voice nor his attire were sufficient for this?

NOVEMBER 6, 1892—Last evening Porel inaugurated his Grand-Théâtre, which is nothing more than the Eden room fitted out with great care.[69] Its dimensions were ill-suited to the contemporary repertoire, as this revival of *Sapho* made clear. Réjane was admirable as Fanny, the role Hading created at the Gymnase. She played the fourth act with great skill—nothing could have been more magnificent.

*　　*　　*

NOVEMBER 20, 1892—An interview with Céard in last night's *Paris* is truly an ingenious study in acidity (I would say in spitefulness if I were not so familiar with the psychology of the writer). This is how the author of *The Meek* vents his gnawing discontent with himself and with his burdensome sterility, and causes Becque to say, with his croaking laugh: "Céard, the failure of the Théâtre-Libre." The article by our former companion in the Rue Blanche is interspersed with conspicuous subtitles: "The Butchershop of Dramatic Art" or "The Grandeur and Decadence of M. Antoine." I consider this unmotivated defection, like Bauer's campaign of aggression, a symptom of the inevitable crisis in the evolution of any experiment. After the general and sincere enthusiasm of the beginning, there is always a shifting battle during which the most violent and doctrinaire factions seek to monopolize the effort for their own ends. I have never wanted to give up the directorship of our movement, and ever since the first production, when I energetically had to resist Byl and Vidal, I have remained firm in my purpose to be the master. I must face this new challenge, as I did Mendès' more adroit interference and Jullien's affectionately poisoned criticism.

---

[69]Porel assumed direction of the former Eden Theatre in October, but it did not actually open until November 12.

NOVEMBER 20, 1892—M. Henri de Weindel, an unusually talented journalist, has begun an extensive inquiry into the present crisis in drama, which according to the directors is severe. I found it entertaining to assemble the opinions of those interested. Koning, who finds himself in a very tight spot, is dissatisfied, and said of us (in his own words):

The Théâtre-Libre! The influence of the Théâtre-Libre! Yes, I know all about it! What has it contributed? *The Kiss* and one or two other plays which would have been received at the Odéon if they had been submitted there—and that is all.

Carré:

The Théâtre-Libre has rendered a service to dramatic progress by destroying a lot of old tricksters who have served their time. . . . The old authors no longer produce much and the new have not yet established themselves. That is probably the reason for the crisis.

Sardou:

We have said so often that a theatrical crisis exists that at last one has broken out. It was inevitable. It is the old story of the healthy person who is told by others every day that he looks pale, who at last falls sick. That is how matters went in this crisis, and now we have a real one.

And as M. de Weindel pressed the master to name the causes of the crisis, the latter answered:

I remain silent. I have my opinion about it, but you won't get it from me.

Dennery proclaimed:

Several young folks have tried to lead us into unpleasant places, to show us overheated cooks. This is not funny—not funny at all. There are two or three of them that have made their debut at the Théâtre-Libre and seem to be catching on with the general public, but they could have made their debuts just as easily somewhere else. The talented ones among the young writers may have been temporarily led astray, but they will come to understand that they are on the wrong track and will return to the old genre and the immutable formulas.

Henry Fouquier mentioned the Théâtre-Libre in the course of an investigation of his own, saying:

It is a revolution which will end like all the rest. It is a confrontation between reactionaries who don't want to give up anything and revolutionaries who want to destroy everything. I await an Augier who will bring all this into focus.

Doumic:

The situation is no longer tolerable. All theatres, from the largest to the smallest, are prey to an inconceivable illness. Yesterday's formula is exhausted—a formula which consisted of portraying characters with the aid of dramatic action, uniting, so far as possible, Scribe and Balzac. Today, this seems a completely hybrid mixture to us. The elements no longer combine. But on the other hand, a new formula is still being sought. The realist disciples of M. Becque and those adept at psychological comedy have not yet produced anything but experiments. They are remarkable experiments—that goes without saying—but they are only experiments none the less. They are hesitant and exploratory, and the bewildered public is naturally disturbed.

Becque:

The public is tired. It wants something new. The new is here. Antoine has come and rendered a considerable service to dramatic art (this cannot be stated too strongly) while accomplishing an admirable task. The directors protest against the young, but they present their works. Wolff, Hennique, Porto-Riche, and the rest will be accepted; each side will give a little; the public will become accustomed to this; the authors will put a little water in their wine; and that will be that. In young Lavedan's play, we naturally would have had the wife go to bed with the

Jew; he has avoided it. This is a compromise, and the public has taken that into account.

Georges Ohnet did not hesitate to declare:

Truth? How ridiculous! If even a novelist tells the truth, people screech like peacocks. If a play is to survive, it must be totally imagined, and at present, this fact is completely ignored. The truth is that all these young scamps want to be more powerful that we elders are. The Théâtre-Libre presents only experiments, and this is very harmful for the young writers.

Meilhac:

I don't think that anything will come of all this. The Théâtre-Libre—what has it presented? Unplayable plays, for the most part. They have well-meaning actors and well-drawn characters, but the actors do not move and the characters do not come alive. Indeed, nothing lives; it is all dull and cheerless. Moreover, the essence of theatre is lacking—the point of departure, the development, and the conclusion.

Gandillot answered (or perhaps murmured, as Weindel says):

It is all a hoax.

Coppée:

We must concentrate on the young; the old are no more interesting than their plays. Their work is over, while the work of the young is just beginning. For my part, I have concentrated on them, and I think that Antoine has done much for dramatic art by permitting the young to show themselves. I think that three or four of them are first-rate —Georges Ancey, Jean Jullien, Pierre Wolff, and, in a quite different way, Lavedan.

When Weindel spoke to him of the Théâtre d'Art which has just been founded, Coppée smiled and said: "No, they are not serious."

NOVEMBER 23, 1892—Last night the Comédie-Française gave *Jean Dariot,* a three-act play by Louis Legendre which I found very entertaining. All the reviewers say that the Théâtre-Français presented this play to prove that it is not afraid of realism, and indeed Mme. Bartet appeared as a seller of newspapers and Albert Lambert as a mechanic. But they were only popular stereotypes as the Rue de Richelieu interpreted them, and the whole thing was an enormous fiasco which no one would dream of attributing to us. They did their utmost to copy our settings and all the small details of our scenes, but when all is said and done, it just didn't come off. Sarcey says: "The whole thing was an unalleviated mediocrity."

NOVEMBER 26, 1892—It is absolutely necessary that the body of the young Duke of Chantemelle be exposed in full view in the last act of Curel's *The Fossils*. His sister reads the will before the whole assembled family while she is next to the funeral bed, and the scene gains all its tragic grandeur from this proximity. The difficulty was that Camis, who was playing the part, could not budge during the whole act, and it was quite long. Our friend Charpentier, the sculptor, therefore cast a mask of his face—a most frightening process. It was quite agonizing for our comrade to have his whole face covered with liquid plaster and to have to wait while it dried, breathing through straws in his nostrils and mouth, but he bore the thing with the resignation of a martyr.

NOVEMBER 29, 1892—Premiere of M. de Curel's *The Fossils*. The work created a sensation even though it was not too well presented— primarily because it asked actors to be romantic, realistic, human, and simple all at once. Mlle. Berthe Bady made her debut. She was rather awkward, but she read Robert's will in an incomparable fashion. She has an admirable voice and a vibrant sensitivity which will not project across the footlights until she has learned her craft. Although the three acts of the play occur in the same salon, a new and original direction by the author obliged us to construct three different settings, since the apartment, as if turning on itself, presented a different face to the audience with each act.

DECEMBER 1, 1892—It was a rare bit of luck that we placed an effigy of Camis in the bed in *The Fossils*. During the last intermission, the monumental chimney of the setting tipped over and reduced his mask to powder. If our companion had been there, he would surely have been killed.

Curel tells me that Paul Perret, the reader at the Comédie-Française, has asked him for a play. It would be a very good thing if the Comédie should open for him, since that theatre was condemned in the papers when it was learned that the house of Molière had refused *The Fossils* at the same time that it was going on with *Jean Dariot*.

* * *

DECEMBER 6, 1892—The Vaudeville has just accepted *The Crisis* by Maurice Boniface, one of the authors of *Aunt Léontine*.[70]

Sarcey devoted the greater part of his column last night to *The Fossils*. After some hearty and largely well-deserved swipes at the interpreters, he said some rather encouraging things about François de Curel. He calls him "a master," and in speaking of the play says that it leaves him "still uncertain, not about the quality of M. de Curel's genius, which is of the first rank, but about his aptitude for the theatre. He has not yet found his medium, although this is not to say that he will not find it. I would swear, on the contrary, that M. Hervieu, author of *The Words Remain*, will never be a dramatist in his life. I am still in doubt about M. François de Curel."

DECEMBER 8, 1892—Curel, furious over Sarcey's column about *The Fossils* (which I personally did not find so bad), absolutely refused to let me take him to the famous critic's home. At Sarcey's insistent invitation, I have gotten into the habit of going sometimes to lunch with him on Fridays. These are his reception days, when it is easy and pleasant to chat with the noted gentleman, who is the most kindly and witty of hosts. He likes to have me bring the young men who have just been presented to see him, and he welcomes them with the utmost kindness, especially if he has condemned their work.

70*The Crisis* was presented April 7, 1893.

I insisted so strongly that at last Curel went with me and we arrived in the Rue de Douai about noon. There was already a large crowd in the dining room, but when I sent in our names, Sarcey came out to welcome us personally. As he greeted Curel, I discerned a lively curiosity in his face, which told me much about the esteem in which Sarcey held the playwright. The critic led in the rather timid and withdrawn Curel, seated him next to himself for lunch, and strove to entertain him with unusual amiability. The two men felt themselves in sympathy immediately, so much so that just now in the cafe, I heard them exchanging terrible jokes with the laughter of schoolboys.

DECEMBER 9, 1892—Luce Colas, also engaged by Carré at the Vaudeville, has made her debut there with great success.[71] I am very happy for her, but many companions have left us, and the troupe is breaking up more and more.

DECEMBER 10, 1892—The *Cercle des Escholiers,* presided over by Georges Bourdon, has presented Ibsen's *The Lady from the Sea.* It is the fourth work by the great Norwegian presented in Paris, for after we gave *Ghosts* and *The Wild Duck,* the Vaudeville staged *Hedda Gabler.* A movement has been launched in support of the Scandinavian dramatist which will be lasting and productive.

DECEMBER 12, 1892—Schurmann has brought us to Milan and Turin to give several productions, which should bring in a most welcome bit of money. We opened at the Manzoni Theatre with *Blanchette,* which was very successful, but a slight shiver ran down my spine as I leafed through the Italian papers this morning. The critics here declare that they will withhold a definitive opinion on us, for—they say—"however excellent Antoine and his company may appear in a peasant comedy, we cannot judge them until after Ibsen's *Ghosts."* Down here the play is called *Spettri* and the role of Oswald is the favorite vehicle of their great actor Ermete Zacconi.

---

[71]Luce Colas made her debut in the play *M. Coulisset* on December 8. Antoine says "also" because Grand, another Théâtre-Libre actor, was now at the Vaudeville.

DECEMBER 13, 1892—We gave *Ghosts* last night at the Manzoni with heart-warming success, but what makes me proudest is that this morning, the papers say that, after Zacconi, we were awaited with great expectation, and that what we did was clearly something quite different, but just as good.

DECEMBER 18, 1892—Every one of our productions at the Manzoni in Milan went well, and we have been equally successful at the Carignano in Turin. Since the Duchess of Aoste faithfully attends all our productions, I had her warned that she would perhaps find *Elisa the Slattern* rather daring, but the Duchess replied that the name of M. de Goncourt and her interest in the productions that she had already applauded convinced her that she should not miss this evening.

DECEMBER 20, 1892—Distributed 5000 francs in fees to my companions.

DECEMBER 20, 1892—Yesterday the Gymnase gave an adaptation of *Charles Demailly* by Paul Alexis and Oscar Méténier. It did not go badly, but there was every kind of opposition and resistance in the audience.

DECEMBER 23, 1892—M. Romain Coolus, a young professor in the Lycée at Chartres, has brought me an unusual one-act play, *The Brazilian Household,* which I am going to put in between the play by Strindberg and the unpublished one-act play by Edmond de Goncourt.

DECEMBER 25, 1892—A great coolness has grown up between us and the Rue de Bellechasse. The success of *Elisa the Slattern* rather overshadowed some play or other by Daudet given at the Gymnase almost the same day, and it has been clear to me that for some time since I have not been very welcome there, despite Daudet's warm and intelligent sympathy.

I have also been growing closer and closer to Zola, so that it has been a good year and a half since I have seen Daudet; then suddenly I received an invitation to dine with him, as I used to. It coincided with the preparation of Goncourt's play at our theatre, and I enjoyed this little revenge for a distressing dropping of acquaintance which I really did not deserve, for I was always very fond of Daudet.

When the table had been cleared and we passed into the master's little study that evening, he called me over to the couch to which he is kept by illness, and said to me: "Well, my dear Antoine, how are things going?" Rather moved, but still a bit reproachful, I responded: "Very well, as always, but I am most astonished to find myself here again!" The handsome face, now drawn and yet somehow glorified by sickness, became sad, and with a look which repaid me a hundred times for the small irritation which I had undergone, he said, without further explanation, in a tone which showed the firmness and tenderness of the good will he had toward me: "Ah yes, my dear Antoine! But you know, alas, we are all bitches."

JANUARY 1893—SEPTEMBER 1894

1893

JANUARY, 1893—While we were rehearsing *The Fossils,* Curel was polishing up another play, which he had submitted to the Théâtre-Français. I was quite sure what the result would be; Albert Carré finally accepted it last November, after a useless six months probationary period. *The Guest* was presented last night, and was very successful.[72] I was not totally convinced that the audience really understood this rather ironic study of motherhood, since Mme. Pasca played it exactly like one of the plays in her old repertoire, and her emotion misled the house about the essence of this misanthropic, egoistic, and withered old woman. Yet whatever the result, even if the battle was not fought on the proper ground, the victory is none the less important, because for the first time an author from our house, perhaps the most eminent, has conquered the elegant public of the boulevards.

JANUARY 2, 1893—Becque is living in a beautiful but completely empty apartment in the Avenue de Villiers. We lunched there on a sort of architect's trestle of white wood in the dining room, furnished only by the two chairs we needed and Rodin's bust of Becque, rising over the earthenware oven. It is the apartment of a solitary old man, and is a bit touching, although he seems highly amused by its paradoxical absence of furnishings.

He had an absolutely revolting dish of macaroni sent up from a near-by restaurant and continued speaking with his usual animation, quite unaware of the terrible thing we were served. I continued to

---

[72]*The Guest* was presented at the Vaudeville on January 19, so this entry should be dated January 20.

listen and to dawdle over my plate as long as possible, imagining the results of eating it. But I could not refuse to eat, and when at last my plate was empty, Becque obliged me by taking the horrible thing away.

JANUARY 13, 1893—Strindberg has written a rather lengthy preface, full of interesting things, for his tragedy *Miss Julie,* which we are going to give. I thought it would be valuable to print this and distribute it to our audience. He includes stimulating suggestions about raking the setting, suppressing the footlights, and lighting from above— clearly showing the German influence that I have long since welcomed from abroad.

JANUARY 15, 1893—Performance of *Miss Julie, The Brazilian Household,* and *Down with Progress! Miss Julie* made an enormous sensation. Everything stimulated the audience—the subject, the setting, the packing into a single act an hour and a half in length enough action to sustain a full-length French play. Of course, there were sneers and protests, but it was, after all, something quite new. *The Brazilian Household,* Coolus' first play, did not seem new at all; Ancey is bolder, and it lacks the direct, almost classic language of *The School for Widows.* Still, its sort of spirit is most entertaining. The audience listened to M. de Goncourt's fantasy with respectful curiosity, but it seemed tame beside such pungent works as the other two, especially since the master had preceded his short play with a rather bellicose preface against Nordic literature:

At this time, when France is so infatuated with foreign literature, when the young dramatists so idolize the Scandinavian theatre, when our contemporaries show themselves so willing to become the literary slaves of Tolstoi or Ibsen (writers whose merit I am far from contesting, but whose qualities seem to me impossible to acclimate to the degree of latitude in which we live), I have attempted a reaction, by writing a dramatic work which others may copy; one which possesses, so far as it lies in my power, the French qualities of clarity, spirit, and irony; and one which expresses what Turgenev has called the cynical irony of this *fin de siècle,* and perhaps of this *fin du monde.*

Yes, I am convinced that this Slavic fog should be left to Russian and Norwegian minds, and not forced upon our lucid intellects. In such a sickly transplanting, the fog is destined to produce only clumsy plagiarisms. And good heavens, if the modern theatre absolutely must have a model, the French at least should turn not to Tolstoi or Ibsen, but rather to the author of the comedies *The Barber of Seville* and *The Marriage of Figaro,* to the author of the drama *Eugénie,* to Beaumarchais.

What a strange thing! This great champion of life and truth, this revolutionary, speaks of the Swedes and the Norwegians with the same incomprehension and prejudice as their inveterate enemies, Sarcey and Pessard!

JANUARY 17, 1893—The reviewers were so surprised by the tone of *The Brazilian Household* that even the most serious critics wondered if Coolus were not trying to confuse them; even Henry Fouquier, ordinarily so level-headed and perceptive, thinks the whole thing is a joke.

Gémier was quite remarkable in his authority and his cold irony in this play, and Arquillière was extraordinary as the lackey in *Miss Julie.*

JANUARY 20, 1893 — Fernand Vandérem has published a subtle and interesting study of Coolus' *The Brazilian Household* in the *Journal;* he seems to be the only one to perceive the bold novelty of the play.

In a recent interview, Dumas *fils* was asked his opinion of all that has happened. He said: "Gimmicks, that's all that's left," adding: "I'm the one who got Villiers de l'Isle-Adam's *The Escape* produced at the Théâtre-Libre"—which is false.

FEBRUARY, 1893—Life is hard; we are in debt and every step forward is painful. Schurmann suggests another rather long tour to

Holland, saying that its certain success will raise funds for me. I accepted his proposal, despite all the disadvantages of these tours and the gossip they stir up. It is said that I am no longer interested in anything but exploiting the Théâtre-Libre financially. Happily, the imbeciles before whom I must keep up a front never suspect where I would be without these tours. How they would shout with joy then!

MARCH 5, 1893—Death of Taine, one of the men to whom I owe the most.

APRIL 15, 1893—For our next production we will give a new two-act play by Courteline, called *Boubouroche*. The first act arrived early and I immediately put it into rehearsal, but I only got the central scene in the second act eight days before production. We have been squabbling all this time. The author wanted to have the character of Boubouroche acted by Arquillière, whom I thought too harsh and, more important, too thin for this great confident and easy-going bourgeois. After much arguing back and forth, I got the author to consent to let Pons-Arlès rehearse the role, and he was so perfect physically for the character that Courteline at last consented to let him do it.

APRIL 29, 1893—Courteline's play yesterday was a triumph; such a delighted audience has rarely been seen. Céard did not take this well, and wrote in the *Evénement* this morning: "*Boubouroche* is a simple joke which would not have been out of place on the stage of some Déjazet or other." All of the other reviewers are enthusiastic, however, and there seems to be a reaction against all the harshness that has been heaped upon me these last months. Lemaître says that *Boubouroche* is an admirable farce, and everybody seems to agree with him.

MAY 10, 1893—We are working hard on Gerhart Hauptmann's *The Weavers,* and I hope to make it one of the most beautiful productions we have ever given. But what expenses! Had it not been for a friend who advanced me ten thousand francs on next season, I could not have given the play.

MAY, 1893—*The Weavers* was an enormous success.[73] It must certainly be admitted that no playwright in France is capable of creating a fresco of this scope and power. The play had great repercussions when it was first given by the Free Theatre in Berlin, where Hauptmann, backed by all the young writers of Germany, got the Imperial ban lifted. Contrary to my expectations, this play of revolt was received at my theatre primarily as a cry of despair and misery. The aroused house cheered it from beginning to end. It is a masterpiece of the developing social theatre, and Jaurès was so impressed that he sent me word that such a production accomplished more than any political campaigns or discussions.

Furthermore, since I have a strong feeling that the end of my task is in sight and that this is one of the last productions I will give, I put all the strength, energy, and resources I had left into it, and I must say that the interpretation was outstanding. Gémier played old Baumert, revealing himself as the great actor I have always known him to be, and Arquillière was splendid, too. The second act was enormously effective. The *Song of the Weavers* served as a *leitmotif*, issuing continuously from the wings. The overrunning of the manufacturer's home in the fourth act generated such terror that the entire orchestra rose to their feet. The last scene, showing the death of old Hilse[74] amid the shooting and shouts of the crowd, was played amidst general acclamation.

Although I have almost decided to abandon the field and no one as yet suspects it, I feel a bitter regret this evening for all that we might yet accomplish. But I no longer have the energy or courage to continue. To get this far, I have utilized every talent and ability possessed by myself as well as my friends—authors and actors alike —but the one thing we cannot create is money. Then, too, I have threatened too many interests and disturbed too many people in important positions to hope for anything other than general satis-

---

[73]The play was presented May 29 and 30.
[74]Played by Antoine.

faction at my ultimate collapse. If I had not committed myself by drawing on next season, I would close down after the next production, which is now in preparation.

JULY 1, 1893—There seems to be no way out of our situation. We have finished the season only by borrowing on next year, and I have no idea what position we will be in by the end of that one. From the artistic point of view, too, I feel that we have come almost to the end of the line, and that our movement is nearly exhausted. For two years I have had to call the foreign theatre to our rescue or fill the gaps between our real demonstrations with sensational curiosities, but this sort of thing has worn thin. *Boubouroche* is really the only thing this season has produced, for the immense reverberation about *The Weavers* merely repeats what happened with Tolstoi and Ibsen. The Théâtre-Libre is in a position where it can be of significance only by nourishing itself on plays written in this country, and the native authors have now left our house to go elsewhere.

What then is the solution? A regular theatre? This would mean assuming frightful risks, while losing all our originality and the most interesting part of our work. We would probably have an audience at first, drawn by curiosity, but it would take years to train them and to become really established.

JULY 4, 1893—As Becque and I were coming back along the Champs-Elysées this evening—a beautiful starry night—he recited to me bits of a one-act verse play which he says he has just finished. It is the tale of a young symbolist poet introduced into a middle-class household, and after each long speech, Becque's powerful laughter rang out gaily in the night.

* * *

AUGUST, 1893—Camaret. I am resting and preparing for next season as much as I can. Nothing important is in sight—so little, indeed, that it will be almost impossible to publish a complete program. I am going to begin again with another Scandinavian, Björnstjerne Björnson,[75] Ibsen's rival, who has written a play about finance that

---

[75]In this and in a later reference Antoine, apparently confused by Scandinavian nomenclature, refers to the dramatist as Bjornson Bjornstern.

is famous almost everywhere. Then I am getting ready to take a turn through the coastal towns and along the beaches to gather a little money, if possible.

AUGUST 15, 1893—Thorel has obtained *The Assumption of Hannele Mattern,* Hauptmann's new play, from him, and we are going to see its premiere this winter in the Imperial Theatre of Berlin.

SEPTEMBER 25, 1893—I have just returned from a trip all the way across France and all along the coast. I am tired, but pleased with the increasingly sympathetic welcome the general public is giving me. This reassures me about the future, when I will have to become a professional actor to earn my living and pay the debts of the Théâtre-Libre.

*　　*　　*

OCTOBER 25, 1893—A heart-rendingly stupid crowd at the Comédie-Française hissed Curel's new play, *Embellished Love,* from start to finish. It was rash indeed to try to get a work of a completely new spirit accepted on these ancient boards. It must be admitted, however, that the play was presented with rare incomprehension. Le Bargy, for all his excitement about the work and the author, apparently lost his way in the course of the evening, and the others seemed overcome by the protests of the public.

NOVEMBER 5, 1893—I received a short note from Mme. de Loynes which asked me to stop by her home. Although she has been a subscriber to the Théâtre-Libre for several years and has attended our presentations with friends from her salon, I thought she was hostile, especially since the *Germinie Lacertaux* affair when Jules Lemaître condemned me so strongly. When I arrived at her house in the Avenue des Champs-Elysées, I found the critic from the *Débats* seated next to the fire. Mme. de Loynes welcomed me most graciously, and asked me if I would be disposed to stage immediately a play by her friend Maurice Barrès, who wanted to have it presented at my theatre because its political character would expose it to censorship elsewhere. I naturally answered yes, and was immediately introduced to Barrès, who was awaiting my reply. He used to be one of those who stopped by the Rue Blanche, but he has never done anything in the theatre, and since then I had seen him only a few times at Daudet's. Moreover, the political events of recent years have certainly not helped to bring us together. Still, it is clearly a godsend to have his first play. Mme. de Loynes appeared quite touched by the way in which I acceded to her request.

NOVEMBER 10, 1893—Yesterday before taking the train to Berlin we gave Björnstjerne Björnson's *A Bankruptcy*. In our present state of affairs, I alone secretly felt how poignant this title was. It is the most pathetic tragedy about money that has ever appeared in the theatre, and the third act was enormously effective. Gémier and I played its big scene, between the merchant and the assignee, very well.

NOVEMBER 12-20, 1893—Here we are in Berlin to see Hauptmann's *The Assumption of Hannele Mattern,* which the Imperial Theatre (the Schauspielhaus) is about to give. Accompanying me are Thorel, who translated the play for us, and Baston, my *régisseur.* Jean Ajalbert has joined us.

NOVEMBER, 1893—We were most cordially received. Gerhart Hauptmann and Sudermann, the most famous theatre persons in Germany just now, formed a sort of welcoming committee, although we asked them to keep such a ceremony to a minimum.

NOVEMBER, 1893—Naturally, I am seeing as many productions in Berlin as possible. Everywhere the staging surprises me, especially in the areas of settings and lighting. The very day of our arrival we saw a magnificent presentation of Schiller's *Joan of Arc* at the Lessing, a classic matinee with an audience composed entirely of girls between twelve and fifteen. They followed the drama with the same studious intensity which everyone here brings to the theatre. Then we saw a very strange production of *The Weavers* on a little stage in the suburbs. The play is not given here with the great spirit of wrath and rebellion that it stimulated at our theatre, and I told Hauptmann that he would be quite surprised if he saw it in Paris.

NOVEMBER, 1893—*The Assumption of Hannele Mattern* is a beautiful poetic work in every respect, and its scenic realization was truly admirable. The director of the Schauspielhaus, the local Jules Claretie, most graciously let me attend a working rehearsal at ten in the morning. I was thus able to see the technical installations in the great official theatre. No theatre in Paris can give one the slightest idea of what is found here, for everything here is underwritten by the Imperial treasury.

NOVEMBER, 1893—The administrator of the Schauspielhaus tells me that rather often during their rehearsals, the Emperor comes in and sits in the balcony, enjoining them not to interrupt their work. He sometimes remains for a long time and readily breaks in to give his opinion. He follows the administrative details of the Imperial Theatre closely, and is quite attentive to the choice of the repertoire, in which he favors plays of a noble or historic nature. He is also very interested in the artists, and quite well informed on the private lives of the actresses, who are forbidden much luxury. They are not allowed, for example, to have a private carriage.

NOVEMBER, 1893—Premiere of *Hannele Mattern*. The reviews are very good. The staging was ingenious, but we will do as well, and at some points, better. The interpretation was what struck me as particularly superior. In the audience were more than thirty directors from other theatres in the German provinces who will take the play away to stage it in their own theatres. Centralization does not exist here; cities like Dresden, Munich, Leipzig, and Hamburg are centers provided with important theatres, better equipped than our most famous Parisian stages.

NOVEMBER, 1893—Before leaving Berlin, I was compelled to attend a sort of banquet at the *Friedrichof*. In an immense room were gathered the authors and dramatic artists of Berlin, novelists, painters —almost all of artistic Germany. The Théâtre-Libre is held in great honor here, for the two young rival German stages were inspired by our experiment in Paris. I was embarrassed by this demonstration, and despite the manifest cordiality of our hosts, I remained taciturn in the face of a series of speeches which began as early as the soup. This apparently caused some surprise. Earlier in the day, a representative from the French Embassy came to see me, a little worried about this ceremony and afraid of an imprudent oration on my part. The functionary in question then attended the banquet in order to report on it to his ambassador.

DECEMBER 2, 1893—Mme. de Loynes, who has proved one of my most valuable friends, now invites me rather often to her Friday dinners, the twelve or fourteen members of which are always very select. I am sure that the generous woman knows that she is giving me powerful support by thus welcoming me into her salon, which is the most exclusive and influential in Paris. Among its members are Lemaître, Roujon, Barrès, Magnard, Henri Houssaye, Arthur Meyer, the sculptor Saint-Marceaux, Alfred Capus, Abel Hermant, and Calmettes, who is the secretary to the editors on the *Figaro*. The other evening I was seated at table next to a gentleman of whom Mme. de Loynes said: "He is an important financier, a great friend of artists, who can give you good advice on your tangled affairs." It was Vlasto, who is, I believe, the director of the Discount Bank. He is a man of unusual elegance and refined culture, and we struck up a close friendship immediately.

Mme. de Loynes leads the conversation in the manner of a great hostess—the hostess of a house frequented by Renan, Emile de Girardin, and all the celebrities of our time. She has a warm and engaging interest in each of her friends, and she follows their enterprises, their plans, and their business transactions with perpetual good advice, strong devotion, and perspicacity. She receives a further small group of noted friends every day at five. These teas are reserved for the most personal matters, and she asks me to come then when I have something of interest to tell her. At these teas she receives the actresses Bartet, Réjane, and Sarah Bernhardt, and with admirable diplomacy, she exercises from afar an enlightened influence in favor of her friends in almost all the great artistic theatres.

DECEMBER 8, 1893—For Barrès' play, *A Day in Parliament,* Magnard, Lemaître, and the author have asked me to put on a closed rehearsal for their friends before the regular presentation in the Théâtre-Libre. This should mean an extraordinary roomful of people.

DECEMBER 9, 1893—This Barrès affair will probably put me in bad with Brieux. Just when Barrès was writing his play, Brieux finished one on the same subject, called *In Gear,* and he wanted me to give him preference because of his association with the theatre. But I had to remain firm in our resolve to give preference to new authors, and besides, the theatrical debut of a writer like Barrès is a literary event that I could not let take place elsewhere.

DECEMBER 16, 1893—Brieux has taken his play to the *Cercle des Escholiers* and they are going to produce it, so everything turned out for the best.

1894

JANUARY 5, 1894—We just gave *The Assumption of Hannele Mattern,* which stimulated great interest. I carefully assembled for it the best setting that I could imagine. The play was not as sensational as *The Weavers,* but it will have its devotees, and this was a lovely and artistic production—which, of course, cost me a fortune. It brings me to the point where I have just enough left to do two or three more good things before going under.

JANUARY 15, 1894—We are rehearsing Barrès' comedy. It is a violent lampoon against the present regime, and this makes me rather uneasy, for it clearly reflects political intrigues of which I strongly disapprove. From a purely theatrical point of view, however, the third act has some fine scenes, and the second, an interesting scene in the Laocoön room at the Chamber. Again, unhappily, the expense will be enormous, and this will do nothing toward putting me back on my feet.

FEBRUARY 23, 1894—The dress rehearsal of *A Day in Parliament,* given before an invited audience from the *Figaro* and friends of the author, was a real Parisian event. The political side, however, robbed the play of all its interest as drama. The last act was fairly effective, since in it Barrès expresses very artistically the agonies of his hero— a deputy, compromised by intrigue, whose moral collapse is most beautifully pathetic.

FEBRUARY 24, 1894—*A Day in Parliament* was received by the Théâtre-Libre audience with interest and without disturbance, but it is clear that we have never aroused so much public feeling, and the controversy about the theatre is great. Yet, on the practical side, Chastanet has just drawn up a disastrous balance-sheet. We can never finish the season.

FEBRUARY 27 to MARCH 19, 1894—Another trip across France to get a little money, but Luguet's *The Missionary,* which is just going into rehearsal, is only the fifth production of the season; there are still three to go! The end is in sight. Our pressing debts are causing us real embarrassment, and we must give in to the inevitable.

APRIL 20, 1894—I lack the material strength to continue. This several-years battle has depleted my resources, and I feel that I no longer have the resiliency I need. I have used every resource and every device in my power, and I am still strangled by a lack of money. Moreover, I lack even a hint that new efforts would be useful, for young dramatists are no longer appearing. The upcoming generation has made its contribution. The most talented ones have succeeded and are now established; from now on, we would be struggling in a vacuum.

APRIL 24, 1894—Toulouse-Lautrec has designed an admirable colored program for *The Missionary* which collectors will fight over some day. I have succeeded in continuing this series of programs for several years, and it will be unique. All the artists of the time will have contributed to it: Forain, Willette, Raffaelli, Henri Rivière, Vuillard, Steinlein, Auriol, Signac, Luce, the sculptor Charpentier, and many others. I even had the pleasure of furnishing a newcomer with an opportunity to show himself in an original way, by setting aside eight programs for H. G. Ibels last year.

APRIL 25, 1894—*The Missionary,* which we just presented, is quite unusual in form. It is a story in five scenes, interspersed with comments from a reader seated on the forestage, who turns the pages of a book as the play progresses. He reads bits of it aloud, and bridges into the scenes unfolding on the stage. This new approach delighted the audience, and, in the difficult part of the reader, I was subjected to the jests of the house for the entire evening. At one point during the uproar, I was even struck in the face by a fistful of sous— a most symbolic gesture. It was this brutal action which decided me, at that very moment, to abandon the Théâtre-Libre. The wretches in the theatre did not know this, and they would probably have been ashamed if I had dared to stop the performance and suddenly reveal to them what I had decided.

MAY 6, 1894—Fortuné Henry,[76] the anarchist who was just guillotined, has made it known through his lawyer what happened on the evening of February 12. Apparently his first intention was to go to the Théâtre-Français, where the premiere of *The Mouse*[77] was being given, and to throw his bomb into the orchestra. When he arrived, however, the line at the ticket-window for cheap seats discouraged him from going in. He then went down the Avenue de l'Opéra, his bomb in his pocket, looking for a chance to get rid of it. Crossing the boulevards, he came up in front of the Café Américain about seven-thirty, but just as he was about to throw his projectile through the windows, he recognized me dining with some friends, Mendès and Gailhard. Remembering a visit with some friends to the Théâtre-

---

[76] The first name of this anarchist was actually Emile.
[77] I have been unable to trace this play. The work actually premiered on the date in question was Pailleron's *Barnstormers.*

Libre to see Alexis' *Mlle. Pomme,* he decided against an explosion at this place. It was thus that, turning into the Rue Halévy, he came to the Saint-Lazare Station, and at last threw his bomb into the cafe of the Hôtel Terminus, which was full of people taking aperitifs.

MAY 22, 1894—Edmond Rostand's *The Romantics,* at the Comédie-Française, is a huge success. All in all, it is a delightful thing.

JUNE 15, 1894—Several months ago, Larochelle, who is the son of a former actor-director and devoted to the theatre, came to offer me his services. I saw nothing to be gained at the time from such an association, but the idea later came to me, since he is interested in the Théâtre-Libre, to offer him the opportunity to become my successor. I asked no money from him. In exchange for the three productions still due to my season subscribers which he has promised to present, I guaranteed him my personal assistance as an actor. I required only that he give the two plays already accepted, Emile Fabre's *Money* and Caraguel's *Where There's Smoke.*[78] I turned over to him without charge my warehouse at la Villette, with all the settings, properties, and costumes it contains—a considerable amount. He will assume leadership of the theatre in the Rue Blanche, and I will be responsible for all the debts already incurred. This agreement, which we just signed, was not too badly received by the public and the papers, who at last understood what a struggle I have had. Indeed, many were quite astonished, believing I had made a fortune.

JULY 1, 1894—Having made these arrangements, I turned to settling my debts. I can do this, of course, only through my own efforts, which will not be easy, for although I have established a reputation as an actor at the Théâtre-Libre, I have gained very little sympathy among the current theatre circles. I have fought too much with persons in important positions, with the directors, indeed with the whole trade, to hope that anyone would hire me. An impresario has just brought me his plans for a six- or eight-month tour of Europe, where

---

[78] Both plays were presented the following year, Fabre's on May 6 and 7, and Caraguel's on October 24.

I might gain some reward for my great labors. The amount he guarantees me is rather modest, but it is enough to keep my companions alive (for they too need to get back on their feet), while allowing me to meet my scattered debts and free myself from the Théâtre-Libre's creditors. My comrades—Gémier, Luce Colas, Barny, Arquillière, and all those who were always so devoted—readily agreed with me. We will leave in the autumn for six months, beginning in Belgium, then going on to Holland, Italy, Germany, Austria, and Russia. We can give two hundred presentations and return to Paris completely through with the matter.

JULY 10, 1894—I have gathered together all the creditors of the Théâtre-Libre, arranged for staggered payments, and signed bonds for dates corresponding to the dates of payment guaranteed by our manager. All is in order, and I am beginning to breathe more easily. There are cities like Berlin in our itinerary where we can remain almost a month and where success seems assured.

Besides the discouragement of this terrible end to the season, I had literally nothing to allow me to get an essential few weeks of rest at Camaret, since all the resources I could count on had already been exhausted by the Théâtre-Libre. I thought of that Vlasto, with whom Mme. de Loynes had so graciously put me in contact, and screwing up my courage, I went to the Discount Bank to explain my difficulties to him. The charming gentleman heard my tangled confession with a smile, and then rang and had five thousand-franc bills brought. He told me that this was quite simple, that money is a commodity like any other, and that he was only doing his job by approving a note which his assistant asked me to sign. It was an unusually tactful gesture, for I was certain that the financier had put this on his own expenses and that he was personally obliging me. He graciously added that deep down he envied me, for I was happy with so little, and that I was much more fortunate than he because his position does not allow him take vacations.

JULY 21, 1894—*Tabarin's Wife,* which we first gave, has entered the repertoire of the Comédie-Française, with Sylvain in the role of

Tabarin. I was very unhappy to see that in the new version Mendès, probably so as not to offend the new interpreters, has suppressed the lovely dedication which he put in the first edition.

AUGUST 28, 1894—We are spending all our time now in polishing up the plays we are going to give. The troupe appears joyous and confident; we are to open in Brussels on September 3. It seems that the business manager has contracts in almost every major city of Europe and he tells me that things look very promising. Chastanet, my administrator, who has been devotion itself right down to the end, will do what is necessary in my absence in the way of liquidation. We have agreed that at each date of payment I will send him the necessary amount from my personal earnings. It brings this business to a happy ending that I could not foresee several months ago.

SEPTEMBER 6, 1894—We were supposed to take the 8:50 train this evening for Brussels, to open tomorrow at the Parc, which has already announced our coming. We all arrived in good order at the Gare du Nord, and our business manager had just finished handing out tickets, when an unknown person came up to me and said: "Monsieur, I have come to seize your luggage, and I will not release it except on payment of the sum due one of my clients by your business manager." I turned to our mahout and said: "Very well, old chap, pay him and let's be on our way," but he refused to do it, and stood arguing with this bailiff, who seemed quite intractable. In vain I pointed out that we had to be in Brussels for tomorrow's performance and that such a beginning was very disturbing; the manager persisted, and said that we should reconvene tomorrow morning. Clearly, he has no funds in reserve, and he is leading us across Europe trusting to chance. The bailiff, understanding our predicament, said to me: "Try to get this matter straightened out. Here is my address; I will receive you tonight and you can still leave tomorrow morning. Perhaps this is just a passing difficulty and everything will work out all right yet." My comrades, as disturbed as I, drifted off one by one to come back the next morning at the announced time. I remained with Arquillière, discussing this prospect of the ruin of a plan undertaken with such difficulty.

SEPTEMBER 7, 1894—I did not even go back home—there was no point in waking up the house—but roamed about all night with Arquillière. It was clear to me that like most business managers, ours had at hand only traveling money and the several advances that he had made us, and was relying on the first receipts to finance him further. Since I did not think that he would be able to find the three or four thousand francs he needed during the night, I sought to find where I could obtain this sum. The hour was late, and everyone is out of Paris just now. I suddenly remembered having recently received a visit from the director of a Berlin theatre where we will soon appear, and we rushed over to his hotel in the Avenue de l'Opéra. He did not come back until about two in the morning, and I stopped him on the sidewalk to tell him my business. I asked him to advance us what we needed for our departure, for which he would soon be reimbursed out of our receipts in Germany. This good German, who had always seemed friendly, even a bit obsequious to me, appeared somewhat distressed by this story. He not only pointed out to me that I was not responsible for finding the money for the trip, which was reasonable enough, but he also refused my request. I understood and we went away.

It was two-thirty in the morning. I had to find the means to allow us to leave before eight, for if it were learned in Paris how our tour began, the people with whom I had made my arrangements would be immediately disturbed. Besides, the default of not appearing in Brussels on the announced date might well damage the Théâtre-Libre and its company. I hurried through the streets, looking everywhere. Then I thought of Gailhard, the director of the Opéra, with whom I have dined several times a week for years, and who has always been very friendly, even offering to help our theatre in financial matters. I said to Arquillière: "We are saved!" Gailhard lives in Levallois in a fine house in Arab style which I knew from having dined there once or twice. It was three in the morning; our problem was to see him as soon as possible and get this money, for which I was now ready to give my right arm. But we could not go wake up the good gentleman in the middle of the night, and we waited for dawn. My request would seem less preposterous about seven. At six-thirty we were at his door, waiting for the concierge and the servants to wake up. At last about seven I screwed up my courage and had Gailhard awakened. He came down in his dressing gown, rubbing his eyes, but immediately hospitable. I sadly told him my story. "But," said Gailhard, "why do you want me to make an advance for something which concerns your manager? You have a contract. If you suffer any damages, you will be reimbursed for them."

We went back crestfallen to the Gare du Nord, where we found everyone rather worried. The business manager was not there—only a short note from his *régisseur* asking us to meet about one o'clock at the Court of Injunctions, where we were asked to surrender our trunks. Ruin. We wandered aimlessly all morning, until it was time to go to the court. Our man was not there yet. I explained our frightful situation to the judge, who was very sympathetic, but unable to help. At last I ran like a madman to the manager's home, where I found him in a state of collapse. I showed him what frightful circumstances he had led me into, and he promised that we would leave without fail this evening.

SEPTEMBER 8, 1894—We are in Brussels at last and all has gone well here. My hopes are reviving a bit; the receipts are good and we are going on to Germany.

EPILOGUE

For six weeks we wandered from city to city, with the receipts good at times and bad at times, as is the case with any tour. The impresario paid us regularly enough. Every evening I distributed their portions to my companions and sent what was left to Chastanet. We paid off our first obligations, for Germany was quite profitable—Dresden, Leipzig, Cologne, Hamburg, and especially Berlin, where we gave more than twenty performances. I felt strongly, however, that our leader was not making any money and that he was disturbed. The truth was that after leaving Germany, where our success was assured, he did not really know where to take us. We stagnated for eight days in Aix-la-Chapelle. Then he dragged us into Italy, through Milan, Turin, and at last here to Rome. Our opening evening was brilliant, with the Valle Theatre filled from top to bottom with elegant society, but we were impolitic enough to give *Blanchette,* a peasant play which did not interest the audience, and we were consequently virtually boycotted for the violence of our repertoire. Our manager was so concerned the last several days that he no longer gave me my daily wages, and I distributed the little money I had left among my companions.

Last evening as the curtain went down on the last act of *The Fossils,* when we were all on stage, I was handed a note from our business manager which informed me that I had repeatedly violated our contract, that he refused all responsibility, and that he was leaving without us. On his return to Paris, he would ask the courts to settle our case. This was the ultimate calamity. Here I am left in the lurch in Rome with fifteen or sixteen persons, and I can expect no help from Paris where my notes are coming due at this very moment. All my companions are taking this in the best possible way, with admirable devotion and unselfishness, despite the worries that beset them too. We informed the police in Rome the same evening; they sympathized with our disappointment, but could do nothing. The following morning, I went to the French Embassy, where the consul promised to protect me by his verifications from any possible claims of our business manager.

Here ends the odyssey of the Théâtre-Libre. Having set out seven years ago from my garret in the Rue de Dunkerque with forty sous in my pocket, to rehearse our first production in the little wine shop in the Rue des Abbesses, I at last find myself in Rome, with almost the same sum in my pocket, surrounded by fifteen companions as dejected as myself, with a hundred thousand francs of debts awaiting me in Paris, and with no idea of what we will do tomorrow.

INDEX OF NAMES
MOST FREQUENTLY MENTIONED IN THE TEXT

CLARETIE, Jules (1840-1913), director of the Comédie-Française, 54, 69, 80, 83, 115, 139, 169, 171, 190.

CUREL, François de (1854-1928), dramatist, specialist in thesis plays, 183, 187, 192, 194, 195, 201, 202, 209, 210, 211, 214, 220.

DARZENS, Rodolphe (1865-1938), poet, archivist of the Théâtre-Libre, later director of the Théâtre des Arts, 43, 48, 63, 89, 128, 131, 133, 161. [Plate VI]

DAUDET, Alphonse (1840-1897), novelist and dramatist, 19, 20, 21, 26, 34, 52, 54, 67, 96, 101, 109, 114, 122, 132, 140, 149, 160, 161, 162, 167, 212, 213, 221.

DESCAVES, Lucien (1861-1949), dramatist, much prosecuted for his writings, 39, 53, 58, 59, 60, 62, 65, 77, 136, 141, 142, 157, 160, 161, 162, 163, 191. [Plates VI, VII]

DUMAS *FILS*, Alexandre (1824-1895), novelist and dramatist, 3, 26, 58, 61, 103, 144, 145, 171, 174, 178, 190, 216.

FOUQUIER, Henri (1838-1901), politician and journalist, 20, 21, 22, 24, 46, 56, 72, 99, 100, 132, 147, 188, 193, 204, 207, 216.

GONCOURT, Edmond de (1822-1896), author, critic, and diarist, with his brother Jules (1830-1870) a precursor of naturalism in literature, 3, 9, 26, 34, 38, 44, 52, 71, 86, 91, 95, 96, 97, 98, 99, 104, 105, 106, 107, 109, 110, 114, 122, 123, 124, 126, 129, 132, 140, 149, 159, 160, 161, 162, 165, 166, 167, 168, 171, 177, 178, 198, 212, 215.

GOT, Edmond (1822-1901), actor, famous for comic roles at the Comédie-Française, 7, 24, 28, 31, 69, 108, 112, 116, 144, 165, 176, 201.

HENNIQUE, Leon (1851-1935), novelist and dramatist, 10, 16, 18, 19, 20, 21, 22, 38, 45, 51, 76, 86, 94, 104, 124, 126, 127, 161, 191, 199, 207.

IBSEN, Henrik (1828-1906), Norwegian dramatist, major source of inspiration for the new drama of the 1880's, 85, 121, 122, 129, 131, 133, 134, 136, 140, 142, 185, 195, 202, 203, 211, 216, 219.

JULLIEN, Jean (1854-1919), dramatist and critic, the critical spokesman for the Théâtre-Libre, 38, 45, 53, 54, 55, 76, 105, 112, 113, 129, 130, 131, 142, 148, 153, 164, 176, 186, 199, 204, 205, 208. [Plates VI, VII]

LAVEDAN, Henri (1859-1940), dramatist, specialist in comedies of manners with social themes, 39, 59, 60, 62, 65, 66, 77, 127, 135, 207, 208.

LEMAITRE, François-Elie-Jules (1853-1914), critic, dramatist, and politician, 3, 29, 47, 105, 114, 130, 132, 146, 168, 175, 187, 217, 223, 224.

MAGNARD, Francis (1837-1894), journalist, editor of the *Figaro,* 63, 98, 120, 127, 132, 137, 162, 163, 169, 223, 224.

MENDES, CATULLE (1842-1909), poet, novelist, and dramatist, one of the Parnassians, 2, 6, 28, 30, 31, 32, 38, 45, 46, 48, 51, 57, 64, 71, 74, 76, 80, 90, 91, 92, 93, 101, 102, 125, 132, 137, 146, 162, 165, 197, 203, 205, 226, 229.

METENIER, OSCAR (1859-1913), artist, novelist, and dramatist, 26, 27, 28, 29, 30, 33, 39, 45, 51, 56, 60, 61, 99, 112, 122, 124, 126, 127, 199, 212. [Plates VI, VIII]

PESSARD, HECTOR (1836-1895), journalist and drama critic, associated with the *Liberté Gaulois,* the *Temps,* and the *Soir,* 102, 110, 114, 147, 161, 163, 164, 165, 169, 216.

POREL, DESIRE-PAUL PARFOURU, called Porel (1842-1917), actor and director of the Odéon, the Gymnase, and the Vaudeville, 3, 21, 22, 28, 35, 36, 42, 71, 86, 95, 96, 109, 110, 113, 122, 124, 126, 146, 157, 174, 176, 186, 196, 205.

PORTO-RICHE, GEORGES DE (1849-1930), dramatist, a specialist in the subtle analysis of amatory relationships, 58, 71, 87, 88, 94, 103, 108, 109, 120, 174, 199, 207.

REJANE, GABRIELLE-CHARLOTTE REJU, called Réjane (1856-1920), actress, one of her country's greatest comediennes, 68, 70, 71, 95, 96, 126, 174, 205, 224. [Plate XIA]

SARCEY, FRANCISQUE (1827-1899), critical spokesman of the conservative late-nineteenth-century theatre in France, 3, 9, 10, 22, 28, 33, 35, 38, 41, 48, 49, 50, 66, 76, 78, 80, 93, 99, 107, 112, 116, 117, 118, 126, 127, 128, 129, 130, 134, 135, 137, 140, 148, 149, 155, 156, 157, 158, 165, 168, 170, 172, 173, 175, 176, 188, 195, 196, 209, 210, 211, 216.

VIDAL, JULES (1858-1895), artist, novelist, and dramatist, 9, 11, 16, 20, 22, 23, 33, 34, 38, 88, 205. [Plate VI]

VILLIERS DE L'ISLE-ADAM, PHILIPPE-AUGUSTE (1838-1889), novelist and dramatist, 2, 38, 43, 48, 76, 114, 216.

WOLFF, ALBERT (1835-1891), journalist, critic for the *Figaro,* 40, 41, 63, 67, 92, 95, 98, 126, 127, 134, 136, 137, 138, 139, 140, 141, 179, 186, 189.

WOLFF, PIERRE (1865-1891), dramatist, nephew of Albert Wolff, 134, 135, 137, 141, 143, 159, 178, 179, 189, 197, 202, 203, 207, 208. [Plate VIII]

ZOLA, EMILE (1840-1903), novelist, dramatist, and critic, the father of naturalism in literature, 3, 6, 9, 10, 11, 12, 15, 16, 17, 18, 19, 20, 21, 25, 26, 33, 38, 54, 55, 56, 60, 62, 65, 66, 67, 74, 84, 91, 92, 96, 104, 108, 109, 113, 121, 122, 123, 128, 132, 138, 139, 156, 162, 164, 171, 178, 212.

LIST OF PLATES

*The plates follow; in each case credits are
given in the accompanying captions.*

PLATE I — Antoine in 1889. In the background is a poster advertising *The Power of Darkness*. (Matei Roussou, *André Antoine*)

37, Passage de l'Elysée des Beaux-Arts (Place Pigalle)

MERCREDI 30 MARS 1887

à 8 heures très-précises du soir

Première Représentation

Jacques Damour | Mademoiselle Pomme
Pièce en 1 acte, en prose | Comédie-farce en 1 acte, en prose
Tirée de la nouvelle de M. Emile ZOLA | par DURANTY
par M. Léon HENNIQUE | et M. Paul ALEXIS.

La Cocarde | Un Préfet
Comédie en 1 acte, en prose | Drame en 1 acte, en prose
par M. Jules VIDAL. | par M. Arthur BYL.

NOTA — Cette invitation étant **rigoureusement personnelle,**
prière de vouloir bien retourner, avant la représentation, les places dont on
ne disposerait pas.
A. ANTOINE.

PLATE IIA — Invitation to the first production of the
Théâtre-Libre. (*André Antoine*)

PLATE IIB — Paul Alexis. Drawing by Métivet. (Rodolphe Darzens,
Le Théâtre-Libre Illustré)

PLATE IIC — Emile Bergerat.
Drawing by Métivet. (*Le Théâtre-
Libre Illustré*)

PLATE IIIA — The stage in the Elysée-des-Beaux-Arts. (*André Antoine*)

PLATE IIIB — The auditorium in the Elysée-des-Beaux-Arts. (*André Antoine*)

PLATE IVA — *The Power of Darkness* at the Théâtre-Libre. *(André Antoine)*

PLATE IVB — *Elisa the Slattern*, the Courtroom scene. Antoine is standing. *(André Antoine)*

M. Janvier

Mlle. Barny

Mlle. Luce Colas

M. Arquillière

PLATE V — Actors and actresses of the Théâtre-Libre. Drawings by Métivet. *(Le Théâtre-Libre Illustré)*

PLATE VI — "A Reading at the Théâtre-Libre," painted about 1890.
(André Antoine)

Key to left half of painting:

1. Mlle. Barny
2. Vidal
3. Ancey
4. probably Descaves
5. possibly Méténier
6. Alexis

Key to right half of painting:

7. Darzens
8. possibly Luce Colas
9. Jullien
10. Mévisto
11. Antoine
12. probably Louise France
13. Arquillière

Lucien Descaves

Georges Ancey

Plate VII — Dramatists of the Théâtre-Libre. Drawings by Métivet. *(Le Théâtre-Libre Illustré)*

Jean Jullien

Oscar Méténier

Pierre Wolff

Eugène Brieux

PLATE VIII — Dramatists of the Théâtre-Libre. Drawings by Métivet. *(Le Théâtre-Libre Illustré)*

PLATE IXA — Antoine's retreat at Camaret. *(André Antoine)*

PLATE IXB—Antoine in *Blanchette.* *(André Antoine)*

PLATE XA — Program by Ibels for *The Fossils.* *(André Antoine)*

PLATE XB — Program by Toulouse - Lautrec f o r *The Missionary.* (E r n e s t Maindron, *Les Programs Illustrés des Théâtres et des Cafés-Concerts)*

PLATE XIA — 1904 production of *The Woman of Paris* (left to right: Grand, de Féraudy, Réjane, Antoine). *(André Antoine)*

PLATE XIB — Antoine in 1941. *(André Antoine)*